Inky Water

The Bluefield Beach Series
Heather Grey

Contents

Dedication		VI
Author's Note		VII
1.	Lillian	1
2.	Jackson	10
3.	Lillian	17
4.	Jackson	25
5.	Lillian	32
6.	Jackson	44
7.	Lillian	52
8.	Jackson	62
9.	Lillian	70
10.	Jackson	79
11.	Lillian	88
12.	Jackson	101
13.	Lillian	110

14.	Jackson	120
15.	Lillian	130
16.	Jackson	138
17.	Lillian	148
18.	Jackson	155
19.	Lillian	166
20.	Jackson	178
21.	Lillian	187
22.	Jackson	197
23.	Lillian	209
24.	Jackson	220
25.	Lillian	230
26.	Jackson	242
27.	Lillian	249
28.	Jackson	261
29.	Lillian	274
30.	Jackson	281
31.	Lillian	291
32.	Jackson	297
33.	Lillian	302
34.	Jackson	309

35. Lillian   317

36. Jackson   323

Epilogue   329

More by Heather   335

Content Warnings   336

About the author   337

Acknowledgements   338

To all the versions of myself that came before this one.
Thank you for getting me here.

Author's Note

Inky Water contains mature content and is suited for those 18 and older. A list of content warnings can be found on my website, or at the back of this novel.
Bluefield is an imaginary town in Canada; the spelling in this book reflects Canadian English.

Chapter 1
Lillian

ASPEN:

Don't miss me too much

Call if you need anything

LILLIAN:

Thanks...Mom

ASPEN:

Oh, you keep me young

"Yes, Mom, I found the place alright. The key is where I remember it."

I turn the key in the lock and jiggle it slightly. Turning the handle on the large oak door, I am immediately engulfed in the familiar smell of childhood. A mixture of fresh-cut grass, mothballs, and sandy lake air, more comforting than a warm blanket on a cold winter's day.

"Are you sure you don't want your father and me to come stay with you? I'm sure you will get too lonely up there by yourself." My mother breaks me from the daydream as I place my bags at the door and turn on the kitchen light.

"I'm sure, Mom. Lonely is fine with me. I need quiet for work. Plus, you guys have your trip planned. Don't worry about me, enjoy your retirement," I respond, trying to keep my tone constant.

I know that she cares, but we have had this conversation more times than I would like. My mom can't understand why I would want to spend my summer alone at our family cottage.

I can't understand why anyone wouldn't want to.

"Okay, Lillian, please call if you need anything, or text your father. He's always on his phone, so he'll respond right away. We love you."

I chuckle, picturing my dad 'working' on his phone, most likely spending his day playing Hearts or Solitaire. He retired last year, so I'm not sure what work she thinks he's ever doing.

"I love you guys, too. I'll call soon."

I take another deep breath in as I hang up the phone, trying to exhale the stress I'm holding in my shoulders. The itch in my nose tells me there might be a layer of dust I don't remember from childhood. A quick cleaning needs to be added to the agenda for the day.

Making my way to the living room, I cast my eyes out at my favourite view, the beautiful Lake Huron. It's just as amazing as I remembered, probably because it is the background on my phone and computer.

This time of year, the sun still sets to the south, but by the end of July, we will have a picture perfect sunset directly in front of us. This section of the lake is home to sandy beaches. The farther north you get along the coast, the shore turns to rock as it reaches past Georgian Bay.

My grandpa once said the lake is almost the same size as the entire state of West Virginia. Though I've never fact-checked him on that, it seems believable.

We aren't able to see the other shores on all three sides.

On a bright sunny day, the water is crystal blue like a Caribbean ocean and no matter how deep you get, you can always see to the bottom.

There is something a bit different about it this time, though. There is a giant tractor of some sort on the neighbour's lawn. It wouldn't be such an eyesore if it wasn't bright orange and surrounded by dirt.

From the looks of it, there is a very large structure replacing the Waldens' quaint cottage. When my grandparents told me the Waldens next door had sold their cottage, I didn't think that the new owners would tear it down, but my drive up here should have been a tell that this town is changing.

There are a lot more large, new cottages than there once was. I know we can't stop change, but a part of me wants to hold on to this place and the happy memories from here.

Bluefield, Ontario. During the winter months, it is described as a quiet town with the majority of the population being seniors living out their retirement years in peace.

In the summer, it is a tourist destination, pulling in all ages of beach goers and boaters, for day trips or summer vacations. It also happens to be where my grandparents' cottage sits empty for most weeks of the year.

When I was a child, my parents would bring my brother and me here for a week or two each summer, and somewhere between our sand castle competitions and the never-ending amounts of ice cream consumed on Main Street, this place became my sanctuary.

So, finding myself here, at the age of twenty-seven, with a major deadline looming, isn't in the least bit surprising.

Living in the city is all I've ever known.

I grew up there, went to school there and bought a condo there, but something about my grandparents' cottage feels more like home than any place in the world.

Choosing to ignore the giant orange problem in front of me, I put my things upstairs and spend the rest of the afternoon cleaning the place from top to bottom.

The sooner I'm settled, the sooner I can figure my life out.

My stomach growling brings my attention to the clock. I realize that not only have I missed dinner, but the grocery store in town is already closed, a small town downfall. Accepting that a chip truck poutine dinner is my fate, I make the short walk into town to settle my stomach.

When I get to Ron's Chip Truck, parked next to the bakery in the exact spot it has been my whole life, I see none other than the man himself.

"Hi, Ron, how are things? How was the winter?" I ask.

"Oh my, do I need new glasses or is that Lillian Shaw before my very eyes?" His dark skin has weathered throughout the years, but his caramel eyes still hold the warmth of an old friend.

"You don't wear glasses, Ron, but yes, it's me. I'm back!" I motion to my body to display I am, in fact, in front of him. Ron quickly steps out of my eyesight as he makes his way to the side of the truck and out the back door. Wiping his hands on his apron, he then welcomes me in a warm embrace.

To most tourists around, this might seem like an overly affectionate welcome for a customer, but thanks to the summer of 2003 when my brother, Ben, refused to eat anything but hotdogs for three months, Ron now feels more like family.

"Are you here for the summer, or just passing through?" he asks once he has returned to the truck to start the order I didn't need to make.

"For the summer." I think. I know I'm on a deadline, but my plans are not concrete for the first time in my life.

I've always been a planner; it's where I find comfort. I started to plan my own birthday parties when I was six to ensure I knew exactly what to expect when the day arrived, so when I presented my parents with my fifteen-year plan at age fifteen, no one was surprised.

I had it all laid out for me: graduate high school, attend the University of Toronto, major in English Literature, graduate with honours, get signed on with a publishing company, move in with my boyfriend, buy our apartment, marriage, two-point-five kids. My own fairy tale. So, sitting on a chip truck bench alone, recently single, with what feels like the worst case of writer's block imaginable, was certainly not part of that plan.

I never let myself think of a plan B or C, because planning properly meant executing things properly. Success.

No need for backup plans. No anxiety.

So maybe I'm a bit of a control freak. Or maybe it's a coping mechanism.

"One order of poutine, heavy on the curd, for my favourite customer." Ron plops a plate of cheesy goodness in front of my face. "Just don't tell Ben you're my favourite, it would bruise his ego."

"Please, my brother's ego could use some bruising," I respond.

My older brother Ben has never been accused of having confidence issues.

Captain of the lacrosse team, class president, had five girls ask him to prom. Charming, you know the type, I don't think I need to go on.

Of course, he's also super nice and a great dad, and I love him very much, but being his younger sister was sometimes a lot. I can't count the number of times girls I barely spoke to wanted to be my partner for group projects, hoping we could work on it at my house and they could worm their way into my brother's heart or something.

I don't understand how they rationalized it, but I avoided anyone who wanted to be my friend suddenly, or anyone at all for the most part, just to stay safe.

If people can't see you, they can't judge you, right?

Or they can only judge the parts that you choose to show.

Maybe that's why I love Bluefield so much: less people, less eyes. The city can be too much some days. Even though my entire life I have technically been a city girl, it's always felt a bit forced.

Especially when I look at my best friend, who seems to have been born for the role.

Aspen and I could not be more different. If I wasn't one half of the friendship, I don't think I would understand how it functions.

We met in preschool when a boy in our class, Duncan, stole the toy I was playing with. She promptly pushed him over and gave the toy back. When the teacher tried to scold her, I stepped in to take the fall and that was it.

Twenty-three years of friendship later and she feels more like a sister to me at this point.

She's wild when I'm reserved, loud when I'm quiet, and sometimes unhinged when I'm thoughtful. She loves hard; a true ride or die.

As though I've summoned her with my thoughts, my phone chimes with a message from her.

ASPEN:

Billy!! Alive? Well? Rowdy?

LILLIAN:

Hello to you too. I would say yes to the first two, but I'm not sure how you expect me to be rowdy alone in Bluefield

ASPEN:

Boys exist in Bluefield, don't they??

LILLIAN:

I would assume so, but I don't need any distractions right now

ASPEN:

I think that's exactly what you need

I think this might be my best idea ever-rrrrr. I am such an idea girlie

LILLIAN:

Your ideas often lead to trouble

ASPEN

That's the point. I love trouble.

That she does, Aspen is the only person who has ever convinced me away from areas of control. I can say every social gathering I have ever attended was thanks to her, and they didn't always end in trouble, but more often than not, they did. Luckily, my parents love Aspen, probably as much as they love me, so the punishment was never severe.

They were probably thankful she got my nose out of a book and into the dance studio.

Aspen insists on calling me Billy. It started out as Lilly, but I didn't like when she called me that. Aspen decided to get more creative with Billy, meaning beautiful Lilly.

Apparently, I was only allowed to veto one nickname, so she's been calling me Billy for most of our friendship. The only upside to her weird rules is that she is the only one allowed to call me by this nickname, which is more than fine with me.

After sufficiently filling my stomach with Canada's best poutine, I say goodnight to Ron and head back to the cottage.

The temperature has dropped quite a bit since the sun has gone down and it feels like there may be a storm coming in tomorrow. With this in mind, a quick nighttime dip in the lake is just what I need to calm me down before bed.

The water is quite cold. It's still spring, so the days haven't been warm or long enough to truly warm the lake water yet. My relaxing dip feels a bit more like a polar bear plunge, but it gets the job done of being refreshing enough to get a good night's sleep.

And I really need to get a good night's sleep.

Tomorrow I will end my creative block, get a lot of work done and get my life back on track. Tomorrow I will create a new plan.

Chapter 2
Jackson

GORD:

Things good?

JACKSON:

Yes. Everything is ready to break ground tomorrow. I met with all the trades today. Expectations have been laid out and everyone seems excited to get started. I think this project is going to be great.

GORD:

I'll check back in a couple of days

JACKSON:

Okay. Talk soon.

Well, I think that might break the record for the longest text conversation with my father. I'm astounded by the fact his second message had more than three words.

The bar of expectations that I have set for communicating with my father is very low.

A man of few words, unless he is giving you a verbal spanking, that is.

He's always been this way, unfortunately. The commitment to his job was always more important than the marriage to any of his wives, my mother included.

I unfortunately ended up as collateral damage in their divorce. Since my father was the only reason she moved to Canada, the second the divorce was finalized, she returned to Florida and I was left with him.

For whatever reason, my dad insisted he get full custody of me, and my mother didn't care to fight, so it was simple enough for them.

I've always assumed my birth was not planned, or at least she had very little interest in being a mother.

I probably will never get the answer to that as we have no relationship now. Simple as that.

For eight-year-old me, it was anything but simple.

My only saving grace as a child was that my father's sister, her husband and my two cousins lived in the same neighbourhood as us in Toronto. I basically lived at their house. My cousin, Simon, is the same age. He's felt more like a brother than a cousin or a friend for my whole life.

When I was younger, I couldn't wait to grow up, get out of my father's house and be my own man. So, working for him certainly wasn't what I had imagined for my future. The problem was, construction sites were my babysitters for a lot of my childhood, making a career in architecture feel like a natural choice.

My father, Gordon Mane, owns Mane Construction. They mostly deal with large new builds and renovations in the upper-class neighbourhoods of Toronto.

After completing my master's degree, my father made it very clear there wasn't a spot in the company for me without any experience. That wasn't a problem at all because I wanted nothing to do with him or his company.

I was twenty-three and still fighting to become my own man and resenting him for how my childhood was shaped. I worked for a firm out of Ottawa for almost five years, and found a lot of success there, but I still felt like I hadn't found my place.

So, this spring when my father shockingly offered me a position on a new project in Bluefield, I decided to give it a shot.

I haven't decided what I think I'm going to get out of this, but it beats feeling stuck. Maybe this is an opportunity to improve my relationship with my dad? That's not likely considering I will be in Bluefield and he will be in Toronto, but it will give me a chance to show him what I'm capable of. He always said Mane Construction could be mine someday, but he wouldn't hand it to me if I didn't deserve it. This is a great opportunity to prove myself.

If I don't take a chance, I can't expect to feel a change.

The Bluefield project is a bit out of the norm for Mane Construction. The company's typical clientele has shown a great interest in lake houses and cottages, so we are currently buying great properties with not-so-great cottages, tearing down the current structures and replacing them with much larger, state-of-the-art summer homes. The waiting list for the properties is already becoming unmanageable, so to say there is pressure to deliver is an understatement. I'm working with a new crew filled with some local tradesmen and current employees, and taking on the role of architect and project manager.

I know this is going to be a learning experience with a steep curve, but my father isn't someone who expects that mistakes happen. I need to hit the ground running to prove myself to him, the Mane construction employees, but most importantly, myself.

As all of our properties are teardowns, I will be staying at the Bluefield Inn for the foreseeable future.

It's a rather charming large red-brick home in the centre of Main Street that has been converted to hold ten guest rooms and a small dining space for breakfast and lunch. I couldn't help it, but the first day I arrived, my architectural brain went wild.

The interior is still leaning into its original colonial style and doesn't fit the character of the rest of this beach town. I would love to round the firm lines of the doorways into arches and sand down the wood on the floors and baseboards to their natural colour. Overall, give the place a softer look and feel while maintaining enough of the original charm.

I've been here for exactly one week and have eaten every meal either at The Inn or the chip truck on Main Street.

The chip truck is exactly where I am headed now as my stomach is quite unhappy that it has been neglected since breakfast this morning. The five cups of coffee are not sufficient and are sitting pretty heavy in my bloodstream. I'm either good to run a marathon or about to crash from a lack of nutrients in my system.

My morning runs have been a struggle recently and the heavy carb meal I'm about to eat isn't going to remedy that. Too bad the food is too good for me to really care.

The chip truck is interesting, certainly not something you would find in the city, which makes me kind of love it. Named simply Ron's Chip Truck, after the owner, the building looks like it was probably a shipping container that has been refurbished to look more like a street food truck.

The white exterior looks clean, but the window baskets filled with pansies add a cozy charm. The area beside the truck houses a plethora of picnic tables surrounded by mature trees, all lined with gingham tablecloths in white and blue.

There's comfort in a ten-item menu where you know everything is good, consistent and fried. As I approach the truck, Ron gives me a nod and then pulls out my usual order of a burger and fries from the counter. It's been a week and I think I have become a regular.

I chuckle to myself while taking a seat on the pine picnic table farthest from the truck so fewer people will notice I'm dining alone, again. Ron plops himself down across from me, as he has the last couple of days. I am probably one of his last customers of the day, so I'm not sure if he's this friendly with everyone or if he's just taking a load off.

Ron gives off a warm feeling. He's probably the same age as my grandparents would be if I had any, based on the salt and pepper black hair that is loosely tucked under his branded hat.

"Jackson, how was your day?" Ron asks as he leans forward,

placing his elbows on the table.

"Good, good... Too productive actually. Although, you are saving my life with this burger because I missed lunch today."

He rubs his hand on his round belly that's covered in a grease-stained t-shirt. "I don't think I've missed a meal in my life. Is there such a thing as being too productive?"

"Come on, Ron, I know you love working hard. There's no way you make one of the best burgers I ever had without putting in the work."

He shakes his head, laughing a little. "Oh, that's where you've got me all wrong, son. I am a man with dumb luck." His eyes crinkle at the sides as he looks into the distance. "My wife brought all the good in my life to me. She always knew how to dream and execute. I was just along for the ride."

"That doesn't sound like dumb luck, then. That sounds like a smart lady."

"Oh, that she was, but dumb luck brought her to me. And I'm thankful every day for it. But that's a story for another time." He slaps the table and stands, wiping his palms on his apron.

When his eyes meet mine again, there's a light that has returned to them after it was momentarily lost at the mention of his wife. "Well, son, I will see you tomorrow? Take care and eat lunch tomorrow, please."

I nod in response.

As Ron returns to his truck to close for the night, I feel like I'm dragging through this meal just to avoid returning to The Inn.

My nightly routine consists of a shower and watching whatever movie Netflix recommends on my phone until I fall asleep. At least that's what I've done every night this week, and I don't see it changing anytime soon. I'm a pretty social person, so being in a new town without an office, co-workers or friends is leaving me a bit uneasy.

I know I could try to make plans with someone on my crew, but I am trying to balance being friendly and being professional. I need everyone to respect and trust me, and I don't know that drinking beer with them on a weeknight is the way to achieve that. I'm not sure if that's the reason I'm clinging to every interaction with Ron. Our conversations have become the highlight of my day, but it might just be him.

He's easily one of the nicest people I know and I'm not too proud to say when he calls me 'son,' I smile inside a little. Or a lot. No daddy issues here, of course. None at all.

When I finish up the rest of my meal, I know going back to my room is the smart and only move I can make right now. Another movie alone it is.

The light at the end of the tunnel is that my boat is being dropped off at the marina this weekend, and to say I'm excited is an understatement.

It's a small Bayliner that I use mostly for cruising and, occasionally, fishing when I need some quiet. Quiet is not what I need. I need an outlet and I need it now.

My dreams have consisted of redesigning almost every building on Main Street since I can't turn my brain off at night. I either need friends here or a hobby. Preferably both, but for now, I will settle for just my boat.

Chapter 3
Lillian

ASPEN:

Proof of life request

LILLIAN:

It's been less than 24 hours, I'm alive

ASPEN:

Oh, thank god.

"You are smart."

"You are creative."

"You are good at your job."

"Please, please, please, brain. Think of something."

I've been staring at a blank Word document for three hours already, willing myself to come up with something, anything. I just need to start.

Starting should be easy, right? You know, I just need a character, or a lesson, a theme, a title even. Any one of those things would be helpful.

I have none of them.

Writing children's books should be a fun, creative job, yet somewhere in the last year it's felt like a math equation I keep repeating with different variables. This shape + this shape – the problem x the heartwarming lesson. Solve for y, add some colour and done. Cute, marketable, safe.

And that's always been enough, because with everything else in my life feeling a bit out of my control, safe should feel right. I need the safe; I'm clinging to the safe.

But the safe also feels suffocating.

A change of scenery may help.

Yes, it will definitely help. And we are going to ignore the fact that being at the cottage was supposed to be the change of scenery. I need different scenery. Outdoor scenery? Is the word scenery starting to sound weird? I'm sure if I say it out loud, it would at this point.

The air is still crisp in the mornings and the grass is covered in dew as spring makes way for summer. Soon the streets will be filled with tourists donning sun hats and bathing suits, but for now, a sweater and a warm cup of tea are still required in the early mornings. Pouring my green tea into a travel mug and placing it in my backpack, I hop on my bike to head towards Main Street.

Most of the shops are just opening for the day. With light chatter from the few early birds out for a walk, the town is the perfect picture of peacefulness.

This time of day is my favourite.

Being able to get the necessities from town with little human interaction is a blessing in any tourist destination. It's not that I don't like people; I just like people I know and trust. I know that people aren't walking around judging me, but there is a part of my brain that loves to feed that delusion a bit too often.

For some reason convincing yourself that no one thinks about you as much as you think about you is a hard concept to wrap your head around.

Locking my bike to a tree in front of The General Store, I walked up the path to the front door.

The bell above me rings, prompting the man, or should I say boy, behind the cash to look up. He must be a high school or college student working here for the summer.

"Good morning, miss, is there anything I can help you with this morning?"

His dimples are nearly popping out of his face with the grin he gives me. I'm sure the ladies love that smile, but I think it's at least seven years too young for me.

"Hi there, I'm just going to grab a snack before I head to the park to get some work done." I tap my tote bag, hoping it's obvious that I'm acknowledging my computer that's in there.

He nods his head once, his large smile seemingly getting even bigger. "Well, if you need anything, anything at all, my name is Sam and I'm here to serve you."

Kind of a strange kid, but I bet the old ladies love him. I'm pretty sure this is him trying to flirt with me. Again, a minimum of seven years too old for that.

After grabbing a bag of trail mix and paying, I grab my bike and make my way to the park at the end of the street. Aside from an elderly couple sitting on a bench at the far side of the park, it seems I have the place all to myself.

I find what must be the largest maple tree in the whole town, and I spread out the blanket I packed and pull out my tablet and computer. More technology equals more productivity, probably.

An artist I am not, but sometimes doodling helps me get a story going in my head. All the illustrations for my stories are done once the manuscript has been approved by someone in a different department, so these will never be seen by anyone's eyes but mine.

I spend the next couple of hours changing between a silly drawing of a scrappy-looking dog and a flower. Not only do I have no idea how those two would exist inside my book together, but frankly, the dog is looking a bit too much like a pirate for my liking. Not ideal.

I'm starting to feel like I need to stage an intervention with myself.

The next time I convince myself changing scenery will break me out of this rut, someone needs to stop me. And damn it, scenery still sounds silly in my head.

Thankfully, not a common word in a book for children ages two to four.

A dark shadow appears above me as the figure approaching blocks the sunlight sneaking through the trees. Once my eyes adjust, I realize it's Sam from The General Store. Did I forget something in the store?

"Hey... Sorry, I didn't actually catch your name earlier." He states this like it's super unusual. I don't think it is. Probably because I don't tell most strangers my name.

"Oh, it's Lillian."

He smiles at my answer, not replying further. I take a closer look at him during the silence. I wasn't paying a lot of attention when we were in the store, but now that we are outside in natural light, I see a light smattering of freckles across his cheeks.

Considering his job takes place indoors, he probably plays sports outside. If I had to guess based on his unusually large muscles that fill out his otherwise lanky frame, he probably plays football.

"Did I forget something at the store or are you just passing through the park?" I ask, a bit confused as to why he approached me.

"Oh, no. You just mentioned you would be in the park, so I thought I would stop by while on my break and see how you are doing." He gives me another dimpled smile, like there's some secret we share that I should know about. I don't.

"No, I'm all good here, just working. Like I said I would be."

And he's staring at me, smiling. I know my social skills can be a bit lacking, but I'm pretty sure this is getting weird and it's not because of me.

I am totally calling Aspen about this tonight. She would know if this was my fault.

I look down at my tablet and pretend I'm very busy working. Maybe he will get the clue and leave.

But since the sun isn't reappearing from behind his head, I don't think I am going to be that lucky.

Clearing my throat, I look back up at Sam's smiling face. It doesn't even seem like he's really looking at me, it's more like he's some smiling doll that is looking through me. I'm starting to get the creeps.

So, as any sane woman does in this situation, I'm going to fake a phone call.

"Oh, hi, Mom," I say, picking up my phone and holding it to my ear.

"Yes, right, I totally forgot I was supposed to call you back."

"Oh, yes, the windows. I will go do that right now."

"Okay, love you, too, bye." Ending my fake phone call, I stand.

"Sorry about that." I start to gather up my things. While Sam stands there, not even trying to act like he isn't listening in on my phone call.

"I need to head home. Left some of the windows open and it looks like we're getting our first summer storm this evening. Don't want any of that getting inside."

Sam finally steps away, nodding his head.

"Of course," he says. "I should head back to work, my break is almost over, but it was really great hanging out with you."

"Yes, okay, you, too." I guess. With my blanket, computer and tablet all safely back in my tote, I hop onto my bike as quickly as possible without drawing any attention to myself and get the hell away from Main Street, and Sam.

Even though the phone call was not real, the summer storm is. And boy has it come in ferociously. The oak and maple trees surrounding the cottage have started to lose leaves and acorns, adding to the loud wind. The noise rivals a rock concert.

Normally, I quite enjoy watching storms blow off the lake. Once you see the clouds rolling in, it only takes minutes before the raindrops dance off the surface of the lake. Normally, I would grab a book and a nice blanket to curl up by the window. Normally, I wouldn't have been distracted by a strange teenage boy and would have remembered I have almost no groceries in the cottage, and I missed lunch.

I have two options.

One, eat stale saltine crackers and peanut butter for dinner.

Two, call ahead an order from The Dancing Dog, a restaurant on Main Street, and brave the storm.

Option one is very enticing, but I haven't eaten enough to sustain myself today and if the storm continues through the night, I will be in the same spot come morning. At one point in my life, a spoonful of peanut butter would have been a great idea for dinner, but I am no longer a starving university student. Getting my life back on track involves the small things, too, like food.

With that in mind, I place my order for dinner, the nice hostess says it will be ready in fifteen minutes, and I just hope I can find a spot to park close to the front door.

As I drive down Main Street, I swear the sky has opened. I'm not sure it would be physically possible for it to be raining any harder.

Thankfully, there is a spot three car lengths away from The

Dancing Dog. Not too bad considering the next closest is ten cars away.

Rain hood on, I make my way to the restaurant. I only have to wait five minutes before I'm handed my food. I re-secure my raincoat to my body and contemplate putting my bag of food inside my coat, too. I think that's a bit overkill for my two-second sprint to the car and the bag is a bit too warm against my skin. I take a deep breath and then step out of the restaurant.

I run smack dab into a very soaked someone.

Chapter 4
Jackson

Have you ever forgotten a raincoat in the middle of the worst storm you've ever experienced and then run into the prettiest girl you've ever seen and knocked her dinner all over the ground?

That is very specific

But, no. Can't say that I have

That makes one of us

Shit.

Shit. Shit. Shit.

I should have been looking where I was going, that's for sure.

I should have been wearing a raincoat, or a hat at the very least. Anything to block the rain from my eyes.

But I didn't, and now this blonde-haired angel with striking blue eyes is staring at me like I killed her kitten.

Not to mention, I think I have mashed potatoes in my shoes. Shit.

"I am so sorry. This is all my fault. I wasn't looking where I was going, obviously. And now your dinner is ruined," I stammer out, not breathing until the end.

"That was my dinner," is all she replies, dropping her gaze to the ground where her meal will be laid to rest.

"Yes, again, I am so sorry. Please let me replace your food."

"Oh no, that's not necessary. It was an accident." She takes a step away from me, like she's going to walk away without any food. Without thinking, I grab her elbow, stopping her. The rain continues to pour around us, but I don't care about getting wet anymore.

"Please let me," I insist.

She looks at me and then to my hand that is still holding onto her. I quickly let go as I realize I held contact for longer than is polite.

She mumbles something about peanut butter under breath before looking back at me.

Her eyes are piercing. They are a deep blue that I'm sure would rival the current colour of the lake, and there are gold flecks just around the outside of her irises. I don't think I've ever paid attention to anyone's eye colour this closely, so I hope I haven't been staring for longer than is socially acceptable. Between the staring and awkward elbow holding, I am not making a good first impression.

I took the mandatory etiquette classes in high school. I have never been socially awkward in my life, but maybe I'm a late bloomer.

I move my gaze away from her eyes upward, to her hair. She has soft blonde curls that are mostly sticking to her face because of the rain. I wonder if they would spring back into place if I ran my fingers through them. I'm tempted to reach out and touch them, but thankfully stop myself.

Etiquette and manners, don't touch strangers.

"Can I buy you dinner?" I try again.

"Um," she stammers, looking back down at the ground. "I guess."

She only sounds about sixty percent confident in that answer, but I'm not going to let this opportunity pass. Slipping past her, I open the door to the restaurant and gesture for her to go in ahead of me.

Once inside, I explain to the hostess what just happened, and get them to remake my new acquaintance's meal and add it to my bill. My food is already ready, but there's no way I'm leaving her here alone. Not only is all this my fault, but I also wouldn't mind learning her name.

"I'll wait with you," I offer, even though it's not up for discussion.

She looks startled, like she forgot I was standing beside her.

"That's not necessary. You're already buying my meal. I can wait alone."

"No way," I respond, trying to ease her discomfort with a subtle smile. "I'm in no rush to eat alone."

She only nods. I wasn't expecting her to offer to eat with me, but a part of me is disappointed anyway. I don't want to get caught staring again, so I follow her eye line down to her shoes which, damn it, also have mashed potatoes on them. I cringe, vacillating between apologizing more and keeping my mouth shut because I think I'm making her more uncomfortable.

She looks so tiny beside me. I'm not a huge guy, about six foot two. But she can't be any taller than five foot three, max, so I hope she is not feeling intimidated by me right now. Taking a slight step away from her to give her some more room to breathe, I try to school my thoughts and let us stand in semi-comfortable silence.

Unfortunately, I can't stop myself from talking in situations like this. My aunt always said I was a charmer, and I just can't stop until whomever it is seems to be happily charmed.

"So, are you here for business or pleasure?" She whips her head up towards me at that. I cannot believe that just came out of my mouth. I sound like a creepy man who escaped from the old folks' home.

I think she might be trying to fight a smile. I guess laughing at me is better than nothing. I'm not sure how to recover from that one, but she thankfully responds before I can make things worse.

"I guess a bit of both. I'm, um, working while I'm here, but my work isn't here." She pauses, reviewing her words. "Did that make sense to you? 'Because I think I just confused myself."

A man could get high off of the small smile gracing her lips and the little way her nose is crinkling with confusion.

"You're getting work done while you're here. But you are not here for work, nor do you work here?" I ask, and she bites her lip, nodding.

"That is correct."

We both stand there for a couple of awkward moments before she asks, "What about you? Business or...?" She trails off, her smile growing ever so slightly. She's making fun of me and I love it.

"Business, mostly. I do intend on enjoying the lake while I'm here, but yeah. Business."

"That's nice."

And we're done.

I think she just ended this conversation in the nicest way possible. I'm not sure what I'm about to say, but as I open my mouth, the hostess returns with her food.

I'm a bit disappointed she doesn't have a reason to stay and talk to me, but I did also ruin the first iteration of her dinner, so I don't want to keep her longer than necessary.

As we make our way back outside, I notice the rain has let up and now is more of a steady drizzle.

If I had waited ten more minutes for dinner, I would probably be dry right now. But I can't find it in me to regret being soaked.

Just as she's about to turn away from me, I say, "Sorry again for all of this. I hope you have a good night..." I pause, hoping she will fill in the blank.

"Oh, Lillian. My name is Lillian."

Lillian.

I like it.

"Well, it was nice to meet you, Lillian. I'm Jackson. I hope to see you again soon, and I will try my best to keep our clothes clean if we do." Not smooth. I get it, brain. I need to stop trying.

"Goodnight, Jackson."

As Lillian turns away, I can't help but think I want to hear my name from her lips as many times as I can.

I don't even remember the walk back to my room, nor am I sure what I ate for dinner. I can't keep my mind off Lillian.

She's different than the women I normally go for. Not in a bad way by any means, but the girls I dated in high school and the ones I had agreements with in university were all decently similar.

Confident, outgoing, they pursued me, that type. In all honesty, it was mostly easier that way.

All my life I've been working to be where I am today career-wise and to overall be a good man. I haven't wanted to put any time into dating, at least seriously. I have a couple numbers in my phone that I use when it suits me, but I am very much a single bachelor.

Lillian.

I am fully aware that whatever conversation we had tonight was certainly lacking in my charm. I don't know what happened, my brain was not computing on all levels.

As much as it was all a bit of a disaster, for some reason I want to see her again.

It's not like every girl I talk to throws herself at me, but this is the first time I've wanted to chase someone who seems like they would rather I didn't. Hmmm. Interesting. Is this an age thing?

I am only twenty-seven, soon to be twenty-eight, but maybe something changes biologically the closer men get to thirty?

Doubtful, but no matter what I do for the rest of the night and through the entire next day, I can't stop thinking about Lillian.

It's become such a problem that I've been compiling a list in my head of things to ask her the next time I run into her. And trust me, I will make sure I run into her. These questions include:

What does she do for work?

How long will she be in town for?

Where is she staying?

What does she like to do for fun?

Is her hair naturally that curly?

Can I touch it? Creepy.

Does she want to hang out with me? Okay, that one sounds desperate, even in my head.

Does she like boating?

If yes, does she want to go on my boat?

Yeah, I sound creepy. But this is where I'm at now. I am thankful that it is Friday and I will have all weekend to get things settled with my boat and see if there is anything to do in this town besides work.

So far, I am thinking no. It appears the tourists won't be out in full force until the end of June, which leaves the general population at an average age of seventy. I'm not going to be ageist. I'm sure the seniors can get into trouble, too.

Maybe they will let me join.

And then, of course, there's Lillian. I wouldn't mind getting into some trouble with her.

Chapter 5
Lillian

My call with Aspen on Thursday was a bit of a struggle for me. Although she did agree that Sam from The General Store is a strange person. She thinks he must have a crush on me; I think he's probably just lonely or bored. Regardless, I am going to give him a wide berth for the time being.

The part of the call that was unpleasant was when I told her about Jackson.

See, she's the type of person that wants every detail. She would have been more than happy to have me make a recording of the conversation for her to analyze. Well, she certainly didn't get that, or anything close, because I think I blacked out. I have no idea what I said for the entire twenty minutes I was in his presence. The only things I am sure of are: I need to clean mashed potatoes off my shoes, I looked like a drowned rat, and his name is Jackson.

Okay, that's a lie.

I also know Jackson is beautiful. Is it weird to call men beautiful? Who cares, because he is. I don't want to sound like a cliché, but three words. Tall. Dark. Handsome.

And his voice, smooth like marble. Which is fitting considering he could be a Greek god, chiselled from marble in Olympia. Yum.

And due to all of those descriptors, not only do I not remember what I said, but I'm sure it wasn't a whole lot anyway. Hot guy equals brain shut off.

This has always been a problem for me. I was a shy kid, turned shy teenager, which surprise, surprise, made me a shy adult. The only area of my life this doesn't affect is my career. It's almost like I cosplay a functioning adult in a career setting and then promptly turn it off the second I get home or off a work call.

I've only had one real boyfriend and he gets most of the credit for us even being in a relationship. I met Christopher in one of my first-year university lectures when he asked me to join his study group. I didn't even find it that strange when we were the only two people in it, I just thought no one else was showing up. I think it took me three months before I figured out that he was flirting with me and then another two before I agreed to hang out in a non-academic setting. Being study buddies, turned friends, made the rest easier. Christopher was also career-focused, so neither of us prioritized our social lives, and that suited me well because I never wanted a social life. Everything progressed naturally for us.

We dated all through our four years at university. Moved in together and both got hired on at his family's publishing company. The literary agent and the author. How cute, right?

Everything was great, until it wasn't. At least, that's what I thought.

After coming home from a trip to New York, he ended things. He said he wanted to do some soul-searching and couldn't do that while in a relationship with me. Nine years we were together. I'm thankful he didn't give me the "it's not you, it's me," but hearing someone say they won't be able to find themselves while being in a relationship with you stings.

The sad part is, I wasn't heartbroken.

I packed up my stuff, moved into an open unit in the same building and kept working. This all led me to realize I don't think I like my life much. I followed my plan seamlessly and yet I wasn't terribly happy.

Unfortunately, this realization brought on a nasty case of writer's block. Thus, the scenery change, etcetera, etcetera.

Even with my failed relationship behind me, talking to men? Not a skill of mine.

Aspen liked Chris; she didn't love him. Her words, not mine, so when I mentioned my interaction with Jackson, she was offended that I didn't even ask for his phone number. She thinks our collision should have warranted an exchange of insurance and personal information. I did make it clear we were not in our vehicles, but her only response was 'minor details.'

The only commonality between my best friend and me is our choice of creative careers. Aspen has always been a social butterfly. I think she was friends with every person in our grade all through school, part of any club that would let her in, and captain of the dance team. I was friendly, but not friends with anyone but her, and only attended meetings or events if she forced me to.

I think our differences make the friendship that much better.

As much as I would like to spend my Saturday thinking about Jackson, I put him out of my mind. Guys with faces like that aren't interested in girls who forget how to talk in public.

Even though I got almost no work done this week, I am forcing myself to not work over the weekend. I am hoping maintaining a routine will allow my brain to be on when it needs to be and off when I allow it.

Turning it on is still a problem.

One of the things that comes from realizing you aren't happy with your life, is not knowing how to spend your time. Should I be making changes everywhere? If there are too many new variables, how do I know which aspect fixed the funk? Spending the weekend deep cleaning the cottage seemed like neutral territory. All the cleaning solutions here smell like bleach and I am avoiding The General Store for a couple more days because my interaction with Sam is still making me feel a bit weird inside, so a trip to the grocery store across town was warranted.

I had no Jackson sightings all weekend.

I'm not sure if that makes me happy or sad. I am happy there weren't any chances to embarrass myself. But I also wouldn't have minded a peek or two of him out and about. Maybe if I see him doing normal people things, I will remember that I can act normal next time I see him.

By Tuesday evening, I started to go stir crazy.

There is a very cute bookstore in town that I think may be the cure.

Like most bookworms, I've always found comfort in bookstores. They're always quiet and warm and there is no expectation to socialize.

As a child, my parents often joked that they were wasting money on day camps and summer programs. I would have been just as happy to be dropped off at a bookstore all day and left alone.

The weather is unusually warm for this time of year, but perfect for a bike ride into town.

After locking my bike out front, I grab my tote from the basket and head inside.

I am instantly assaulted with the smell of books, old and new. This store has a nice combination of bestsellers and classics. They even have a section at the back titled "Leave a Book, Take a Book" where you are able to get a used book for free as long as you leave one of your own. I love the concept, though I never participate.

I have an unhealthy relationship with all my paperbacks and haven't been able to give any up yet. I am an avid re-reader, so I think that justifies my hoard of books at home.

There is a girl behind the counter that I have seen here a

couple of times over the years. She's got the whole piercings, dark hair and eye makeup look going on, which she rocks. I think my grandma has mentioned that her family owns the shop.

I can't imagine anything greater than growing up in a bookstore like this one. Maybe the grass is always greener, but not when it comes to books.

After she finishes with an older gentleman buying a book about World War II, she waves me over to her. I am feeling a bit more confident than usual being surrounded by books, so I put one foot in front of the other and try to channel corporate Lillian in hopes I don't embarrass myself and can keep shopping here in the future.

"Hi there, I'm Julia. Is there anything I can help you with?" she asks.

"No, I'm just browsing. I love this place, figured it would be a good almost midweek pick-me-up," I responded.

"If you need something to improve your day, or week, I have just the thing for you. Fair warning, it's not a book," she says with a mischievous smile. Her eyes drift towards the back of the store and I follow her gaze. Among the psychological thriller section is none other than Jackson. I feel my cheeks redden immediately.

Julia catches my blush and gives me a knowing smile. "Yeah, talk about godly genetics. We don't get a lot of guys like him around here."

And he reads, I think to myself.

"And he reads!" she says, mirroring my exact thoughts. I can't help the small laugh that comes out of my mouth. At least I'm not the only one not immune to Jackson's good looks. And a guy that reads, a solid twelve out of ten.

He must hear our chatter because he looks over his shoulder towards us and locks eyes on me.

"I'm not one to call dibs, but that smolders he is giving you says he's all yours anyway." Julia raises her eyebrow in question.

"I've met him once before," I tell her. "Nothing happening there. I'm surprised he even remembers me."

"It looks like he remembers you just fine because he's headed this way. Quick, pretend we aren't talking about him." She throws her dark hair over her shoulder and pretends to type on the computer, leaving me standing here awkwardly.

"Hey, Lillian. How have you been?"

I turn slightly towards him and try not to blush. "I've been doing okay. How have you been?" I can see out of the corner of my eye Julia is trying to not look like she's watching us. She's not hiding it very well.

"Good, good," he says. Lifting the books in his hand, he adds, "Just getting some reading material. Outside of work, I've had a bit of free time here."

"Oh, that's good. Reading is good." I cringe. I swear my vocabulary is currently at level with a second grader.

Julia thankfully steps in. "Can I ring you through or are you still browsing?"

"Oh, um, actually, I think I'm going to keep looking around a bit more." He looks at me for a moment and I think he wants to browse with me? Hoping I'm not totally off base, I ask, "I'm just browsing, if you want to join me?"

He gives me a relieved smile and gestures with his hand towards the nearest aisle. I'm excited I read that situation correctly, but the feeling quickly vanishes because I've now opened myself up to more conversation with Jackson. I'm mentally preparing for the embarrassment I'm sure to feel soon.

As I comb through the books to my left, pretending to be interested in the latest Stephen King release, Jackson stops directly in front of me and turns.

"Sorry if I'm intruding on your time. I've spent all day in front of my computer and I wouldn't mind some human interaction. I caught myself listening to Marge at The Inn's bingo drama earlier and decided I needed to get out."

"And you choose a bookstore as your socialization spot?" I ask, lacing humour in my voice so he doesn't take offense.

He smiles and says, "I know, right? Was my next spot a library, or even the cemetery? Truthfully, I was just wandering and stumbled upon this place and thought I should get some reading material. I can say that I'm certainly glad I did because I found you here."

I try not to blush, but I must be because Jackson smiles, and his teeth are perfectly straight, because of course they are. I wonder if he had braces or just hit the genetic jackpot. I'm betting on genetics.

"Well, if human interaction is what you want, then let's interact," I say rather awkwardly.

He ignores my blunder and asks, "So are you into horror? Maybe we should hit up the cemetery after all." I look at him, beyond confused, so he gestures towards the book in my hand. I quickly put the book down.

"Honestly, no. I don't like scary movies very much either

unless I watch them somewhere I never have to go again. Does that make sense?"

He starts to walk towards the next aisle and I follow.

"Yeah, I get that. Linking the scary movie to a place would make it spookier. I don't mind horror, but I'm not big into gore. Give me ghosts any day."

I visibly shudder as a chill runs through me thinking of ghosts, trying to wrap my sweater around myself tightly. We are now in the romance section, certainly a guilty pleasure of mine, but not my favourite of all the genres, which is what I tell Jackson.

"I have never read a romance book. Should I try one?" he asks.

"Only if you want to. Some of them are cute, but there are also dark ones, too. Maybe you would like those better?" I offer.

"Dark how?"

I am red as a tomato as I say, "Like being kidnapped by a mafia prince. But in a good way."

He grabs a book from the shelf to our left. "What about this one? It has haunting in the title. Ghost romance?"

I smack the book out of his hand without even thinking and say, "No, don't start there." He looks at me a little stunned but recovers well.

"Maybe a sports romance? You look athletic," I say, grabbing a book I've never read with a hockey stick on the front cover. I put it on top of the others in his stack and then walk out of this section as quickly as I can without sprinting.

Thankfully, I know where my favourite section is, so I make my way towards the poetry while Jackson follows behind me.

"Is it safe to assume you like poetry?" Jackson asks.

I nod while focusing on the spines in front of me. I don't need to buy any new books, but I love looking.

"Which is your favourite?"

"I can't say I have one. I'm a bit of a mood reader with every genre. I think with poetry especially, you want to read to suit your mood. Or sometimes I read to change my mood. A good poem can definitely do that. At least for me."

Jackson looks more interested than I assumed he would.

"That makes sense. I can't say I've read a poem since grade twelve English class, but I'm about to read a hockey romance, so I am certainly open to broadening my reading palate." He scans the shelf a bit before grabbing a small book. "Gord Downie wrote a poetry book? Sign me up."

"I can't say I have read any of his work, but you can let me know how you like it."

While he continues to browse this section, I take note of the conversation we have had so far. It is honestly not going too terribly. Aside from the book-throwing earlier, I would give myself a seven out of ten for this interaction, and I am proud of the conversation I have held.

There must be a bookstore fairy somewhere working her magic in my favour.

There is one more section I want to check out before I leave, but I would rather not venture there with Jackson. I try to sneak away while he reads a bit of the book in his hand, but by the time I make it to the children's section, he is right behind me.

As casually as I can, I grab a couple of my most recent books and then swiftly head towards Julia at the cash register. I basically throw the books on the counter, hoping Julia can bag them quickly.

The bookstore fairy has failed me because Jackson asks, "Do you often buy children's books and try to hide them?"

Trying to be as vague as possible, I say, "Sometimes."

He nods to himself, clearly understanding I am not going to offer any more information, and pretends to look away while I make my purchase. Julia gives me a questioning look, so I shake my head, trying to dismiss this whole interaction. I don't want her asking questions that I have to answer in front of Jackson.

I thank Julia and then wait for Jackson to buy his books. I would like to leave this store as soon as possible, but that is not a reason to be rude to someone who spent thirty minutes listening to me talk about books.

With our bags in hand, we exit the store to dimly lit Main Street. I know I've made this awkward and now my rating of my performance has lowered from a seven to a four.

It's not that I don't want Jackson to know I write children's books, it's just that...

Actually, that is exactly it. I like my career, and outside of the current block, I am good at it, but I don't like talking about it for some reason.

Thankfully, all my work is printed under L. Shaw, so it would be hard for him to connect the dots right now.

Knowing I need to end this before it gets worse, I start unlocking my bike while Jackson stands there staring at me.

Jackson looks like he is about to say something, but I stop him with a wave over my shoulder as I mount my bike. Before he can compute what has happened, I'm halfway home.

This might have been a bit rude, but panic is not my friend, and I know I would have stuck my foot in my mouth if I stayed any longer.

When I get back to the cottage, I unload my purchases, leaving the children's books next to my computer. Hopefully re-reading some of my own work will help get the creativity going in my head.

The rest of the week unfortunately drags on. Knowing Aspen will be spending the weekend has me counting down the hours most days. I need out of my head and she is one of the only people with the skills to accomplish just that.

Chapter 6
Jackson

My boat arrived last week. It is now clean, fueled and docked at the marina in town.

I met my slip neighbours as well. Rick has a similar-sized vessel, but his is fancier. He said he has a family of five and they live in London (Ontario, not England), so they spend most weekends in Bluefield. Overall, he was a very friendly guy, asked about my work and family. We don't have a lot in common, which is fine, but I'm still not used to sharing personal information with strangers like everyone seems to in Bluefield.

I couldn't tell you the names or occupations of any of the people I share a floor with in my condo building in Toronto. Small towns are weird. Rick seemed shocked that I owned my own boat.

I don't think it's that unreasonable for my age. I don't have any dependents and I've managed my money well.

Obviously growing up well-off has given me a head start, but I've worked hard for everything I have now.

Both personally and professionally.

I know most people my age wouldn't be in the position I am at my father's company. But experience isn't always everything. I dropped everything and moved myself to some random town to make sure I could be as hands-on as possible for this project. I may have been my father's first choice, because he wants me to prove myself, but I have a suspicion I might have been his only choice.

Most of my colleagues wouldn't have packed up and relocated over an hour from home for four months.

I am blessed to say the crew on my site has warmed up to me. I think they appreciate that I don't micromanage like my father has been known to do. He is a firm believer in "if you want something done right, do it yourself." That is not my style, and it has worked out for me so far.

Since my interaction with Lillian on Tuesday, I have been trying to figure out what went wrong. It seemed like we were both having a good time, and then suddenly she was hiding the children's books she wanted to buy and acting flighty. I've considered that she might have a child and doesn't want me to know.

As soon as I saw what section we were in, I did double check she didn't have a ring on her left hand. It was thankfully empty, but that doesn't mean she's not a single or unmarried mom.

Or maybe she likes the simplicity of a children's book. Both scenarios are fine with me. But it doesn't seem like she has kids in town here with her, and from our conversation about her likes, dislikes and love of poetry, her reading at an elementary school level seems far-fetched.

I was on cloud nine when we were in the poetry section. She seemed almost at ease with me for the first time, and overall, I remembered how to have a conversation with her. Big step up from the restaurant encounter.

I felt like I got my charm back and then poof, she was gone.

Is this the chase some people talk about? I don't think I like it. I'm willing to put the work in if that's what it takes to get her to talk to me, I just feel like I'm missing something.

I've never had to or wanted to put this much effort into something with a girl before, but I remember guys in high school talking about chasing after girls being half the fun. But Lillian isn't acting like she wants to be chased. If anything, I think she's indifferent towards me.

Even if our encounter ended on a weird note, I can't say I'm discouraged. The short time we have spent together felt good. She's shy, but I think I like it. When she does talk, it's not to fill space.

She has interesting perspectives and opinions that I want to hear.

I've decided I can't live off takeout only, so I need to stock some non-perishables in my room at the Inn. I also need to stock up on emergency food for the boat. On my way to the grocery store, I remember I need to call my cousin Simon for a catch-up. We normally see each other multiple times a week, either in the building we both live in, or we will meet at the gym or our neighbourhood pub.

"Hey, man, your hair turned grey yet?" he greets me. Simon is convinced that because the main population of Bluefield outside of the summer months is sixty-five plus, I'm destined for a retirement home.

"Nope, still brown and lush, my friend. No need to worry about me," I say with a chuckle.

"Good to hear, good to hear. I hadn't heard from you for almost a week, so I was worried the technology in your phone may be too advanced."

Simon thinks he is a lot funnier than he is.

Knowing I need to stop this because he will go on for hours with his jokes, I say, "I actually need some advice."

"And you came to the master. My young friend, that was smart of you."

He is only a couple of months older than me but loves playing the young card. He has an older sister, so he has decided I should be filling the role of younger brother in his life.

"You accused me of being elderly a minute ago and now I'm young. Which is it?" I ask. "You know what, never mind, I don't want to get off topic again... I met a girl."

He waits for so long to respond that I check to make sure the call hasn't dropped. "Are you still there, Si?"

"Yeah, I'm here. I just don't know what advice I am supposed to give. You met a girl and what?"

"Well, I'm trying to get to know her, but I'm not really sure how. You've dated quite a bit, what are the beginning steps?"

"Beginning steps?" he questions. "Are you trying to tell me that Jackson Mane, my cousin Jackson, lady killer Jackson, is trying to pursue something beyond a casual hookup?"

"When you say it like that I sound like a sleaze." I duck my head a bit in my car, suddenly feeling like everyone in the grocery store parking lot is judging me.

"You aren't a sleaze, per se. But you have a bit of a reputation. I mean, you've never had a girlfriend, but you also are never short of female companionship. That's kind of your thing," he says.

Just because it's true doesn't mean it's something I'm overly proud of. I hadn't thought much about it until now. It was just my normal.

"Well, maybe I don't want it to be my thing," I say grumpily. "Can you give me advice or not? I don't want to be judged for the consensual situations I have been in previously. All parties knew the score. No one was ever looking for something more."

"Ok, ok. No need to get upset. I can help, maybe. Or maybe I'm not actually the best for this."

"What do you mean?" I ask. "You've had plenty of girl-friends."

"Well..." he starts. "None of my relationships last more than a month or two, which I'm mostly okay with. That's the amount of time it takes for me to realize it isn't going to work, so I end it.

If you want my advice on short relationships, that's my specialty. If you see real potential with this girl…Maybe don't listen to me. I obviously haven't figured it out yet."

That isn't super helpful for me, but at least he's self-aware.

"So maybe not, then. She's a bit gun-shy, so I need to think this through before I do anything." I take a deep breath to centre my thoughts.

"Define gun-shy."

"I think I can confidently say that she is shy, period. But she's also flighty. The last time I saw her, she just took off without much of a goodbye. And then there's the whole, I forget how to talk around her. Sometimes I'm charming and then other times I feel like I have no control over what's coming out of my mouth. The whole situation has me feeling like I am treading water and I'm not sure if I'm sinking or swimming at this point. But I can't stop thinking about her, even though I've literally talked to her twice ever, so I don't know her that well, but… I don't know, dude, there's just something about her. Not to mention she is also so damn pretty, I feel like I'm creepily staring at her half the time. It's all just…I don't know. I don't know."

Simon breaks out into a fit of laughter. "You've got it bad, my man. Boy, do you have it bad. I wish I could be more helpful, but I don't want to give you bad advice and then you end up mad at me. Sorry, dude, you are on your own."

I huff out a breath. That isn't what I wanted to hear, but I respect his honesty. I would rather him not send me astray, so I guess it's back to the drawing board. Not that there's anything to even put on the board. I have no idea how to track her down. Aside from wandering Main Street all day, every day until I see her again, I'm going to have to leave it up to fate. I just hope our next interaction ends better than the last.

"Wait." Simon breaks my train of thought. "Is this the girl you dumped food on?"

"Yeah, that would be the one. Her name is Lillian, by the way. We don't need to refer to her as 'the girl' anymore."

"Okay, testy. You already sound protective over the girl. *Sorry*, I mean Lillian. This is going to be so interesting." As Simon continues chuckling to himself, I realize I've been sitting in the parking lot for almost thirty minutes now.

Needing to end the phone call, I say, "Well, thanks for your help, I guess. I'm going to spend the rest of the day on the water, hopefully clear my head. I'll call you sometime next week."

"I want an update as soon as there is one on the lovely Lillian. Talk soon, brother."

I pocket my phone and head into the store for some chips and pop.

With sustenance acquired, I am out on the open water. I may be biased, based on my current location, but not many bodies of water are nicer than Lake Huron. The sandy beach mixed with an undisturbed horizon can rival most Caribbean vacations. Today is all about exploring for me. I haven't spent much time on this lake by boat, so I want to make sure I get a feel for the area and other boaters on the lake. Then I plan to anchor near one of the job sites that's on the water, mostly because I can.

What is the point in owning a property on a private beach if I never use it?

Chapter 7
Lillian

"I'm here, Billy!" Aspen yells, plowing through the front door, her bags flying everywhere as she body slams me to the ground. I think sometimes she forgets that all the kickboxing she does every morning means that her seemingly slim frame is not frail and I can barely breathe under her bicep.

"Asp. Can't. Breathe."

"Oh, don't be so dramatic," she quips, while removing her limbs from on top of mine. "I missed you and I have exciting news about LB."

"What is an LB?" I ask while collecting her discarded bags. Considering she's staying the weekend, the three large suitcases seem a bit overboard.

"LB is not a what, he's a who. Duh. Lover Boy... Jackson? Come on, girl, keep up. Small-town life is bad for your brain," she huffs out.

Oof. Aspen and her nicknames. I'm not even going to bother fighting her on this one. "Okay," I concede. "What is this new development?"

"Have you seen the signs around your neighbourhood?" she asks.

"Like street signs? What are you talking about?"

"No, not street signs, my sweet, sweet friend. Construction signs!"

I'm not sure I understand her enthusiasm. Should I be excited about all the construction surrounding me?

"I mean, yeah, there's a lot of renovations and rebuilds happening, but other than the noise and ugly equipment, it doesn't really affect me."

Grabbing my shoulders with each hand, she shakes me side to side. "Mane Construction! Mane!"

What is she talking about? I feel like we aren't even speaking the same language right now.

"Aspen, I have no idea what that means."

Rolling her eyes, she responds, "Okay, I know this is more in my domain than yours, but come on. Jackson Mane. There's no way you meet a hottie named Jackson while his father's construction company is everywhere and it's not him!"

She stares at my confused face before breaking out into laughter. Like dropping to her knees laughter. Have I ever mentioned my best friend is a bit dramatic?

Once she catches her breath, she stops rolling on the floor and says, "Billy, you are like the worst Toronto private school girl ever. Jackson Mane hosted the best parties. If you were cool, you were at those parties. And if you wanted to be cool, you made sure to get an invite. Come on, girl." I grab her hand and pull her off the floor, directing her to follow me upstairs as I lug all of her bags.

"Okay, we both know I was not cool, so I'm not sure why you are surprised. I had one friend, and it was you," I respond.

"You are mistaking popular for cool. You were cool. Everyone liked you. But we are getting off topic. Lover Boy is Jackson Mane. This is great news," she pleads.

"I don't know how you think this is great news. I have a crush on a party boy. This is the worst news ever," I cry, flopping down on the bed in one of the guest rooms.

"Well, first off, glad you are finally admitting you do, in fact, have a crush on him. The first step is acceptance. And second, from what I remember, yes, he was a party boy, but he was nice, never unruly or out of control like some of the guys he hung out with. Nothing like his jerkface cousin. From what you've told me, Jackson seems interested in you, and this isn't high school. There is no reason this can't be something great for you."

"Okay, okay, let's not get ahead of ourselves here." If I don't slow Aspen's roll now, she'll have our entire wedding planned by the end of the night. She is great, but maybe not the best wingwoman. She has no chill, always full speed ahead. "So we know his name, that's great. Maybe a bit stalker*ish*, but we will call it great. I think the logical next step is to do nothing, because nothing is happening. I've run into him a couple of times around town, had some chats. We are acquaintances at this point, not even friends, so let's just drop this for now."

Aspen rolls her eyes at me but then smiles and pulls me up from the bed. I know this isn't the end of this, but I appreciate her backing off for now.

She then dives in on an update of her work. She's currently working for a big interior design firm in Toronto that she kind of hates. Most of her clients are great but boring. She is a big believer in money can't buy taste. I know very little about all of this, but I do agree with her that white and beige houses do seem a bit boring.

She worked for this company every summer as an unpaid intern and then was hired on right after graduation.

They are the "it" company apparently, but they are killing her creativity. For someone as full of life as Aspen, her whole life she's felt like people are trying to dim her. I can't imagine her any way but herself. She's one of the very best people I know.

After letting her settle in a bit, Aspen demands we wash off the work week in the lake. Although it is still a bit cold for my liking, the weather this week was as gloomy as my creativity. Today is beautiful, so we head down the stairs to the sandy beach. Setting our towels down, I strip off the oversized t-shirt that was covering my simple black bikini and we both run screaming into the lake.

Yup, it's cold.

Aspen immediately dives under the water, somehow emerging looking just as good as before, while I'm sure I resemble a drowned rat. Aspen's long, thick brown hair is always impossibly straight while still somehow holding the right kind of volume on top. The hair with her high-cut red one-piece is giving her that Baywatch look.

Then there's me.

People have always said they are envious of my curls, but I have worked for years getting the combination of hair products right to ensure I don't look like Shirley Temple. All those products mean I refuse to dunk my head in the lake. Some may say it's vain; I'm saying it's better for the health of the lake that it isn't exposed to what I have going on.

I tie my hair on top of my head, and then we venture out to the second sandbar where we bob up and down for a while, enjoying the calm evening.

Being early in the season, we don't have to worry about too many boats disturbing the wake.

As soon as the thought leaves my head, a speed boat goes flying past us, a bit too close in my opinion, blaring country music.

It pulls up in front of the Waldens' cottage and cuts the engine.

Now, I don't want to be a Karen, but if this is some college kid thinking he can party on his boat all night, I will sic Aspen on him. I hate confrontation, but I do love order and rules.

While glaring at the boat, trying to figure out what they are doing, Aspen squeals as one of the waves the boat created while weaving around us plows directly over mine and Aspen's heads.

Drowned rat, nice to meet you.

We both come up sputtering and coughing water. This catches the attention of Mr. Annoying Boat. I can see him look over his shoulder, and just as I was expecting him to shout an apology our way, he waves and smiles. Yup, just a wave.

Aspen grumbles something not very ladylike under her breath and then yells, "No, it's cool, we're not drowning. Carry on with your night."

That forces a laugh out of the boater man's lips. He at least has the sense to look sheepish as he yells, "Sorry," in our direction.

Now that I am sufficiently soaked, and the peace we were enjoying is gone, we both swim our way back to the beach, flopping down face-first on our towels. Catching our breaths, neither of us move until the setting sun is blocked out by a figure behind us. Aspen giggles, causing me to look over my shoulder at... Holy mother Mary, Jackson Mane is standing behind me.

I discover three things at this moment.

One, Jackson Mane likes country music.

Me, too.

Two, Jackson Mane is not a very polite boat driver.

I guess he can't be perfect.

Three, Jackson Mane is seeing me look like a drowned rat for the second time.

Why me?

"Hey, Lil." He grins, not looking the least bit apologetic anymore. Aspen reduced to a giggling teenager beside me, repeats his greeting under her breath for only us to hear. Jackson takes a step back, tugging at the hair on the back of his neck when I don't reply. Now that I'm drawn away from his face, I not-so-subtly trace the lines of his chest muscles, leading me to his—oh, of course, there are at least six muscles on his stomach. There might be eight, but the lines leading below to his swim trunks have temporarily distracted me.

Yup, he was carved from marble.

Aspen finally breaks the awkward silence and pulls me out of the daydream. I'm sure by now Jackson has taken note that I've been ogling him.

She flips onto her butt and I follow suit.

"Aspen Arthur." She holds out her hand. "Nice to officially meet you, Jackson Mane." If he's shocked that she knows who he is, he doesn't let it show as he takes her hand in a friendly shake.

"Aspen, nice to meet you, too. Although, I'm sure you've been inside my house before, so maybe nice to see you again would be more appropriate."

Is he flirting with her? Noooooooooo. I mean, Aspen would never go for him regardless, but I would love not to feel invisible here. He's still staring at her, and I swear there is a twinkle in his eye.

This is where I die. Death by twinkle.

Aspen gives him a bit of a confused look, then turns her head towards me.

Oh, hey guys, yeah, I'm still here.

She widens her eyes and I realize that I haven't said a single word. I've been silent since he appeared. Dear lord Lillian, no wonder he's not paying attention to you, you've forgotten how to talk.

"Hi," I say, a bit more quietly than I intended.

I put a lock of hair behind my ear and then remember what it looks like. I quickly readjust the bun on the top of my head, hoping I'm making it better, not worse. I know there is no hope for it and drop my hands, defeated, at my sides.

Jackson doesn't seem to notice my internal panic as he says, "Sorry about the waves and cutting so close to you two in the water. I hadn't seen anyone swimming around here since I've been here, so I wasn't paying as much attention as I should have been. Completely my mistake, I shouldn't have assumed there wouldn't be anyone around."

I can see the sincerity on his face and in his tone.

"It's okay, we also assumed there wouldn't be any boats around, so it may have been hard to see us," I offer.

That seems to ease his guilt and that winning smile returns to his face. I know a minute ago I was begging for him to give me attention, but now I feel like I might melt under the warm glow that is Jackson Mane.

God, even his name is kind of hot. Is that possible? Can people have hot names? Lillian Shaw is so *not* a hot name, that's for sure.

"So, Jackson Mane," Aspen cuts in. "What are you and your boat doing over here? Are you stalking my dear friend?" She points to me.

Aspen may be team Jackson and Lillian, but that doesn't mean she won't give him a hard time. She does so with every single male she encounters. It's kind of her thing.

Jackson doesn't seem put off by her questioning at all. "I own— Well, technically my father's company owns the cottage right there." He gestures towards the Waldens' place, proving Aspen's theory to be true. This also means he's been next door this whole time and I didn't notice.

Without thinking, I blurt, "The noise. You're responsible for the noise."

Smooth.

"I mean, I'm in the cottage next door," I say, pointing behind us. "It's normally quiet this time of year, so the construction has been different."

Aspen gives me a pitying nod that I'm choosing to believe means "great save" and not "stop talking" because apparently, I can't stop.

"The noise doesn't bother me, it's just there, you know? Noise."

Normally I can hardly talk in front of this guy and now I can't stop. Noise is starting to sound weird like scenery still does.

Aspen grabs my hand and squeezes while giving me a slight shake of the head. I know for sure that means stop. So stop, Lillian.

I look back up to Jackson and his smile has dimmed slightly, but it's still there. He chuckles a bit under his breath. It almost sounds nervous. He goes to stuff his hands in his pockets that don't exist and reroutes them to his hips in a very Captain America kind of way. He could be related to Chris Evans; they both have a lot of muscles.

"If it's been too noisy, I am sorry... There isn't a whole lot I can do about it, but let me know if it's affecting your working hours." He pauses, seeming to regain some confidence. "I will say, I am happy to find out we are technically neighbours. What are the odds?"

I'm not really sure how to reply to this and Aspen, being the best friend a girl can ask for, knows that if we keep talking about noise, I may never recuperate.

"So you have a boat?" she asks.

"Yeah," he responds. "I'm keeping it at the marina for the summer while I'm here. Figured I'd need something to keep me busy since there isn't a whole lot to do here."

"Maybe you could take us out sometime?" she asks with a glint in her eye. I'm not sure what she's planning, but she is most definitely up to something.

Jackson looks thrilled by this idea. "Of course. How long are you in town? We could go out this weekend for sure."

"Sunday afternoon would be perfect. I have to head back into the city Monday morning."

"Does that work with you, Lil?" he asks me.

I muster up a small smile and nod, still not trusting my voice or whatever words could potentially come out of my mouth.

"Great, awesome. Sunday afternoon. I should get your number in case anything comes up, but I'll just pick you guys up from here?" he asks, pulling out his phone and looking back and forth between the two of us.

Aspen takes the phone when she sees I have no intention of moving from my spot. "I put Lillian's number in. Makes more sense in the long run."

Yup, she's planning our wedding.

Chapter 8
Jackson

I have a date today.

Apparently.

Cool. Very cool.

I can be cool about this.

Except I may or may not have ever been on a real date.

And by that, I mean I have never been on a real date. Don't get me wrong, I've taken girls out for dinner, but the end goal was also established ahead of time, so aside from making a reservation at a nice restaurant, I've never had to put any effort in.

But I can handle this.

I will handle this. I left things to fate and what would you know, not only am I hanging out with the girl I'm crushing on today, alone, I now know where she lives and I have her phone number. Everything is coming up Jackson, baby.

Her comments about the construction noise did throw me off a little, but her rambling was pretty cute. I am going to try and see if we can possibly keep the louder machines from running during certain times of the day so it's not as constant, if possible. If not, maybe I can gift her noise-cancelling headphones or something.

Regardless, I feel like I'm back in the game.

I spent all day yesterday cleaning the boat again. This beauty has never looked better. I also stocked up on snacks, both sweet and salty, as well as a variety of beverages ranging from water, still and carbonated, to plain old beer.

I even bought a wicker basket to put everything into. I think I saw that in The Notebook or something, so hopefully Lillian likes it.

I stocked the boat with fluffy towels and every range of sunscreen that was available at The General Store.

The kid at the counter, was super weird, but he did pull more product from the back, so I can't complain much. I am going to rock this date.

I am ninety-nine point nine percent sure Lillian does not think we are on a date.

She has apologized for Aspen bailing on us no less than thirty times, and I only picked her up five minutes ago. I'm not sure what story Lillian got as to why Aspen suddenly had to leave for work, but Lillian seems frazzled by it all.

Never fear, I am on my A-game today. Feeling good, the charm is intact, I can totally turn this all around in my favour.

Once Lillian is situated in the seat behind me, I set off away from shore and cruise at a low speed.

One of the problems with boating around is that it isn't the best way to have a conversation, so I figure we can move around for a bit to ease into things and then I'll drop anchor somewhere and we can chat while we eat our snacks.

Lillian seems peaceful where she sits, and I am trying my best to keep my eyes in front of me and not glued to her body.

When I pulled the boat in front of her cottage and she made her way into the water, she still had on some sort of mesh dress over her bathing suit. At some point in the last ten minutes, the mesh has been removed, and good riddance to it because my god, her body. She has on a black two-piece suit that seems to only have the required amount of fabric needed and not a scrap more.

It isn't what I was expecting her to be wearing, but as I try to keep my tongue in my mouth, I can't say I have a bad word to say about it.

There are a lot of strings and ties everywhere keeping her breasts, a perfect handful, in place. What has most of my atten-tion is the lack of fabric heading towards her ass.

It certainly is all eyes on her when she dives into the lake after I drop anchor.

We float around a bit and make general small talk. She tells me about some of her favourite childhood memories in Bluefield, most involving Aspen or her brother, especially the one summer when his obsession with Ron's hotdogs led to him now banning the meat from his house completely.

I fill in the gaps with stories about Simon and I causing trouble at his family's place in the Kawarthas.

I do find it interesting that she has little to no reaction when I mention Simon.

When I texted him about running into Lillian and Aspen, he had a lot of questions about Aspen. I guess they have some sort of history, or he knew her in high school, I'm not really sure, but his interest was piqued.

Either Lillian is good at hiding her thoughts or she and Aspen did not have a similar conversation about Simon. It isn't my place to say, so I will keep his thoughts away from her.

Once we have drained most of our energy treading water, I lay out some towels on the front of the boat and grab all the snacks and drinks I bought. I'm not sure if Lillian is impressed or shocked by my level of preparation.

"Wow, you really went all out. I guess you bought enough for three people. Sorry again about Aspen." I feel a bit awkward because I bought everything with only the two of us in mind, but she doesn't need to know that.

"It really isn't a problem. I'm glad we have this time to get to know each other more," I say as I crack open a can of sparkling water. Lillian is sticking to flat, so I will try to remember that for next time.

"This is relaxing, isn't it?" I ask, hoping to steer the conversation away from Aspen. Lillian takes another sip of her drink and then adjusts her sunglasses.

"Yeah, it's nice. Thank you for taking me out today," she says with a small smile. I was hoping for a bit more enthusiasm, but beggars can't be choosers.

With Lillian's sunglasses on, I'm having trouble getting a read on her. Staring at myself in the reflection is a step down from her striking blue eyes.

We sit in comfortable silence for a bit. I can't say it's very common for me to feel comfortable in silence with most people, especially when I barely know them, but Lillian has such a calm presence, I feel like I could let the day get away from us and not even notice.

"So," Lillian begins, after some time has passed and most of the food is gone, "you're working on the renovation at the Waldens' old place. Is that your only job right now? Wait. What is your job, besides me just grouping it in 'construction' in my head?"

The smile on my face is arguably too large for the topic of conversation, but something about Lillian asking about me has me overly excited.

I don't know if I'm starved for attention here or just desperate for hers.

"I'm an architect, technically. That's what I went to school for, and it's what I've been doing since graduation. This project is a bit different because I'm also managing everything. I have foremen on most sites, but the overall project is on me."

I pause for a moment, trying to decide how much I want to explain. I figure that if I'm trying to get to know her, I should let her get to know me.

"We have around ten properties that have been purchased over the last couple of years that we are doing complete renovations on. Unfortunately, that involves a wrecking ball in a lot of cases. Most of the infrastructure in these cottages needs to be replaced and it's more cost effective to start from scratch. That, and the buyers we have lined up want a lot more square footage in their cottages and luxury finishes than would be possible if we did a simple flip. We have more clients interested than properties, so I am hoping to meet with some of the Bluefield town council about zoning on some undeveloped land soon."

"Wow, that's really interesting. I'm not going to lie, I was shocked to see the Waldens' place flattened, but also not surprised." A look of worry on her face flashes across her face.

"There was always worry that a storm would break something off their cottage and end up going through one of our windows." We both laugh at the thought of that.

Now I know this is the point where I ask her about her job, but I won't. The last time we talked about her working here, she was evasive and seemed uncomfortable, which I don't want.

I think keeping the conversation on me until she volunteers more information is probably the best plan of action moving forward.

I decide to tell her more about some of my favourite jobs and funny stories from when I was first starting out.

"Like most cocky twentysomethings, I tried to put every unique architectural challenge into one of my first jobs. When

I took a step back before sending the design to my supervisor, I could see that I created a house that not only was not structurally sound, it looked like something a Disney villain would live in." We both laugh at my blunder, and it feels good.

Overall, she seems interested in what I have to say about myself, which is refreshing. A lot of the women I normally spend time with want to talk about pop culture or gossip and we normally skip the getting to know each other portion of dates. When I took on this project, I had no idea it would lead to meeting such a genuine person like Lillian.

"I am so glad we ran into each other here. Or I guess, I ran into you, that is," I say, hoping she understands I value her time. "How convenient is it that we both are here for the next couple of months and we met within a week of arriving? I am genuinely excited to get to know you this summer and hopefully spend more time together."

Now this is the moment where I think I should try to ask her out again, but somewhere in the last thirty seconds, she's replaced her carefree smile with something fake.

When she doesn't say anything, I ask, "Is everything okay?"

She clears her throat and says, "Oh, I am actually not feeling well. Maybe I'm getting motion sick. Can you take me home, please?"

She quickly starts cleaning up our picnic and makes her way towards her seat before I can truly register that this date is over.

Sensing her urgency, I haul the anchor up and start the boat, with her cottage as the destination we head towards. I had it in my mind that I would have her try steering the boat for a bit. Maybe I would stand behind her and help her control the speed.

Really, I want to do anything to get closer to her and convey that I am very much interested in her beyond friendship.

Looks like that ship has metaphorically, and literally, sailed as I approach the shore near her cottage.

The second I slow our speed; Lillian is jumping out of the boat and swimming to shore. She doesn't say anything, and as much as I want to follow her, I don't. She has my number, so hopefully I can find out if she's feeling okay later.

Chapter 9
Lillian

Convenient.

I hate that word.

That's what Jackson called us getting to know each other. Well, not in that exact sentence, but that was the meaning behind it, I'm sure. After that, I mostly shut down.

I told him I wasn't feeling great and probably got too much sun, so he took me back to my cottage. He probably knew I was faking it considering I jumped off the boat the second we were close enough for me to swim home.

I needed to get out of there before I either said something to make things even more awkward or cried.

It seems I've made a habit of leaving suddenly with him.

A simple wave over the shoulder and I'm gone. Probably not very convenient of me.

Do you know what that problem with convenience is? One day something is convenient and then suddenly you're twenty-six and have no idea what to do with your life.

Making friends with a guy in your classes is convenient.

Making your schedule match your new boyfriend's is convenient.

Getting a job at your boyfriend's family's company is convenient.

Moving into an apartment with your boyfriend to save money is convenient.

Staying with your boyfriend for years and floating through your own life is convenient.

Damn it, I don't want to be convenient!

Okay, maybe I'm projecting some of my issues with my last relationship onto my friendship with Jackson, but I don't want to end up in this same position in three months or three years.

It's probably best to cut my losses now.

Now most people would say, "Hey, maybe don't stay in a relationship out of convenience and your problem will be solved."

But the thing is, I didn't know that's what I was doing.

Aspen thinks we were basically friends with benefits who lived together. The more I think about it, the more I agree with her. When we were both home, we hung out. Our sex life was fine, not great, but he travelled a lot and I didn't often miss him. I was busy living my life.

I mean, we worked for the same company for many years and never once even tried to eat lunch together.

In hindsight, I think the best way to describe it was that we loved each other, but we weren't in love with each other.

And now I'm not sure how I feel about Jackson. He's nice and thoughtful, and boy is he good-looking.

At one point, I didn't even try to pretend I was listening because I was staring at his body and I didn't care if he knew. I'm not sure how he has a full-body tan when summer hasn't even started, but that smooth skin surrounded by so many muscles caused a glitch in my brain. Even after he jumped in the lake, his light brown hair was still perfect. I would have assumed he spent time on it in the morning, except the longer pieces on the top seem to sit in a perfect swoop all on their own. I am a bit jealous and a lot into him. Physically, that is.

If only I could be vain and say that was enough. I know it's not. I never thought I would say this about a guy that seems to be interested in me, but... I think he was trying too hard.

He's charming, there's no doubt about that, and the passion he had when talking about work was refreshing, but everything else was so surface level and a lot of nothing.

I know I'm shy, we've been over this. I still felt like I was open to being more a part of the conversation than I was able to with all his talking. It's great that I now know so much about him, because he is very forthcoming with details, but the scales seem uneven now. What does he know about me that has him wanting to spend his free time with me?

Maybe it's only physical for him.

And if that's the case, that sucks.

Maybe we should just be friends.

He's a nice enough guy, but the whole day left a strange taste in my mouth.

It's probably for the best; there's no way I'm his type anyway. I do want to give him the benefit of the doubt on a friendship level. This was supposed to be a group activity that basically turned into a date.

Which brings me to the issue I have with my so-called friend, Aspen.

There was no work emergency. I would have believed her if she got an email and said she needed to go back to the city. But that's not what happened.

There was a phone call with lots of yelling.

She threw her clothes around the room while she packed.

Fake tears when she hugged me goodbye.

And then a smile on her face as she ripped out of town. Not to mention the brand-new bathing suit she left for me on my bed.

Yeah, she set me up.

Of course, I'm not actually mad at her. Everything my best friend does is with the purest intentions. This just backfired a little, but it's not her fault. It's probably mine.

I have officially overwhelmed myself and need to take some

space from all of this. A quiet night with my book, followed by a quiet week working alone, sounds like the perfect solution.

I think I put too much emphasis on the quiet and jinxed myself. It's been two days since the boat day date thing and I'm feeling better about everything. What has me worried, however, is the loud noises coming from what used to be the Waldens' cottage. I may be overreacting, but I think I should let Jackson know what's going on.

It is currently 11 pm and I can't imagine anyone is still working. Especially because it is pitch black out there. But there is a lot of banging and clanging happening.

I debate texting him. A phone call might be overreacting, but what if there is a problem and he sleeps through the text and I could have done more? If he's asleep and misses the phone call, then I still did everything I could, so there can't be any hard feelings, right? Yeah, a phone call it is.

After two rings, he picks up. "Hey, Lil?" The gravel in his sleepy voice sends a chill down my spine. Why is that attractive? For a moment, I can't remember why I'm even calling.

"Hi, Jackson, sorry if I woke you, but there is a bit of an issue next door. Well, it might not be an issue, but there's a lot of noise and I don't think anyone is supposed to be there, given it's nighttime. I mean, maybe there is. Who am I to say what hours you let your crews work? Anyway, I wanted to call you so that you knew. I hope I didn't wake you because it might be nothing, but if it's something, then you should know. I..."

Thankfully, he stops my ramble. "Hey, hey, calm down. I just dozed off, so no harm there. I was hardly asleep and I'm glad you called."

I take what I am sure is my first breath since he answered the phone.

"There shouldn't be anyone on site at this time of night. For starters, I would never want to hinder your sleep, and it also isn't safe. I'm glad you called. I would ask if you see anyone over there, but I would rather you stay inside until I get there. I'm heading out the door now."

I hear the click of his truck unlocking and the engine start. I guess he got up and dressed as soon as I called.

"Okay, sounds good. Let me know if everything is okay, I guess. I really hope I'm not getting you out of bed for nothing."

"Better safe than sorry, Lil. Thank you for calling, I'll talk to you soon."

Once we both hang up, I head downstairs to make some tea and watch from the kitchen window. There is no way I am getting any sleep until I know whether I overreacted or not. I may want to catch a glimpse of Jackson, too.

I am a bit excited that I got to talk to Jackson, so maybe I'm not as set on just friendship as I thought. Calling Aspen on the phone certainly doesn't give me butterflies.

Just as a pair of headlights come around the bend, all noise next door abruptly stops. As I press my face up to the window, trying to see if there is anyone moving around, I see Jackson exit his truck and hide the fact that he's laughing at my sleuthing. Yeah, he just caught me with a piggy nose against the window.

Cute.

He disappears for a couple of minutes and I can see his flash-light shining all around the property.

Just as I sit on the couch, so it doesn't seem like I'm watching him, a knock sounds at the door. Even though I know it's just Jackson, the sound startles me more than it should. Quickly, I make my way to the back door to let him in, only there's no one there. I step out the door and look around, assuming Jackson took a step away for some reason, but he's not there.

A chill runs down my spine, and it is nothing like the giddy one I felt earlier.

Just as I am about to head back inside, I hear footsteps approach and Jackson appears from the side of the house.

Before he can say anything, I ask, "Did you knock at this door a couple of minutes ago?"

Frowning, he says, "No, I was just in my truck checking if I had any floodlights. Did you see anyone?"

"No, there was no one there when I opened the door. Maybe I'm just spooked and there was no knock," I offer. I am almost certain I heard a knock, but I don't want Jackson to think I'm making a big deal about this. This isn't about me.

"Did you find the source of the noise?" I ask, rerouting the conversation away from me.

"Yes, I did, unfortunately." He pulls up some photos on his phone. I see a large machine, but I don't know what to look for.

"What am I looking at?" I ask, a bit awkwardly. I don't think I could tell you the difference between a crane and a dump truck truthfully.

"Oh, sorry. This is one of our skid steers. We mostly use it to haul dirt around, but this one will be out of commission until I can replace all four tires."

Looking closer, I see the issue. There are no tires.

"Did someone...?" I ask, letting him finish my sentence.

"Remove all four tires? Yes, they did. Can't say I've ever had this happen before. If they had been slashed, I would have said it was probably teenagers, but this is a bit more technical for a prank. I'm going to have to call the police in the morning to put this through insurance."

Jackson drags his hand down his face and rubs the scruff on the side of this cheek. Taking a closer look at him, he seems more tired than he did last time I saw him. He mentioned that this job is more responsibility than his dad has given him before. This can't be helping with the pressure.

"Will this delay this job or your others at all?" Knowing little about the machine, I can't tell if this is catastrophic or not.

"Honestly, not really. It's more of an annoyance than anything. We have this same machine on a site a couple of streets over, so the crews can share them if we need them. I just hope this isn't the start of something more. I'm going to do another walk around and then hit up all the other properties to make sure this was a one-off. I'm sorry this all kept you awake."

"It's fine, I was just reading. Do you want a tea or coffee to take with you?" I ask, unsure how late he will be up tonight.

"No. I'll be okay, but thank you. You should head to bed and make sure you lock your doors. I know people don't always do that in small towns."

Before I can react, Jackson takes a step towards me and plants the lightest peck on my cheek. He gives me a small smile and a "goodnight" before retreating towards his truck. It isn't until his headlights disappear that I realize I'm still frozen in place, alone in the dark.

Shaking myself out of the daze, I quickly head back inside, locking the door that I wouldn't normally lock. Jackson was right; our cottage is down a private road and it isn't something we've ever worried about.

Even after I'm snuggled in my bed, I still feel a sense of unease about tonight's events, one that even Jackson's kiss can't erase.

Chapter 10
Jackson

GORD:

Why am I hearing about issues in Blue-field from someone who isn't you?

JACKSON:

Because I have it handled

GORD:

If I hear otherwise, you can expect my imminent arrival

Don't test me

JACKSON:

Ok.

Things could be going better. I spent most of the night driving around with a flashlight, checking on the ten active sites we have.

For the most part, I don't think there were any other issues, but I'm not around enough to know if something is missing. I sent a message out to all the most trusted people on each site to do a machine and supply inventory first thing this morning, just to make sure I haven't missed anything.

I also made a call at 7 am to the local police, as I need to send their report for my insurance company.

How my dad has already heard about this, I don't know. I obviously have someone working here that is more loyal to him than to me, but that's the least of my worries right now.

When I spoke to the dispatcher on the non-emergency line, she said a constable would be out sometime this morning. Apparently, they only have a couple constables covering Bluefield and the surrounding area for most of the offseason, and they haven't been sent the extra summer bodies yet. This isn't an emergency, so I'm not upset about waiting, but if this was a real crime, I would hope the people of Bluefield wouldn't be expected to wait.

I called the foreman, Frank, and had him direct everyone that should have been at the Waldens' to other jobs so that nothing is touched before the police get here, and so those jobs stay on schedule. Now I just need to wait for the police.

When I saw that Lillian called last night, I didn't know what to expect. It was late enough that I knew she wasn't trying to hang out, so I was hopeful for a late-night chat. Although having theft occur on the job is not ideal, I appreciate that it's given me an excuse to see Lillian.

I wanted to give her space after our date, but was starting

to worry that she was going to ghost me. Having not seriously dated much, I don't know the common timelines or when I should be calling. I may or may not have put in a Google search in a moment of weakness and the dating thread I found made me feel like a dweeb.

I'm about to pull out my phone and check the time for the fifth time in the last two minutes when Lillian appears in front of me as I sit alone on a random crate.

"Need a pick-me-up?" she asks, holding a cup of coffee towards me.

I graciously take the mug. "You are a lifesaver. I think I could drink ten of these and still be tired."

Lillian gives me a genuine smile and says, "I don't know if my conscience will let me supply that much caffeine, but you are more than welcome to my coffee maker at any point today."

"If you find me in the kitchen at 3 am with the house hippos, just ignore me. I'll scurry away when I'm done," I say, chuckling and hoping she gets the joke.

She does, and it gets a genuine laugh from her. I don't think I've heard her laugh because I would remember a sound like this. There's something melodic yet calming to it, like a field of wildflowers swaying in the breeze. And with her standing there, the sun still making its way overhead, the lake behind her, small waves rolling in, I wish I could capture this moment and keep it with me forever. Lillian has enchanted me; I just need to get this wildflower on the same page.

With everything going on, it's probably not the most ideal time to be pursuing anything with anyone, and yet I can't help but feel like someone like her doesn't come around very often and I do not want to miss my chance.

After we settle a bit, she says, "Canadian television was strange in the 90s. I haven't thought about house hippos in a long time. But seriously, how are you doing? Is this going to mess everything up?" She waves her arm around us and toward the skid steer.

She seems genuinely concerned, so instead of putting on a brave show, I tell her how I'm honestly feeling. "I'm decently stressed about this. I'm choosing to believe this was a one-off and just some bored kids getting into trouble. Best case scenario, we are back up and running tomorrow."

"Staying optimistic is good," she says. "I'll keep my fingers crossed and the coffee hot. I need to get inside and get some work done. You know where to find me if you need anything."

She points her thumb over her shoulder as she takes a couple of steps backwards. I look down at my phone as she turns away so she doesn't see the lost puppy dog look in my face. When she's almost at the door, I look back and catch her looking at me. A light blush rises from her neck to her cheeks when our eyes meet, and she gives me a shy smile before rushing through her door.

I internally fist pump to myself. She didn't run away, showed genuine interest in me, offered to let me into her cottage, and the blush tells me I at least affect her in some way. The rest of the day could be absolute crap, but I think I would still go to sleep with a smile on my face thinking about Lillian.

I answer a few emails from suppliers on my phone when I hear tires coming around the bend. Looking up, I see a police SUV pull in beside my truck and a guy around my age steps out.

Holding his hand out to shake, he asks, "Jackson Mane, I assume?"

I shake his hand and nod.

"It's good to meet you," he continues. "I'm Constable Dylan Peters. I understand there was some vandalism here last night. Can you explain what happened and show me the damage?"

I gesture towards the skid steer and he follows. As he takes some photos of the machine and its lack of tires, I walk him through what happened last night, from my call from Lillian to checking my other sites this morning, and he makes notes.

Once he has everything recorded on his phone, I ask, "What are the odds this was some rowdy teenagers?"

"I'm going to be honest with you, there aren't many teenagers that live here full-time, and we haven't had any other incidents reported around town. With that being said, there hasn't been a lot of growth in Bluefield in recent years, so maybe this was their first opportunity to get into trouble. If it were already tourist season, I would also suspect a drunken tourist, but this is a bit aggressive for even them."

That optimism I was feeling before has faltered slightly. Although Constable Peters is telling me what I had assumed, it still leaves a lot of ifs and maybes on the table.

Constable Peters could probably tell because he offers to dust for prints.

Shifting from one foot to the other, I think about it, but I don't think it would give me any peace of mind. "I don't want to waste your time. With the size of my crew, you're going to get a lot of prints. I mostly needed you to come out for the insurance claim, but I appreciate it."

He nods and then seems to be watching something over my shoulder. I follow his line of sight and catch the curtain of one of the windows on Lillian's cottage falling back into place.

"You got a nosey old woman for a neighbour?" he asks with a chuckle.

"Um," I begin, not quite sure how to answer because he couldn't be more wrong. "Not exactly."

"I'm going to head over there and ask her a couple of questions. See if she saw anything else and hopefully give her some peace of mind, so she isn't calling you every time something goes bump in the night."

"I'll go with you," I quickly offer. He gives me a questioning look, but I ignore it.

It's not that there is any reason he can't talk to Lillian alone, but to be honest, he's a good-looking dude. Peters is about my height, but he definitely spends more time in the gym than I do. I know I don't have any claim to Lillian, but apparently, I am now some sort of jealous fool, so I want to at least be there if suddenly they fall madly in love.

I quicken my steps so that I make it to the door just before him, knocking twice and then opening the door like this is something I do all the time.

"Hey, Lil?" I call out, hoping she doesn't think I'm some weirdo who walks into people's houses. I know she offered me an endless supply of coffee earlier, but I can acknowledge that I may be pushing it a bit with my sudden entrance to her place.

Lillian's head pops out from behind a wall that I assume is the kitchen, and her eyes dart between me and Constable Peters before she squeaks and gives us a very forced smile.

Before I can say anything more, Constable Peters steps in front of me, nodding his head to me. I'm guessing he now understands my vague answer when he thought she was a kooky old lady.

"Good morning, ma'am. I'm Constable Peters, but you can call me Dylan," he says, like we are suddenly in some old western. I don't know if it's in my head, but he sounds a lot more like a cowboy than he did five minutes ago. She shakes his hand before taking a step towards me, so close that our shoulders are now touching.

"It's nice to meet you, Constable. I'm Lillian Shaw." The fact that she didn't call him by his first name and has sought me out for comfort, even if it wasn't intentional, gives me the boost of confidence I needed. Now I'm glad I was a bit insecure because Lillian seems even more shy with Peters than she was with me at first.

Peters gets straight to business, asking Lillian what happened from her point of view, and she tells him in a very factual way, even through her nerves. I can see her fidgeting with her hands behind her back, so without thinking, I grab both of her small hands in one of my larger ones, giving her a small squeeze and holding them still. Her shoulders drop and it looks like she releases a breath that was being held in.

Constable Peters clearly picked the right profession with how observant he is as he tracks my movements to where my hand has now disappeared and raises one eyebrow in my direction. I shrug the shoulder not touching Lillian's ever so slightly because why not? Offering her comfort and giving him the hint that I would rather she isn't available for him at the same time?

Some would call that efficiency.

Once Lillian has given as much information as she can, which isn't that much because she smartly stayed inside while whoever was out there, I give one more squeeze to her hands, before reluctantly letting go and offering to walk the constable out. When we make it to his SUV, he gives me a look more serious than any so far, putting me on edge.

"I don't want to add to any town gossip," he starts, completely confusing me. "But I know some people around town are not very happy with the demolition of what they consider historic cottages. I have no reason to believe the vandalism has anything to do with what I've heard, but if you are able to add any security measures to your site, it might be worth it. Just in case."

I guess because I'm not a local, I don't know about any of the town gossip, so his comment takes me back a bit.

Defensively, I say, "Most of my projects are not structurally sound. We are buying properties that would cost too much for the owners to fix themselves."

Raising his hands to calm me down, he says, "I don't agree with them. You don't have to worry about that. As I'm sure you've noticed, Bluefield's residents tend to be mostly of retirement age and beyond. They aren't the most supportive of change and they love to gossip. I wouldn't worry too much about it. I wanted you to be made aware."

Taking a deep breath, I can appreciate the heads up, so I tell him, "Thank you for letting me know. I'll see about some cameras or motion-sensored lights."

We shake hands and he gets into his vehicle to leave. Before he pulls away, I catch him rolling down his window. He pauses a moment before saying, "Not a nosey old lady for a neighbour at all." Shaking my head, I back away with a smile on my face as he heads toward town. Lillian is a lot of things. Old? No. Nosey? Maybe. Inside waiting for me with a fresh cup of coffee? I sure hope so.

Chapter 11
Lillian

Okay, so my curiosity got the better of me and I was spying on Jackson and Constable Peters from my kitchen window while they talked. Did I expect to get caught? I thought there was a fifty-fifty chance, but it was a risk I was willing to take. Did I expect them to suddenly enter my cottage for questioning? Not at all. I guess I shouldn't have been surprised. I was so focused on the fact that I made an impulsive decision and offered Jackson a free run in my kitchen, that I wasn't thinking too far ahead.

Jackson took my offer at face value because he waltzed right into my cottage where I was standing in the kitchen, looking all sorts of guilty, I'm sure.

Constable Peters is a very large and attractive man. He has the blond-haired, blue-eyed beach boy look, but far too many muscles to be in the surfer style category.

He also doesn't look laid back at all. I don't know if that's because he was on duty, but his tone and posture screamed law enforcement.

When he told me I could call him by his first name, I think I panicked and promptly forgot what it was. I'm not afraid of law enforcement, but I've always felt you should respect people in positions of power, like Constable Peters, so it spiked my nerves quite a bit. The second Jackson grabbed my hand, I felt instantly at ease, which never happens. With everything he's going through, I appreciate that he was still able to be there for me. Like a rock, everything about him seems so solid all the time; it has a calming effect on me apparently. I was more focused on how his hands were a bit rough, where I'm used to smooth, than what was happening around me. I think I answered all the questions without sounding like an idiot.

I'm not sure if Jackson will have to leave now that that's handled, but on the off chance he doesn't, I start brewing a fresh pot of coffee as soon as he and Constable Peters leave. Just as it is finishing up, I hear the door open, the sound of boots being removed, and then Jackson appears from around the corner with a worried expression on his face.

If he's worried that I'm upset with him making himself comfortable in my cottage, I'm surprisingly not. I don't normally like people in my space, especially here because it's my happy, safe place. I know I wasn't sure if I wanted to continue to see Jackson after our date on the weekend, but this all confirms that I like having him around.

Aspen may have also given me an earful this morning about my issue with being convenient. And by "may," I mean she very much did.

What are best friends for if not calling you out for letting your insecurities self-sabotage?

She put me, nicely, in check, and I now have an open mind again. God, I love that girl.

I assume Jackson is here for some coffee, so I quickly pour him a mug, which he takes with a smile on his face. It looks a bit forced.

"Is everything alright?" I ask. I lean against the counter behind me, putting some space between us so I can really take him in. I don't know how he can still give off the calm, cool, collected aura while still looking tired and worried, but he does.

"Technically, yes," he answers before pausing. "With the police report, the insurance should put the claim through smoothly, but there was something Constable Peters mentioned that bothered me a bit."

That's curious. "What did he say?"

Jackson puts his mug down beside me and then takes my hand. I think it's a subconscious action, like he's seeking comfort from physical touch. I'm trying to not think too much into it, but the butterflies in my stomach aren't on the same page. "Apparently, there are people in town who aren't happy about my company being here. They think we are tearing down these cottages without a cause, I guess."

Unfortunately, I'm not nearly as surprised by this as he seems to be.

"People can be stubborn about change," I offer. "When I first got here and saw the size of the cottage being built in the Waldens' place, I asked my grandfather about it and he grumbled some impolite things about city slickers and their McMansions."

Jackson looks taken aback by that, so I add, "He's harmless. He also complains when his favourite weather person is on vacation and someone fills in. Take his opinion with a grain of salt. My point is, this is a quaint town where nothing happens, even during tourist season.

Any change is going to have people talking."

We are both quiet for a moment while he digests my thoughts. Jackson absentmindedly plays with the fingers of my hand that he's still holding. It tickles a bit.

After a moment, I know why Constable Peters would have told him this. "Does Constable Peters think the vandalism was some sort of sabotage or retaliation because they don't want your company here?"

"Not necessarily." He drops my hand and takes a sip of his coffee. The loss of heat is instant, and I feel disappointed. He continues before I can put too much thought into why. "It could have been, I guess. He doesn't think so, but thought I should have extra security added to all my sites just in case. My dad isn't going to love the added cost to the job, nor are a lot of the people in my crew going to like feeling like I'm watching them, but I'm going to trust that Peters knows what he's talking about. I also don't like that this happened so close to where you sleep, so I think it's worth it. I'll check out the hardware store this afternoon, and order products online if I have to."

I don't want him spending money to keep me safe. If my doors are locked from now on, I'm sure I will be okay, but the fact that he is worried about me causes a small flutter in my stomach. In this moment, I realize Jackson and I have had multiple conversations today and I acted normal. He did, too. Well, I don't know him well enough to say that for sure, but this has all felt a lot more authentic than all our other interactions combined.

Feeling encouraged by this, I offer to help in any way I can. This finally removes the pensive look from Jackson's face and I am graced with a panty-dropping smile.

"What are the odds you're up for a trip to the hardware store after lunch?"

After lunch, when I should be working.

Ha, that's not happening. The mental block is still firmly in place. Yesterday, I wrote an entire story without a plot, theme or lesson. How, you ask? No idea. Nothing happened. But words on the page are words on the page, so we are calling it progress. Progress that I will not be building on this afternoon because I want to spend time with Jackson and hopefully keep that smile on his face.

"After lunch sounds great to me," I say with a smile. This causes a dimple to appear on Jackson's cheek. And swoon. He's cute, end of story.

We make plans to meet in town at 1 pm, which gives me about three hours to overthink everything I've ever said and done.

After trying on every article of clothing in my closet upstairs, I decide that keeping on what I was wearing this morning is probably the best bet. I don't want Jackson to think I changed my clothes to go to the hardware store.

That would be weird, I guess.

Throwing a knit sweater over my floral romper, I decide the weather is just right for a bike ride into town. Having a moment to myself on my bike, smelling the fresh air, will be good to clear my head and ease the nerves that I have acquired since Jackson left this morning. I'm not planning on buying anything, so it's not like I need anything more than the basket on the front of my bike.

The hardware store is at the top of Main Street, close to the park, so I lock my bike to the nearest tree just as I see Jackson's truck pull into a parking space behind the store.

The hardware store was uneventful; Jackson was able to get some floodlights, but no cameras. The store employee suggested checking out The General Store, or else heading out of town to one of the bigger box stores.

We agreed it would be better to not waste time and go to the next town over. The ride was forty-five minutes in each direction, and we mostly listened to music and discussed our favourite artists, concerts and songs. It turns out we both have tickets to see Noah Kahan this fall. Jackson suggested that we make Aspen and Simon switch tickets so we can go together instead. I try to laugh that idea off because I know Aspen would not be okay with that. When one of Harry Styles' new songs comes on the radio, I catch Jackson singing along to it. I think he knows almost every word and I'm almost in tears from laughing. I was firmly Team Niall when One Direction split, so I don't know as many of Harry's songs as Jackson does apparently.

Overall, it was a nice way to spend the afternoon and at the very least, I think Jackson would make a good friend. Since I'm still not one hundred percent sure he is even interested in anything more, I'm happy with friendship. Jackson was able to get everything he needed, so we managed to avoid The General Store, too.

I haven't been back since meeting Sam there. I wouldn't say I am avoiding him, but I just haven't had the energy to mentally prepare myself to deal with his quirkiness. Yeah, quirkiness, that's what we'll call it. I don't need Jackson seeing how awkward I am with Sam's strange mannerisms.

I think Jackson must have enjoyed the afternoon as much as I did because without asking, he brought me to his job sites to drop off the equipment to the crews there, and then we headed back to the Waldens' where I offered to help him.

I am not very tech savvy, but Jackson seems like he is a natural problem solver. He claims to have no experience with security equipment, but we got everything set up just before dinner time.

When I asked him to drive me back into town to get my bike, he suggested we get some dinner, and I am never one to turn down Ron's Chip Truck.

I hope Jackson is choosing to spend this time with me because he wants to and not just because Bluefield will be quiet for another two weeks until the tourists start arriving. The convenient comment is still sitting in the back of my brain, trying to ruin our nice afternoon together. So is Aspen's pep talk.

I know I could ask him.

Clear the air and all.

But I am not at that level of confidence just yet. Our friendship made a lot of progress today. I'm going to say a win is a win and we aren't pushing it just yet.

Jackson parks his truck near the park and puts my bike into the truck bed. I give him a confused look, but he just winks and starts walking down Main Street toward Ron's. I have to almost jog to catch up with his long, confident strides.

I catch Ron's eye and he immediately comes out from the side of the truck to engulf me in a hug. This is his greeting regardless of if it's been ten months or two days. In this case, it's probably been only a week.

"How have you been, my girl?" he asks while releasing me from his arms. "I see you've met my friend, Jackson."

I look over my shoulder to Jackson, who looks a bit sheepish. "I may come here a couple of times a week," he says quietly.

Ron chuckles and whispers loud enough for Jackson to hear, "Sometimes a couple of times a day."

Jackson jokingly pulls me away from Ron. "You are the worst wingman ever, Ron. I thought we were friends."

"Lillian here is my number one. Sorry, Jackson."

My eyes ping-pong between the two men like I'm watching a tennis match. I try to stop the laugh from escaping me, which makes it unfortunately come out as a snort. I'm pretty sure my entire body is blushing with embarrassment as I try to hide the strawberry skin with my hands.

Ron breaks out into a full-belly laugh, at me, while Jackson wraps his arm around my shoulder and hides my face in his chest.

I try not to let my internal freak-out show, but it is certainly happening. Jackson is basically hugging me while still chuckling, and I've all but forgotten about my embarrassment because he smells so good. I got a small taste of the smell earlier in his truck, but we had the windows open, so it was muted. This is full-on and so, so good. He smells like clothesline-fresh laundry, fresh cut wood, probably lumber, and man.

If I could bottle his scent, I would spray it on my pillow at night.

In a totally non-creepy way, of course.

Before I can get totally drunk on all that is Jackson Mane, I gently unwrap myself from his arms, but stay close beside him. Ron gives me a knowing smile, deepening the red on my cheeks, before he makes his way back into the truck to get started on our orders.

Considering Jackson seems to be a regular, I'm sure neither of us need to place an actual order with Ron.

We grab a picnic table while waiting for our food and thankfully, there is no further mention of my snorting. I can't say it's ever happened to me before and I am praying I never do it again in public, especially in front of Jackson.

No one should become a snorter at this stage in their life.

I was hoping all embarrassing tendencies would arise in my teenage years so I could deal with them before meeting an incredibly smart and handsome stranger who I want to spend more time with. And because he is not bringing up my embarrassing moment, I have decided not to make fun of him for his frequency to Ron's truck.

"So," Jackson begins, seeming a bit nervous, and I am instantly on edge. "How is your work going? I don't actually know what you do, and after you spent most of the day helping me, I hope you won't be getting in trouble from your boss."

I wondered how long I could go without talking about work. It's not that I don't want people to know, it's just, well, I'm avoiding thinking about my upcoming deadlines.

I don't want Jackson to think I am slacking. I've seen just how much he puts into his job, so he probably wouldn't want to hang out with someone lazing around.

"I won't be in trouble with anyone, don't worry."

I pause, but Jackson doesn't fill the space. I know he wants more information and at this point, I feel a bit silly. I've made it a much bigger deal in my head than it is. I drop my eyes towards my lap, fidgeting with my fingers sitting there.

"I'm an author. I write children's literature. Aside from hitting timeline goals and meetings with my illustrators and agent, I have control over how I spend my time between deadlines."

Looking back up at Jackson, I see a soft smile form on his lips, and that pesky dimple pops out.

"That is just an interesting job, Lil. I can't say I've ever met a writer of, well, anything, let alone children's books. Super cool."

"I wouldn't say it's cool," I reply. "But I don't mind it."

"Well, I think it's cool. How did you get into it?"

I explain to Jackson my love of reading and writing as a child.

I'd say it was the typical shy kid's experience. That led to a degree in English, being hired by my current publishing company as an in-house author and being placed in the children's department.

"And the rest is history, I guess?" he asks. "Did you always know children's literature was the way you wanted to go?"

I force myself to swallow the saliva building in my mouth. This question always makes me uncomfortable because the answer is simply, no. And that leads to more questions. The explanation involves bringing up my ex-boyfriend with a guy I maybe could try to date in the future. I think that's frowned upon.

I already feel bad that Jackson has had to drag all this out of me. I muster up all the courage I can and channel Aspen's "I don't care what people think" bravado.

"Honestly, no."

Jackson's eyes visibly widen, so I continue before he can ask.

"My friend—" My ex-boyfriend. "—Christopher, I met him in university and his parents own a large publishing company. After we graduated, they hired both of us. He became an agent, and I was placed in an open slot in their children's department. Because I didn't have any published work right out of school, I didn't have much say in where I went. I got into a rhythm with my writing and just stayed, I guess."

There, I feel lighter, and I think I avoided mentioning Christopher in the perfect way. I don't want to be the girl whining about my ex, especially because his parents didn't need to hire me and they haven't treated me any differently after our breakup.

"What are you currently working on?"

The biggest pain in my butt, is what I want to respond, but instead, I say, "My current project is a five-book bundle. It needs to follow the same characters and is targeted at two to four-year-olds. The overall concepts of each book need to stay basic, as most children in that age group are reading with assistance and parents don't want to be covering challenging topics at bedtime. At least, that's what the spec I was given directed." At this point, I've put most things on the table, so might as well keep going.

"I'm in a complete block right now. I don't know what it is, but I have almost zero ideas. I wrote this age group a lot when I was first starting my career and it was fine, but in the last couple of years, I've had a lot more focus on small chapter books for ages six to nine. Those kids are typically in grades one to three, and that's when I remember learning to love reading. They've got access to the school library and they can discover what type of world they want to escape into through books. The lessons I can build in as an author feel important. It's an impressionable age, and finding the balance between fun and education is a challenge that I love."

When I finally stop talking, I recognize I've been staring off into space and our food magically appeared in front of us at some point, but Jackson hasn't started eating. He's staring at me with soft eyes. The level of tenderness in his gaze makes me feel even more vulnerable than I normally would while dumping all that information on someone. I grab my fork, looking down at my poutine, but I don't start eating.

After a moment of more silence, I clear my throat. "Sorry, that was probably more than you bargained for with your simple question. I guess I needed to vent."

Jackson keeps smiling at me but shakes his head. "No, that was great. I love hearing you talk about something you're passionate about. Obviously, your mental block is not ideal, but it just shows you care what content you are putting into the world. You can vent to me anytime."

"If things continue how they're going, you might regret your offer," I say.

"I don't think there is anything I could regret about you, Lillian Shaw."

Chapter 12
Jackson

Any updates on the rocket your hiding down there?

I don't even know how to answer that

Are you talking about Lillian?

Or my….

Dude.

Lillian, obviously. Why would you even question that?

Have you met you?

After Lillian shared the stress she has with her job, we ate in comfortable silence. She seemed decently upset about having a creative block, so I didn't want her to have to keep thinking about it.

If Lillian needs a distraction from work, I will happily fill that role.

We have had such a good day together that I don't want it to end. I don't think it is possible for me to take smaller bites than I am, delaying the end of our dinner as long as I possibly can.

I offered to buy us ice cream, but considering neither of us could finish the large portions Ron served us, I'm not surprised she turned me down.

The warm air from the day has faded as we've sat here. With the sun barely peeking through the trees, I can feel a chill through my long-sleeved shirt. Lillian has bare legs, so it's probably for the best that we end the night. The problem is, I don't want to.

I know Bluefield is relatively safe, my site vandalism aside, but I still insist on driving Lillian home. With her bike already in the bed of my truck, she doesn't have much room to decline, and I am hoping I can get a goodnight kiss by walking her to her door.

When we pull up in front of Lillian's cottage, I hop out as quickly as I can to open her door, putting my best effort forward at being a gentleman. I head to the back of my truck, lowering the tailgate, and we both freeze. Her bike tires have been slashed.

"Oh my gosh," she says, hands covering her mouth.

"Your bike didn't look like that when I put it in here before dinner," I confirm.

"No, I think at least one of us would have noticed, right?" She peeks through the fingers covering her eyes, then drops her arms to her sides, looking all sorts of defeated.

"I'm calling Constable Peters," I say, pulling my phone out of my back pocket.

Lillian grabs my wrist. "Do you think that's necessary? They're just tires."

I take her hand that's grabbing my wrist and weave my fingers through hers. "Lil, it may be a coincidence, but your bike was in my truck and the tires were slashed less than twenty-four hours after tires were stolen off of equipment on my job site. I think Peters should at least know about this."

I squeeze her hand reassuringly, while she thinks for a moment. Meeting my eyes, she squeezes my hand back and says, "Okay. Let's call him."

I make the call and we wait for Constable Peters. We both stand at the back of my truck, staring at Lillian's bike without speaking. The only thing keeping me grounded right now is Lillian's hand in mine.

I want to believe that this was a random accident, but it doesn't feel like it. I know at this point, it's just bike tires—that I intend to replace myself. But if this is something more, and is my fault, I won't forgive myself if anything bad happens to Lillian.

The sound of gravel crunching under tires pulls us both out of our haze, and Constable Peters parks behind my truck and walks over to us.

"Twice in one day. You two must really like me," he jokes.

Lillian awkwardly chuckles, but I don't laugh. I know this isn't a serious crime, but I don't find this situation very funny. Constable Peters must read this on my face as he gets straight to business, asking us where I was parked, for how long and if we saw anyone lurking around.

Unfortunately, neither of us were playing much attention to our surroundings, something I will be fixing moving forward.

"I can see if any of the stores have exterior cameras that caught anything, but I know most of them don't. They typically are trying to catch shoplifters inside their stores. Not much focus on the street or parking lot." Constable Peters gives me a look and I have a feeling I know what's coming next.

"I am more confident than I was this morning that you might have pissed someone off, Jackson. I know it was Lillian's bike, but it's not likely this is a coincidence. I'll dust for prints on the bike, but unless I get any concrete evidence, you'll need to be careful moving forward."

"Yeah, I figured as much," I say reluctantly. Lillian leans against me, offering her silent support.

"Bluefield is getting its shipment of summer constables next week. I'm going to be honest with you, we typically get the people no one likes working with. Beggars can't be choosers, I guess. With that being said, I will be able to send more cars out to patrol. I'll make sure all of your sites make it on the rotation," Peters tells us. This isn't the most reassuring plan, but I appreciate the effort he is putting in.

"Are you staying here?" he asks awkwardly.

I quickly jump in before he makes Lillian uncomfortable. "No, I'm at The Inn for the summer."

"Okay, that's good," he says. "That building may be old, but I think it is also bomb proof. You shouldn't worry about any problems there." He looks to Lillian and asks her, "What are the chances you have a security system at your place?"

"Last night was the first time I have even thought about locking my door," she answers sheepishly.

"Don't worry," he reassures her. "You are not the first, nor will you be the last person to tell me that. Just keep it locked moving forward. I wouldn't say you are a target, but if you're spending time with Jackson, you should also be careful."

First Ron was embarrassing me, and now Peters is giving reasons for Lillian to stop hanging out with me. No one is on my side today.

Constable Peters says his goodbyes, letting us know he will be in touch if they get any prints off the bike or hear anything in town. I turn to Lillian, pulling her into a hug, just in case she wants nothing to do with me and this is the first and last one I get. When I held her at Ron's because she was embarrassed, that felt like a win, but right now I want a real hug.

She lightly wraps her hands around my waist and rests her chin on my chest. When she looks up at me, she asks, "How are you feeling?"

Not exactly what I expected, but a valid question for sure. She's worried about me, but I'm worried about her.

"I'm feeling a lot of things right now."

"Can you give me a couple of those feelings?"

Taking a moment, I really think about it. "Stressed, angry, worried, annoyed." But she's also hugging me right now, so: "Happy."

"Happy?"

"Not about all the vandalism, of course. I am happy that I have you here to keep me grounded. If you weren't holding me, I would probably be spinning out right now." That causes Lillian to blush, which I find very cute. She smiles and smooshes her face into my chest like she did earlier to hide it. For someone who seemed so shy in the beginning, Lillian is a bit of a cuddler.

I pull her towards me as much as I can, so there are no gaps between us. Her grip tightens around my waist, so I know I'm not holding her against her will. I take in the moment, and then the day.

If someone is mad that Mane Construction is in town, then we have a pretty big problem. I had plans to meet with town council members about the potential for a vacation community of new builds we are interested in building.

With the waiting list for our properties growing, we need to get in there before someone else does. I can't say I've ever dealt with angry townspeople before, but this is our first project of this scale outside of a large city.

Unfortunately for me, I will need to call my dad about this. I'd rather he gets all information straight from me, instead of crew gossip. We may have a seventy percent male workforce, but those guys love to talk. I am going to have to make a trip back into the city for this conversation.

With only a call to Gord, I won't be able to tell how mad he is. The man has one tone to his voice, and it always sounds angry. I need to be able to tell if this is causing fist-clenching annoyance or steam-out-of-the-ears rage. I wonder if people who don't work for their fathers have to deal with this kind of thing. Probably not.

Lillian breaks my train of thought by slowly releasing me. Not wanting to say goodnight yet, I let my arms fall off her shoulders, but grab her right hand before she can get too far.

"Are you going to feel okay staying in your cottage alone?"

She hesitates a moment, steeling her spine before responding. "I'll be okay." She nods to herself a couple of times, seemingly trying to convince herself.

"It would make me feel better if I came inside for a minute, just to make sure everything is okay. Can I do that?" I don't want to seem pushy or that I'm inviting myself to stay over. As much as I want to spend more time with Lillian, I also want to make sure she's safe.

Her car was parked in the driveway all day, so it would seem like she was home. But if whoever slashed her tires knew it was her bike, they would know she was in town.

Now that I'm thinking of it, we probably should have had Peters check the place out before he left. I'm not a small guy, and playing hockey growing up, I know how to fight. But this is Canada; carrying a gun is illegal, outside of hunting, so we are unarmed in that aspect. I may need to pick up some dog spray for Lillian at an outdoor store. Pepper spray is also illegal.

I can tell Lillian is more freaked out than she wants to let on, as she doesn't say a word but pulls me through the door into her cottage. We then go from room to room opening all closet and cabinet doors. I wasn't expecting an impromptu tour of the place, but I got one. On the first floor, there is a laundry room when you first enter and a large closet full of beach toys. If you follow the hallway further in, there is the kitchen on your left and the dining room on the right. Both of those spaces open to the living room that faces a whole wall of windows, looking out over the lake. A sliding glass door leads you out to a porch with wooden stairs down to the beach.

A staircase off the dining room takes you upstairs. With the peaked roofline, some of the spaces are a tight squeeze at my six-foot-two height. Surprisingly, four decent-sized bedrooms and a bathroom fit up there. Ninety percent of the cottage, including its furniture, is pine. The cottage does not have the airy beach house feel like the ones Mane Construction is building. This is a cozy cottage in the woods, and I love it.

Once every nook has been checked, and the windows and doors locked, we make our way back to the back door where I should be saying goodbye. I still don't want to, though. But it's getting late and I'm still not sure how Lillian's work schedule works, so I don't want to add any extra stress by keeping her up too late.

I pull her into a hug, because I think I'm addicted to touching her now, and she comes willingly. "Thank you for, well, everything today," I murmur into her hair, maintaining as much body contact as possible. She pulls her head away the smallest bit to look up at me.

"That's what friends are for," she says, and my stomach drops. I certainly don't hug my friends like this. I guess I should take friendship over nothing at this point. I remind myself that we are building on our relationship with each interaction, one step at a time. I may be a bit farther in my feelings than she is at this point. On Sunday night, I wasn't sure if she even wanted to talk to me anymore. I guess this is a better alternative.

With that in mind, I drop a feather light kiss on her forehead and take a step back through the open door.

"I'm not sure what my week is going to look like, but I'll call you, okay?"

She nods her head, wrapping her arms around her waist like she misses the warmth of our hug as much as I do.

"Lock up behind me, Lil," I remind her.

She tries to give me a reassuring smile, but it doesn't reach her eyes. "Don't worry, I won't be forgetting that anytime soon."

I turn towards my truck, waiting for the sound of the deadlock clicking into place before I get inside.

I can hardly believe that less than twenty-four hours ago, I thought there was no hope of anything with Lillian. And as much as the vandalism is turning into a dumpster fire, Lillian is a bright light in it all.

I hope I can get things back on track soon because I don't want to wait if I have any chance at Lillian being a part of my future.

Chapter 13
Lillian

To say I am a bit on edge would be an understatement. Jackson has a lot on his plate, so I haven't told him this, but between the theft next door and my tires being slashed, I'm scared. He decided to explain to his dad the concerns with his project and Bluefield in person. This is his decision, of course, but he said he would probably be back in the city until Monday, having some meetings, leaving me alone. And I know I planned to be here alone for the majority of the summer, but my mind is now spiralling and I have assumed an axe murder is now stalking me. My parents have taken off on a cross-country road trip, driving until they reach Vancouver, so I don't want to bother them too much. Ben has said he will come up with his son when the weather gets warmer. I wouldn't try to convince him to come up anyway. If there is any danger here, I wouldn't want my nephew, Noah, anywhere near it.

That leaves Aspen. Have I ever mentioned I have the best friend in the whole world?

Aspen is currently feuding with her boss, so not only has she said she would come stay with me, but she's taking the day off on Friday, which means since today is Thursday, she will be here after dinnertime.

I made sure to let her know what was going on ahead of time, murdering stalker and all. Aspen thinks I am overreacting. I would agree with her, but that doesn't mean I'm not going to keep believing my own lies.

On a side note, writing children's literature while thinking about murders, is not possible. So that's the creative block update for this week.

□□□

I'm not a big drinker, so on Saturday night, when Aspen pulls out a twenty-six-ounce bottle of tequila, I am a bit apprehensive. The last thing I need is a raging hangover and the anxiety-inducing shame spiral it will cause.

"We are not drinking that whole bottle tonight," I say.

Aspen puts her hands up, stopping me before I can further shoot this idea down. "I can't find any shot glasses, so while we may not be drinking the whole bottle, we will be drinking out of the bottle. I brought lemons if that makes it any better."

That is still not ideal, but to be honest, I kind of need this.

Aspen echoes my thoughts. "We need this. You're paranoid.

I hate my boss. I just want to drink some tequila, put on a face mask, and scream Taylor Swift lyrics." Sitting on the floor between the couch and coffee table, she hands me the bottle and a lemon wedge. "Pleeeeease."

Relenting, I take both, raising the bottle to my lips and taking a way larger sip than I should have. I cough a little as I swallow. Aspen shoves the lemon wedge into my mouth for me, which helps marginally.

Aspen then does the exact same, though I allow her to put the lemon wedge in her own mouth.

Aspen gets her playlist playing through the speakers while I grab some sheet masks from my room. On my descent down the stairs, something catches my eye out the window. I'm probably imagining things, but it looks like a figure entering the treed area beside the cottage. Aspen's right, I am paranoid.

Shaking it off, I rejoin Aspen on the floor. It looks like she has taken a couple more swigs from the bottle. I hand her the tub of mask and she hands me the bottle. For the next hour, we alternate between drinking from the bottle and using it as a microphone, fighting over it during the ten-minute version of our favourite song.

Right as the song ends, a cracking noise draws our attention to the windows.

"What was that?" Aspen asks, as she mutes the music.

"I don't know." Both of us peek over the back of the couch, refusing to get any closer to the window.

"During the day all these windows are killer, but right now, I kind of hate them. We're in a snow globe in here. Have you ever heard of curtains?" Looking around, I agree with her. We have most of the lights on, so we can't see outside, but anyone outside could see in. Total snow globe.

"Okay," I start, "not to make things worse, but earlier I thought I saw someone near the trees, near where the sound came from." I didn't want to say anything in case it was my imagination, but we're in this together now.

Aspen squeals and pulls me down to the floor.

"What do we do?" she asks. "I don't want to go out there, but I also don't want to move."

"We could call Constable Peters?" I offer. "If it's just a raccoon or something, we will feel silly, but I also don't want to sleep on the floor tonight."

"Sleep? Who's sleeping tonight? Because I'm not. The only thing we have to defend ourselves with is a bottle of tequila." Looking at the bottle in her hand, I see that we drank way more than I thought. I am definitely drunk. Not ideal.

"We did hear something, right? The tequila isn't making us hallucinate?"

"It's tequila, not mushrooms, Billy. We heard it."

Fair point.

"So we call Constable McHottie, then?" she asks. When I explained the vandalism issue to her, I mentioned the police constable that was helping us. She asked for a picture of him because I wouldn't verify whether he was good-looking or not. I don't know why she thought I would have a photo of him, but she found her own online and now has a crush on him apparently.

As I look around for my phone, it rings on the kitchen counter.

We both look at the phone and then at each other. Aspen mumbles, "Creepy." At the same time, I say, "I am not answering that."

We both sit, unmoving, while the call rings through to voicemail. I then get two text alerts and another call.

"What if it's Constable Dreamy warning us of a killer in the area?" Aspen has pulled the blanket off the couch and wrapped it around us.

"He doesn't have my phone number, Asp."

I feel her fidgeting beside me and see that she has somehow removed the couch cushions without me noticing and is building a barricade around us. I give her a side-eye because cushions are not going to save us against a knife-wielding killer.

Her mouth opens to argue, even though I didn't say anything, just as there's a loud knock at the back door.

If we survive this, it will be with hearing loss, because I don't think I have ever heard anything as blood-curdling as the sounds coming from both of our mouths.

Aspen, with the lungs of an opera singer apparently, continues her scream as the knocking stops. We are both quiet, waiting to hear more. Whoever is outside knows we are in here. Hopefully, they will leave.

Just as my heart rate begins to decline, there is more knocking, only this time it is coming from the sliding door behind us. Aspen abandons our fort and scurries under the couch. My fight or flight seems to be broken as I sit there unmoving. All I can hear is the blood pumping in my ears. Somewhere in the back of my mind, I swear I hear someone calling my name. It must not be my imagination because Aspen peeks her head out and looks at me questioningly.

I chance a glance over my shoulder and see Jackson's face peering in the door. I don't know whether I want to kiss him or kill him. Regardless, I will my legs to regain feeling as I stand up and let him into the cottage.

The second I unlock the door, both of his hands are on my face as he asks, "Are you okay?"

I'm stunned and confused. Instead of answering, I burrow my face into his chest, holding him around the waist for dear life.

Jackson murmurs soothing words into my ear, but I'm too focused on lowering my heart rate to really hear him as he rubs my back gently. We both make an "oomph," as another body latches onto us from behind me. Peeking over my shoulder, I see Aspen worming her way into our hug until Jackson has his arms around both of us.

A minute or so passes and Aspen removes herself from the hug, looking a little embarrassed. I follow suit, wrapping my arm around her shoulder as we both stare up at Jackson.

The embarrassment quickly fades and Aspen slaps Jackson across the chest and yells, "What the hell were you thinking? You scared us half to death."

Now that my adrenaline levels have returned to normal, I feel just how drunk I am, hiccupping and nodding in agreement with Aspen.

"I called you," Jackson defends. "You hadn't answered any of my texts in a while and I wanted to let you know I was back in town, so I called. You didn't answer, so I thought I would drive by and see if you were home. The lights were on, so I texted and called some more, and when you didn't answer, I got worried. When you two screamed when I knocked, I thought something was wrong, so I ran around to the deck and tried to get your attention." He looks away from Aspen, staring straight into my eyes and says, "I'm sorry. I just wanted to make sure you were okay." He glances back to Aspen. "Both of you. I'm sorry."

I don't know about Aspen, but he is already forgiven. Just knowing he's back in town puts me a little at ease, but then I remember. "Were you around the side of the cottage at all? Like near the trees, maybe fifteen minutes ago, and then also probably an hour ago?"

Aspen clutches me tighter as we wait for his answer. Jackson looks visibly confused.

"No. I knocked as soon as I got here. I wasn't even in town an hour ago. Why, what happened?"

Aspen and I share a look of dread. Either someone else was out there or we reacted over nothing.

Taking the lead, Aspen tells him, "Billy thought she saw someone in the woods earlier, and then there was a loud noise outside not long ago."

I jump in, finishing the story. "We were hiding behind the couch when you called. My phone is in the kitchen, but we were too scared to go get it. Then you knocked and, well, we were scared."

"That wasn't me," he says. "Do you want me to call Peters? I could go do a lap around the cottage and check things out?"

"No." I grab Jackson's hand, even though he hasn't made a move to leave. If there was someone out there, they would probably be long gone after all the noise we made. And if someone is still out there, I don't want Jackson in harm's way.

Out of nowhere, Aspen's laughter breaks up this tense moment. She's laughing like all that just happened is the funniest thing she's ever seen. Full-body, crumpling to the floor laughter.

"Is she okay?" Jackson asks me, as we both stare down at Aspen. She's clutching her stomach and no noise is coming out of her mouth anymore, but her whole body is still vibrating with her now-silent laughter.

"It's probably a weird stress response," I say because I have no idea what she could be finding funny right now. After about twenty seconds, Aspen's body relaxes until she is lying on the floor, looking up at us with a goofy smile on her face.

"I'm ready for bed," she finally says, giggling a little again. Looking at the clock above the stove, I see that it is almost midnight and after everything that just happened, plus the lingering alcohol in my system, I am tired, too.

Even with the exhaustion hitting, the lingering fear is still there, so without thinking I turn to Jackson and ask, "Will you stay the night?"

He looks shocked by my question, so I add, "It's late and we have tons of space for everyone to sleep upstairs." More quietly, I add, "It would ease my nerves a bit."

Jackson squeezes the hand that I am apparently still holding his with. "I'll stay."

Aspen gets up off the floor, looking around at the mess we've made of the place. "You guys clean up down here, I'll get a bed ready for Jackson."

Before either of us can respond, she is bounding up the stairs, taking them two at a time.

We clean up the cushions, blankets, lemon wedges and tequila in comfortable silence. When Jackson picks up the bottle that is now only a third full, he gives me a quizzical look.

"I thought it smelled like a dive bar in here, but I was too distracted to say anything. Aspen's episode on the floor makes a lot more sense now."

I giggle and take the bottle from his hands, putting it in the cupboard over the refrigerator. With everything back in order, I watch as Jackson checks that all the windows and doors are locked, before he turns off the lights and we climb the stairs.

I stop when I reach the top of the stairs, looking straight into the room Aspen has been sleeping in. There she is curled up in bed, looking at me with a silly smile on her face. But that's not why I stopped. Beside her bed, on the floor, is the mattress from my room, remade like it's in a home design magazine.

Stepping into what little space is left to walk around the room, I ask, "Are we having a sleepover?"

She nods her head, her smile growing. "You and I are cuddling, Jackson's on the floor." Jackson barks out a laugh from behind me.

"Why can't Jackson sleep in his own room?"

She sits up in the bed, looking at me like the answer is obvious. "He's like our guard dog. If anyone tries to come in here, they get to him first and he can save us." Her smile reappears and she adds quietly, "Or get killed first."

I'm about to argue that this is weird and unnecessary, because it is, when Jackson squeezes my shoulder. "I've slept on worse. If it makes Aspen feel better, a mattress on the floor is perfect for me."

Jackson gives me a reassuring smile as I hear Aspen mumble, "Swoon," while she snuggles herself back under the covers.

Since neither of them seem to think this is strange, I go with it. I direct Jackson to the bathroom and show him where he can find a new toothbrush and any toiletries he might need. I also grab a pair of my brother's sweatpants that he always leaves in his bedroom and leave him to get ready for bed while I do the same in my bedroom.

Once we are all settled in Aspen's room, she and I cuddled up in her bed, Jackson seemingly content on my mattress on the floor, I can't help but feel a bit silly about everything that happened tonight.

My mind was probably playing tricks on me and no one was in the trees. Come morning, we are going to find evidence of a raccoon or skunk out there that caused the noise and feel ridiculous. At the same time, I can't lie and say that Jackson coming to our rescue didn't feel good. He may be on a mattress on the floor, but he's here. I was the first thing he wanted to see when he came back into town.

Just as I'm drifting off to sleep, I hear Aspen mumble beside me, "I love sleepovers."

Chapter 14

Jackson

As weird as Saturday night was, Sunday was great. I woke up to the smell of bacon and saw I was the only one left in Aspen's room after our strange sleepover.

When I descended the stairs, I found both girls in the kitchen whipping up a breakfast spread including eggs, bacon, pancakes, toast and mimosas. With staying at The Inn and being so busy with work, I don't think I have made a home-cooked meal in a month. I'm not a great cook, but I can handle the basics.

My time in the city was frustrating but productive. When

I explained to Gord that the vandalism potentially isn't some high school kids messing about and actually angry townspeople, he told me to simply "Deal with it." When I asked how he expected me to do that, he said, "Run for mayor or something, I don't care. Get them on your side."

I'm not sure if he doesn't understand how municipal government works or simply doesn't care.

But not only am I not going to be running for anything in politics in a town I don't live in, but I'm sure if I did, there would be some major conflict of interest issues.

Aside from my dad, I met with some existing clients who want to work with me on new projects. As much as I would love to design their new homes, because that is what I like about my job, the Bluefield project has become a lot more work than we originally thought, and I don't think I can take on much more. To keep the clients happy, I offered to work on the first draft of the drawings and then pass them off to someone else to see to completion.

Not how I like to work, but Bluefield needs to be my top priority. If all goes well, I'm hoping my dad takes me off the leash he currently holds over me and I can have more freedom within the company until he retires and it's all mine.

I stayed at Simon's condo instead of my own, even though we live in the same building. As much noise as you have in the city, my condo felt too quiet. It's crazy how car honking and sirens blaring amplifies the emptiness of a room, whereas the trees rustling and waves breaking can fill that same space.

Normally, I would meet up with Simon once a week to catch up, so it was good to see what he's been up to. He pestered me about Lillian, a lot. I may have accidentally described her as a wildflower, and now he's using that as her new nickname. I'll need to fix that before they meet.

He also asked far too many questions about Aspen. For someone who, quote, unquote, didn't have a crush on her in high school, the guy is nosey. I still find it interesting that neither Aspen or Lillian have brought him up to me yet. Whatever he's imagining up in his head, it must be very one-sided.

After we eat, I offer to take the girls on my boat for the afternoon, before Aspen has to head back to the city. I was planning on asking them, but Aspen's text gave me the confidence that this would go better than last time.

Neither of them has brought up what happened last night, and considering their fears stem from events that seem to be linked to me, I am also avoiding all topics. Lillian is obviously more freaked out than she led me to believe, so if she wants to live in blissful ignorance for the day, I will happily join her.

We stop at The General Store at Aspen's insistence. Apparently, she wants to meet Sam, the kid who works there. I'm not sure why, but she and Lillian had a hushed conversation about it.

Those two are very close, and in the short amount of time I have spent with them, I've learned that eighty percent of their conversations are non-verbal. I've caught them finishing each other's sentences. Sometimes they don't use words for this, so I've been a bit lost at times. Half of my conversations with Simon are ongoing inside jokes, so it doesn't bother me.

When we enter the store, Sam's head shoots in our direction and he beams at the girls. I don't really blame him; the kids probably just graduated high school, and Aspen and Lillian are beautiful women. Most of the girls he goes to school with he's probably known his whole life, so anyone new is interesting.

"Hi, Aspen. Hi, Lily," he greets enthusiastically, then nods his head towards me. "Jackson."

I see Lillian visibly shudder when he calls her Lily. As much as she reminds me of wildflowers, Lily really doesn't suit her, and I can tell by her reaction, that she doesn't like it either.

Aspen looks a bit startled, probably wondering how Sam knows her name. From what I gathered before we got here, she had never met him. I wonder if Lillian mentioned her to him before. I wander to the back of the store, leaving the girls to talk to Sam, or whatever they plan to do. After a couple of minutes, I feel someone staring at me from across the store. When I look up, I catch Sam just as he glances away from me, and he doesn't look happy. I realize that both Aspen and Lillian must have left the store at some point, so I quickly make my way to the door and see they are waiting outside my truck, whispering.

"Hey, everything alright?" I ask as I approach the two of them.

"Yeah, we're fine," Aspen says. "That kid is just as weird as Billy said he was."

I look to Lillian and she shrugs. "When I first met him, I couldn't tell if he was strange or if I was being socially awkward. Aspen was verifying which it was for me."

It's pretty obvious that Lillian is shy. I didn't know that she thought she was socially awkward, too. I could have told Lillian that Sam is an unusual character, but knowing that Aspen went out of her way to tell her one way or the other who was making the conversation uncomfortable, has me really appreciating who Aspen is as a person, and more importantly, as a friend to Lillian. I think we could all use an Aspen in our lives to keep us self-aware.

They seem to be done with this conversation as we pile into my truck and head to the marina in town.

At the marina, I guide them to my slip and see the neighbouring boat owner, Rick, cleaning his boat, just like he was last time I was here.

"Can't keep the thing clean?" I ask, jokingly.

He returns my smile and says, "The wife won't step foot on it unless it sparkles and my daughters copy whatever she says, so I'll be here cleaning it until it sparkles for them."

"Smart man," Aspen comments as she and Lillian get settled on my boat. I get us ready to set sail, checking the gas level and giving both the girls a lifejacket. Rick steps in to untie the rope connecting us to the dock before we coast through the marina and out into open water.

Once I've dropped anchor, Aspen puts on her headphones and heads for the bow, telling us, "Not to disturb her nap with our chatter." That is more than okay with me. I now get uninterrupted time with Lillian, something that I am quickly becoming addicted to. Taking a seat on the bench at the rear of the boat, Lillian curls up in the opposite corner, pulling her knees to her chest and grabbing a novel out of her tote bag. Needing something to do with my hands, I grab a spare rope from under the captain's chair and mindlessly tie knots.

Growing up, my dad always had a boat, and when we were on the water, it was the only time we really spent together. I would love to say he taught me everything I know, but that isn't true. When I learned Simon was being sent to summer camp in grade three, I begged to go, too. I think my dad was glad to ship me off for a whole month, so he willingly agreed.

We did the typical camp activities: arts and crafts, swimming, hiking, and canoeing. But our camp offered sailing as well. Simon liked it, but I loved it. I would have spent the whole day sailing if I was allowed. In high school, I got a part-time job at the yacht club in Toronto, soaking up everything I could about boats. Drawing houses is my passion, but sailing was my first love.

Simon and I have a sailboat we keep in the city. The speed boat we are on now, I purchased just for fun.

"Whatcha doing over there?" Lillian asks, eyeing the rope in my hand.

"Mostly just fiddling," I reply, while weaving a running bowline. She watches me for a moment before dropping her book back into her tote and holding out her hands. "Show me?"

After a couple of minutes, she gets that one down, so I continue showing her the fisherman's knot, sheet bend, granny knot, figure-eight, thief knot, and a couple more. Lillian is a fast learner, which doesn't surprise me. I can tell she doesn't half-ass things. She's probably a perfectionist like me.

My point is further proven when she asks if she can take the rope home to practise. I think that's pretty cute. Maybe she likes keeping her hands busy, but I like that she's showing interest in one of my hobbies. Maybe I can convince her to go sailing with me one day.

We sit in comfortable silence for a bit. That is until my stomach makes its presence known. Lillian smirks at me as she gets up to grab the cooler she packed with food this morning. It may be just sandwiches and fruit, but it's another homemade meal that I am not taking for granted. We 'cheers' our sandwiches before I take a big bite of my roast beef and cheddar, groaning. You cannot go wrong with sandwiches cut into triangles on a warm day.

"That good?"

I swallow before I give her my most charming smile.

"Lil, I'm going to need you to cook all my meals moving forward. Between breakfast and lunch today, I've been spoiled. I don't think I can go back to takeout every day."

Lillian rolls her eyes at me, giving me a bit of sass I haven't seen from her before.

I guess she's getting comfortable with me. "Jackson, it's just a sandwich. You're so dramatic." She pauses for a moment before asking, "Why are you staying at The Inn? Why not rent a place for the summer?"

"So, I did actually." Lillian looks beyond confused. "We hired as many local employees as we could for the crew here, but we still have a lot from the city crew that I needed with me. We rented out half the trailer park to house them. I had every intention of bunking with one of my foremen, but when I thought about how much time I was pulling him away from his family, I offered up my room for his kids. His wife and kids have been coming up on the weekends, and once school is out for the summer, they'll stay full-time."

"Oh," Lillian says, shocked by my confession. I didn't tell her to try to impress her, it's just the truth. I gave up my bed and had to find something else.

"Once that was all decided, the only place left was The Inn, and to hold the room for the whole summer came with a pretty price tag. But what else was I going to do?"

Lillian smiles at me, nodding in agreement. Suddenly full of excitement, she grabs both my hands and says, "We could cook together!"

That is certainly not what I thought she was going to say, and my face must say as much because she adds, "I love cooking, but don't like cooking just for myself. Maybe once or twice a week, you could come over and we could make a whole meal, and then you would have some leftovers for lunch the next day."

That sounds like an excellent idea except... "I'm not great at cooking."

Looking slightly concerned, she asks, "Define not great, please."

"I can do the basics. Cook meat on the barbecue, boil pasta, and fry vegetables. There isn't a lot of seasoning going on, nor any embellishments. I've tried following recipes, but if it's not a video, I will mess it up," I admit.

Lillian squeezes the hands that she's still holding, so I adjust them to intertwine our fingers.

"I can work with that," she says.

"You really like cooking?" I ask, as she seems genuinely excited about this idea.

"I kind of love it actually. Everyone in my family loves food, but neither of my parents were great at cooking when I was younger. We started this tradition when I was in high school, that on our yearly family vacation, we would take a cooking class to learn a dish from that country or area's local cuisine."

"That's really impressive."

"Some of them I probably can't recreate as well without the instructor's help, but we all agreed it gave us a lot of new skills and mostly just confidence. In recent years, we've picked our trip locations based on dishes we want to learn."

I would have never thought to take a cooking class while on vacation. My dad used to take trips without me, so I usually tagged along with Simon's family on theirs. When we were younger, we just tried to get into as much trouble as possible. As an adult, I haven't left the country much, spending too much time working.

"What's this year's trip?"

"We're spending all of November in Southeast Asia, splitting our time between Thailand and Vietnam. It was my brother's idea. My nephew, Noah, is only five but requests Asian takeout once a week, so the cooking class is necessary."

"Okay, that is really cool. Wait, your brother has a kid? I didn't know he was married."

Lillian's face turns serious. "No, he isn't married, but he does have a kid. Ben's a single dad... Noah's mom was never a part of his life, but Ben is doing a really great job."

There is obviously more to the story, given the mood change, but I don't want to pry. It's really none of my business. I was raised by a single dad and he wasn't travelling around the world to learn my favourite foods, so props to Ben, he sounds great.

Redirecting the conversation away from serious topics, I agree to Lillian's offer. "Yes, I would love to come over and cook with you. Not only will it probably improve my health, but also my sanity, and you sound like you know what you're doing in the kitchen. So, yes. Please." I feel my cheeks heat a little bit. I swear it's from the sun, but I may be blushing right now.

We make plans to start on Tuesday night. Lillian will send me a shopping list the day before and I will bring all the supplies. She argued we could take turns shopping, but that isn't going to happen. She's supplying the kitchen and her expertise; I'm getting off easy with only a grocery store run.

Not only that, I get her undivided attention, multiple times a week. I'm not going to tell her this, but she is quickly becoming the highlight of my summer.

Chapter 15
Lillian

I have this theory.

Jackson and I are hopeless.

Okay, I know I'm being dramatic. My actual theory is that Jackson and I are just friends and that's all we will ever be. I guess I should be okay with that. It's not like I'm desperate to be in a relationship. I was in one for a very long time and being single is good for me. I think I'm learning a lot about myself. Even though I've got the whole life crisis thing going on, growth comes from being uncomfortable. And not knowing what you're doing with your life feels pretty damn uncomfortable to me.

For the last two weeks, Jackson has come over on Tuesdays and Fridays. We cook, we have a great time, and I would now consider him one of my closest friends.

The issue here is that I am so insanely attracted to everything he does.

I know at first I was apprehensive, but now that I know him, the real version he now shows me, I like him. A lot.

Him being superhero hot is a bonus, but he's also sweet and thoughtful, protective, funny, and nice to everyone he meets. He's the total package, but he might not be interested in more. At first, I was scared he just wanted to sleep with me, honestly. I try to give people the benefit of the doubt, but he did come on a bit strong. Now I'm not sure if he's even attracted to me.

We spend a lot of time together. When we cook dinner together, I always make sure there are leftovers for lunch. Since he doesn't have a mini fridge in his hotel room, he comes over on Wednesdays and Saturdays for lunch. And we tend to spend Sundays on his boat.

Remember that time I entered a nine-year relationship by accident? I guess that is not how it always works. Aspen has been trying to coach me on how to make a move, but I haven't worked up the courage yet.

Sure, we hold hands sometimes, and we typically hug when we say hello and goodbye. But aside from the occasional forehead kiss, nothing. I'm starting to wonder if Jackson is just a super physically affectionate guy. I get that. My family are huggers—my parents practically maul me every time I see them—so basic affection with friends is something I'm comfortable with.

But I want more.

And if he doesn't? I guess I hide until he leaves town and never try to date someone out of my league again.

Kidding. Maybe.

We have plans to make dinner tonight, but it's such a nice night, I want to propose I just make us some sandwiches and we go sit on the pier or something. As much fun as our cooking together has been, I feel like I've been so cooped up in the cottage lately, that I need to get out.

When Jackson arrives at my cottage, I cut him off before he can get out of his truck, opening his passenger side door and getting in with my cooler of food.

"Dinner on the pier?" I ask.

Jackson puts his truck into reverse and pulls back out onto the road.

"You've got it, boss."

Jackson fills me in on his day, and anything that happened since the last time I saw him. Although we are still learning new things about each other, there's a lot of comfort in the simple back and forth conversations.

I do think we need to have a serious conversation soon. You know, about my whole friendship theory. I have also started to feel bad not telling him about Christopher.

I know I don't owe him the entire story of my last relationship. But we were together for nine years. So much of who I am and my life is tied up in that relationship, and sometimes I feel like I'm skirting around the truth, not including Christopher's part in my life. But I don't think tonight is the night. It is far too pretty of a night for anything that serious.

Eating our sandwiches, we sit in silence, letting the waves crash against the pier, and the seagulls overhead create the soundtrack of our evening. Jackson's phone has been buzzing all night, but when I ask if he needs to call anyone or check in with work, he assures me it is nothing. I want to believe him. While I may have been sitting here in what I thought was a comfortable silence, I fear he was lost in other thoughts completely.

I'm really glad I decided not to have any serious conversations with Jackson tonight.

As we finish our food, I can tell he's distracted.

I trust that if he wanted to tell me what was going on he would, so I decided not to push and end the night early.

I know we didn't cook last night, but I haven't heard from Jackson at all today, and he didn't stop by for lunch. I had a sandwich made just in case, but it looks like I'll be feeding the ducks with it instead.

After a very productive morning, I was really looking forward to seeing him. I may or may not have been inspired and wrote a book today. And by that, I mean, I have one story completed and two more mapped out on my boating dog series.

I figured if Jackson is going to be constantly taking up my thoughts, he should make himself useful. And that is how Jack, the sailing golden retriever, was born.

So yes, I want to see Jackson and tell him all about it. I haven't even told anyone from my publishing company yet. I want to make sure Jackson doesn't think this is weird or crazy before anyone on my team starts working on it. I guess I need to go find him.

I could text to see where he is, but he shows up out of the blue all the time. Why can't I? I figure I'll bike around town and look for his truck. If that doesn't work, I can always call him and see where he is.

When I get to Main Street, I see his truck parked in front of The Inn. He isn't normally there during the day, but I'm not complaining because finding him here makes things easier for me. The sun is hot today, and I would be sweating if I actually had to bike all around town to find him.

Just as I am locking my bike to the bench out front, I hear the door of The Inn open.

Looking over my shoulder, I see Jackson emerge and I can't help but smile.

That is, until I see he's holding the door open for a beautiful brunette, and they seem to know each other, as his hand sits on her lower back, guiding her forward. She's wearing a skin-tight short dress, showing off her legs, and boobs and butt.

Looking down at my own clothes, I'm in faded jean shorts and a plain white tank. My hair is a mess on the top of my head because I plan to go swimming this afternoon and didn't want to put any curl product in it. We couldn't look more opposite right now. Not to mention, I'm a bit sweaty from the bike ride, and she looks like she probably smells like roses.

I'm not sure what is going on, and at this moment, I don't

think I want to find out. They are chatting like old friends, or more than friends. I think it's best if my surprise waits.

I undo my bike lock as quickly as I can, keeping my head down to hopefully go unnoticed. Luck is not on my side today because Jackson's pretty friend calls to me, "I love your bike. It's so cute."

I may be shy, but I'm not rude, so I slowly stand up straight and turn towards them. "Thanks," I say with a polite smile, trying to avoid looking at Jackson. He is clearly doing the same as he hardly makes eye contact and says, "Hey, Lil."

I've always liked when he called me Lil. No one else does, so it felt special.

Right now, it feels like a blade through my stomach.

I force the polite smile to remain on my lips and look to Jackson.

"Hi, Jackson."

Jackson's friend looks from Jackson to me and then back to him again, before sticking her hand out to mine and saying words I am not ready to hear. "I'm Veronica, Jackson's girl-friend."

His girlfriend? Did I ever ask him if he was single? Thinking back, I don't think I did. I guess I assumed when you spend as much time together as we do, he would have mentioned it. He's an attractive man, of course he has a girlfriend back at home. Was he setting me up to be some summer side piece? I think I might throw up.

"Oh, it's very nice to meet you," I say, even though it doesn't feel very nice right now. I am so stupid. It all makes sense now; we really are just friends. I didn't throw myself at him like most women probably do, so he saw this lonely shy girl and thought, "Hmm, she needs a friend, I'll be nice to her."

I'm basically a charity case. A convenient one.

Shit.

Well, this is going way worse than I could have predicted.

Why did I think this was a good idea? Yeah, Lillian, go surprise your not-boyfriend who hasn't shown any interest beyond friendship, because remember, you're convenient. It will totally go well for you. I feel like an idiot. This is why I stay in my comfort zone of having one friend. I know I need to say something. I've already been silent long enough that it would be deemed rude, but I'm spiralling.

Jackson looks like he is about to say something, and I don't think I want to stick around to hear it.

Remember back when I first met Jackson and I would awkwardly leave very suddenly? Yeah, I'm doing that again.

I get onto my bike, rather ungracefully, and take off down the street without looking back. This bike is not made for speed, but I push it to the limit all the way home.

Once inside, I immediately turn off my phone, put on my comfiest clothes and curl up in bed with my Kindle. You know who's never hurt my feelings? My book boyfriends.

Anxiety sucks.

Especially when an anxious thought comes true, cementing that your anxiety was justified and you should listen to it from now on. That's where I was at before the emergency session with my therapist this morning. I used to see her often, but with the coping methods she taught me, I have been doing well, and we only meet every other month. I know Jackson having a girlfriend is not the end of the world. But I also know myself enough to know this will cause a setback in my mental health journey, and it's okay to need support to stay on track.

Rational support, that is. I held off on telling Aspen anything until after my session. The last thing I need is her convincing me arson is the answer to my problems.

The best part of my emergency session? It required that I take off for the city. Now I can pretend I'm not intentionally avoiding Jackson. Although all of the unanswered text messages would say otherwise.

Am I being mature? Probably not.

Am I giving myself grace and avoiding him for one day? Yes.

My therapist said I am allowed to take things at my own pace. My problems will still be there tomorrow, and as long as I put in the effort to work through what's going on in my head, my anxiety and insecurity, she supports me.

I can't stress enough the importance of a good relationship with your therapist. I went through a couple before I found the right one for me.

Every person is on their own journey and the healing journey is unique to them. That's what Miranda, my therapist, told me during one of our first sessions, and I couldn't agree more.

So here I am, alone in my condo, giving myself grace. Self-improvement is on tomorrow's agenda. Today we binge Netflix and eat takeout.

Chapter 16
Jackson

I am having the worst week ever.

Okay, that is probably an exaggeration, but it's not going great.

Everything was fine until I got multiple texts and phone calls from Veronica when I was with Lillian on Thursday night.

Veronica and I have known each other for a while. We were friends in university and then when she moved to Toronto after graduation, we remained friends. She didn't know many people and wasn't used to city life, so I showed her around, introduced her to my friends and we stayed in contact.

About six months ago, I think I made a mistake. I slept with her. We've always gotten along well, and she knew about my casual dating status, so when she made a move after a night of drinking, I went with it. Nothing about our friendship changed after that, but we did typically sleep together after we would hang out. That being said, we only hung out five times after the initial incident.

I haven't been very responsive to Veronica's text messages since being in Bluefield. She knew I was heading here for work and would be busy, so she didn't call me out on it.

I honestly haven't thought much about her since being here. We are better as friends. It's less messy that way, and I figured the next time I saw her, I would tell her that.

I didn't think the next time I saw her would be Thursday night when she surprised me by coming to Bluefield and getting a room at The Inn for the weekend. She didn't know I was also staying there, but she figured it would be a romantic weekend for us.

Obviously, I needed to clear up the misunderstanding surrounding our friendship, but I was so shocked, I faked a headache on Thursday night and went to my own room, promising we could meet for lunch the next day.

I then proceeded to sleep through my alarm and almost miss

a video conference with our designer. Of course, we are having problems with the design firm that typically works with our clients, adding stress I don't need right now. That meeting went long, and Veronica had been blowing up my phone all morning.

It was already past noon when we met up to get lunch. I was craving a burger from Ron's, but there was no way I was taking Veronica to one of Lillian's favourite spots.

It feels like a special place to us, and I didn't want Ron to see me with another girl and get the wrong impression.

The wrong impression Veronica had clearly gotten. As we exited The Inn, things went from bad to worse. Lillian was outside.

With everything going on, I hadn't talked to her since I had dropped her off the night before, and I couldn't even tell you if I had missed messages from her waiting on my phone. As soon as I saw her face, I knew things were going to get a lot worse, and they did.

Veronica is not my girlfriend.

She has never been my girlfriend, and she will never be my girlfriend.

After Lillian took off on her bike, I nicely told Veronica just that and sent her on her way without lunch. I couldn't tell you if she decided to stay the weekend or not, and I don't plan on finding out.

Was that the nicest thing to do to someone I had been friends with for years? Probably not. But with her showing up like she did and acting territorial with Lillian, I don't think I want that kind of person as my friend anyway. She knew exactly what she was doing. The satisfied smile on her face as Lillian pedalled away told me all I needed to know about who Veronica really is as a person.

I tried calling Lillian multiple times on Friday, but I got sent to voicemail every time, so her phone was clearly off. I waited until Saturday to stop by her cottage, but her car was gone. When she finally responded to my text on Saturday night, I was both relieved and worried that she had gone into the city.

She doesn't need to be in Bluefield for the summer. It's a choice she's making; one that she could reverse at any time.

I will be here until Thanksgiving most likely, so if she chooses to never want to see me again, she can do that quite easily.

I really hope that isn't the case since this is one big miscommunication. As much as I would love to blame Veronica for this entire situation, I think she was only the catalyst. I have been dragging my feet when I should have told Lillian everything. That I like her, want to date her, have no idea what I'm doing. That I'm scared.

That is also why I haven't really made a proper move. It's not that I think she will reject me. Although, she could. But putting myself out there and then screwing it up? Terrifying. Sitting in this in-between isn't much better though. So although I will not be thanking Veronica any time soon, if I can get Lillian to talk to me again, she may have helped give me the push I needed.

Lillian didn't say when exactly she was going to be back. The weekend could mean midday Sunday, Sunday night, or Monday morning.

Would it be creepy if I just camped out at the Waldens' and waited for her to come back? I hope the answer isn't yes, because that's exactly what I plan on doing.

I know my parents' divorce messed me up a bit, but what I didn't acknowledge until now is that aside from movies, I don't really know anything about relationships, or how to handle conflict within them. I didn't get to witness my parents argue and make up. I don't think my dad even knows the meaning of the word compromise.

I contemplated calling my Aunt Caroline, Simon's mom, but for one, she would lecture me about being stupid and I already know I am. And two, I'm almost twenty-eight years old. I should probably figure this out on my own.

So here I am, sitting in my truck facing Lillian's cottage.

I brought snacks and a blanket. If I end up here all night, then so be it, but I want to clear the air as soon as possible.

It has only been three days, but I miss her. And if I've hurt her, which at this point, it's safe to assume I have, I want to make it up to her. The thought of her being hurt has been giving me stomach pains all day.

After three hours, every email ever sent to me has been responded to, I created a new filing system within my inbox, and have won four games of Hearts. I'm about to start my fifth game when headlights break through the trees from around the bend. Lillian's white BMW pulls into her driveway, where she sits for five minutes unmoving. My truck is turned off, so I don't think she has noticed me yet, and if she has, she's too focused on the conversation she's having with herself to acknowledge me.

Even though there haven't been any issues since her bike tires were slashed, I don't want her to think that I'm some weirdo lurking about, so I get out of my truck and approach her car slowly. I listen to see if she's on the phone with someone, but I don't hear anyone respond to her. It does seem like Lillian is, in fact, having a conversation with herself, or maybe giving herself a pep talk.

Her shoulders rise and fall slowly as she takes a deep breath and grabs the handle to open her car door. She takes one step out of the car and spots me standing there watching her, like the weirdo I was trying not to be. With a high-pitched squeak, she falls back into her car and shuts the door quickly.

By that reaction, I think it's safe to say Lillian was avoiding me, and I should have waited until she told me she was back.

What I should have done and what I am doing are not the same thing, and I don't have it in me to be apologetic about it. Lack of communication got me into this mess; I am not putting off the hard conversations anymore.

With that in mind, I reopen Lillian's door and grab her hand. She seems too shocked to react, so I take the opportunity to pull her out of the car and right into my arms. I always hug her when I see her, and I'm not letting that change. There is a chance this will be the last hug we will share, so I'm taking everything I can get right now.

She stays stiff in my arms for a moment, and then relaxes into my hold. My heart is beating so fast that with her head resting on my chest, she probably feels like she's at a techno concert. I hold her for as long as she lets me, which always feels too short. When she pulls away, I look down at her sad, tired eyes. It seems as though she didn't get much sleep either, which makes me feel even worse.

With a soft sigh, I say, "We need to talk."

She nods her head, taking a step back and breaking off the

physical contact we still had.

I follow her into her cottage and head straight to the couch. I would love some caffeine right now, but I would rather get straight to business than let us procrastinate.

Lillian sits on the opposite side of the couch. She brings her knees to her chest, resting her chin on top of them. I would like to pull her closer, but I can't bulldoze her need for space just because the distance fuels my insecurities.

Wanting to get right into it, I say, "Veronica is not my girlfriend."

"Does she know that?"

Fair question.

"Yes, she does. And I'm not sure why she thought it was okay to say or think that. She was a friend."

"Just a friend?" she asks, face remaining impassive. I've never seen this side of Lillian before and it kind of scares me.

Taking a deep breath, I give her the truth. "We've been friends for a while. Earlier this year, those lines of friendship blurred a bit." I cringe internally. "They blurred a couple of times. But we hadn't spoken since I came to Bluefield. I had no idea she was going to show up here or act like that."

"Did she know they were just blurred lines and not the beginning of a relationship?"

"I thought so. But I've been wrong a lot recently. She never vocalized it, but I also didn't tell her either way." Apparently, I don't need to call my aunt after all. Lillian is going to make sure I know I'm stupid without the lecture. "We didn't talk about it. I tend to just not have the hard conversations and assume everyone is on the same page."

"Clearly," she says under her breath and immediately blushes when she realizes I heard her.

I'm not sure if it's to save myself, or if I think blurting statements out about myself is the way to solve my problems, but the next words out of my mouth are, "I've never been in a relationship."

Lillian's eyes snap up to mine. "Never?"

"Never," I say. "I've gone on dates and that sort of thing, but there was never a title or commitment involved."

Saying it out loud makes me feel gross. I might as well rent a billboard that says, "Jackson Mane is a walking red flag." And since I want this to be a two-way conversation, I ask, "What about you?"

Lillian hesitates a moment, chewing on her lip. "I've had one boyfriend." I release the breath I was holding.

One boyfriend. That makes my lack of experience seem not so bad. That thought bubble immediately pops when she continues.

"We dated for nine years, through most of university. And then we lived together until we broke up. Which was in January of this year."

Shit. Nine years is not a light and fluffy relationship. They lived together. They were common-law. She was in love. Is she still in love? Shit. I'm chasing a girl who might be in love with someone else. I'm just the puppy who's been following her around for a month and a half.

Shit.

"Are you over him? Like is that relationship done, done?" The hesitation in my voice is very evident, but I don't have it in me to care right now.

"Very done," she says with a serious tone. "It should have ended sooner. Christopher and I spent almost a third of our lives together. I will always have love for him. But I haven't been in love with him for a long time."

Okay, I can handle that. Spiral temporarily paused. Back to blurting out statements.

"I like you, Lil. I don't want to sound like I'm in grade five, but I like like you. I want to date you. I'm focused on this." I point between us. "Us. I want to see where this could go."

Lillian scoots closer to me. I grab both her hands and hold them in mine, reveling in the fact that she's letting me touch her.

"I like you, too, Jackson."

Yes!

Wooooooo!

Internal fist pump.

"But..." She trails off, and no...

But? No buts.

Please. No.

"But?" I ask, when she doesn't immediately continue.

"But my head is a mess. The whole thing with Veronica brought some insecurities back that I need to deal with. I am just now feeling like I've got a handle on my job again, so I don't want to commit to anything more at this very moment."

Okay.

Okay. I can handle this. "This very moment, like not never, but you just need a bit of time?"

She nods her head cautiously.

"And we can keep hanging out while you deal with everything going on in your head?"

She nods her head again, a small smile forming on her lips.

"Oh, thank god." Without thinking, I grab Lillian's cheeks with both my hands and haul her mouth to mine. This is, in fact, the opposite of giving her time to figure her head out, but I am so relieved I can't help it. The kiss ends as quickly as it starts, but every second of it feels right.

When Lillian pulls away, her entire body matches the pink of the sun currently setting over the lake. It's probably the cutest she's ever looked, but I'm not going to force her to embrace it. I pull her onto my lap so she can hide her face in my chest. We sit here for a while, basking in us.

Because even if there isn't officially an 'us,' I will do everything I can to ensure there is one, when she's ready.

Chapter 17
Lillian

I almost drift to sleep in Jackson's arms, but my phone ringing somewhere in the cottage wakes me. I quickly jump off the couch, startling Jackson, who also looks like he was about to fall asleep. I grab my phone from where my purse is sitting on the entry table by the door.

Looking at the screen, I see my brother is calling.

"Hey, loser," he greets, which unfortunately is completely normal for our conversations.

"Hey, Ben. Is everything okay? It's pretty late for you, old man." If he's going to call me names, I'm going to sling them right back. What else are little sisters for, right?

"Oh, shut it. I have a quick question. Your boyfriend is in construction, right? Like, he can fix things?"

I pause, because how does he know about Jackson? I look over at the man in question, making sure he can't hear my brother's side of the conversation. The last thing I need is him hearing Ben call him my boyfriend after I just said I wasn't ready for that.

Ben continues, clearly reading my mind, "Aspen."

"When were you talking to Aspen?" I ask. Since we've been friends forever, it wouldn't be that weird for them to be talking. He's basically her brother, too. But she hadn't told me they had talked recently, which she normally would.

"She and Noah were video chatting the other day and she was telling him all about your boat day. Now I either need to buy Noah a boat or your new boyfriend needs to take him out on it when we come next month."

Okay, that makes more sense.

Noah has a huge crush on Aspen, even though she's basically his aunt at this point, so they hang out once a month and video call almost weekly.

I'm not sure why she thought telling my five-year-old nephew I have a boyfriend was necessary, but Aspen doesn't always have a filter.

I can tell Ben is getting frustrated with our conversation or my lack of response.

"So can he fix things or what?" I look behind me to Jackson, who is polite enough to pretend he's not listening. I'm now confident he can't hear Ben, but he can hear my side of the conversation.

Whispering to Ben, "I mean, he's not my boyfriend, but yeah. He isn't very hands-on with his job, but he has tools and the knowledge, I guess?"

Taking a deep breath, his voice turns serious. "For the sake of my sanity, we are calling him your boyfriend. I'm not explaining to my five-year-old hookup culture. And you're my little sister, so gross. But I need you to get him to replace the rotting boards on Mrs. Langley's porch. She tripped last week and I don't want her hurting herself."

"Oh, yeah, I can ask. Not a problem." Hopefully, that eases the tension my brother seems to be feeling.

Mrs. Langley is an older woman who has lived in town her whole life, I think. She has a granddaughter, Alexandra, who hung around us when she was younger because she was friends with Aspen's little sister. I haven't seen her in years, but my brother formed some sort of friendship with Mrs. Langley and he always makes a point of checking in with her.

It's a bit weird, but sweet.

"Thank you, Lillian. Just have the bill for any materials and labour costs sent to me. Don't let her try to pay for anything, but if she offers you her peanut butter cookies, please put some in the freezer for me."

That makes me laugh. Their friendship was probably formed due to her incredible baking skills, and her cookies are the best, so who am I to judge?

"Will do," I say. "I'm with him right now, so I'll ask. I don't know his work schedule, but we'll get it done as soon as we can."

This catches Jackson's attention and he gives me a quizzical look while pointing to himself.

"It's late. Don't tell me you're with a boy, Lillian. I don't want nightmares. I'm saying goodnight before I puke." God, he's so dramatic. "Goodnight, loser. Love you."

"Love you too, old man."

As soon as I hang up the phone, Jackson is right there.

"Who was that? And were you talking about me?"

I take his hand and guide him back into the living room. "That was my brother and yes, we were talking about you." I raise my eyebrows, adding to the drama. Jackson looks seriously stressed about this. "Oh, calm down. He asked for a favour actually, so you don't need to worry. But you do need to help fix an elderly woman's deck."

"Is this some sort of test? Do older brothers ask their sister's male friends to do community service to get their blessing? Is that a thing?" The worried look on his face is quite cute, but after the conversation we just had, I am not going to torture him.

"No, nothing like that. He genuinely needs someone with your skillset to help him," I assure him.

He visibly relaxes into the back of the couch, laying his arm along the back so he can draw small circles on my arm. "Okay, I can handle that, not a problem."

I settle into the couch further, allowing his fingers to lull me into a sense of calm. What a whirlwind the last couple of days have been. From the low on Friday, to the sadness of Saturday, to now. I feel like I have whiplash.

It would have been so easy to tell Jackson I'm all in and I

want to be in a relationship. He's put his cards on the table and was quite honest. But after a lot of self-reflection over the last forty-eight hours, I'm not there. I want to be there. I am not there yet.

My reaction to the incident on Friday with Veronica basically highlighted I am not ready to be in another relationship. I had a doomsday reaction. Some of the things I thought about myself were not nice. And I need to be nice to myself before I can be nice to others. I projected the lack of trust I have with myself onto Jackson. I ran before he could clear things up, and then I hid.

It wouldn't be fair to him to enter a relationship when that was my reaction.

The fact that he's willing to wait while I work on myself is a relief. He doesn't have to do that, but he seems eager to be on this journey with me, which is more than I could ever ask for.

When I was speaking with Miranda again this morn-ing—she's a hero for taking my call on a Sunday—she reminded me that even though I was in a long-term relationship, I still have no idea what I'm doing.

Okay, so she didn't put it exactly like that, but that was the gist of it.

Christopher and I rarely fought, hardly ever had conflict, and brushed a lot under the rug. It's not surprising our re-lationship was pretty lackluster near the end. We had passion for our careers and not a lot else. If it wasn't about work, our conversations were facts, no debates, no feelings. Turns out you can live with someone successfully for years without knowing how to communicate.

I feel like in the span of an hour, Jackson and I have already surpassed the level of communication I am used to. I hope this will set us up for success. Because let's be honest, I like like him, too.

As I've been staring off into space, I can see out of the corner of my eye that Jackson is looking at me, quite lovingly actually. Trying not to blush, I turn my head to meet his eyes.

"What?" I ask.

"Can I ask you a question?"

That makes me a bit nervous, but, "Okay…"

"You mentioned earlier you had a handle on your job. What did you mean by that?"

I'm sure my excitement is palpable as I tuck my knees under my butt so I can turn and face him properly. "I completed my first book and have plans for all the others!"

Jackson matches my level of excitement. I want to tell him all about it, but honestly, I am so tired.

I haven't had much sleep the last couple of days and if I want to continue with my productivity tomorrow, I need to get to bed soon.

"Can I rain-check the work update till tomorrow? I'm so ready for bed."

"Of course," he agrees, getting up from the couch and slowly heading towards the door. I don't blame him for delaying leaving. I am dead on my feet, but after three days apart, leaving feels hard. I lean against the doorframe while Jackson stands on the small porch.

"Before you go, there weren't any issues over the weekend with vandalism or anything?" I ask.

"No, everything was very quiet around here. Thankfully."

"I'm glad to hear that." And I mean it. It's almost been three weeks now since my tires were slashed and I feel like I can relax again. I am still locking every entryway to the cottage, but I probably should have been doing that all along. We stand in silence for a minute, neither of us trying to end the conversation. It makes me want to giggle, but I hold it in.

"Goodnight, Lil." Jackson pulls me towards him like he's going to hug me, but moves at the last second, giving me a goodnight kiss.

It's slow and sweet and oh so right. If Jackson wasn't actively holding me, I would be in a puddle on the floor. I get lost in the kiss. Just as his tongue touches my lips, I remember that I'm not ready for this yet. But what great motivation kissing Jackson Mane could be.

I pull away before we can get too lost in it. Jackson has a dopey and slightly guilty look on his face. He knew exactly what he was doing with that kiss.

"Goodnight, Jackson."

He plants one more kiss on my forehead and walks backwards towards his truck that's parked next door.

I'm not sure how I didn't notice it when I first got here, my mind was too preoccupied to take in my surroundings.

Once he's out of sight, I close the door and lock up for the night. It's not until I'm all tucked into bed that I allow the butterflies in my stomach to truly take flight. Kicking my feet with a giggle into my pillow, I can't help the smile on my face.

Chapter 18
Jackson

UNKNOWN:

Don't eat all my cookies

JACKSON:

Who is this?

Mrs. Langley is a hoot.

When I showed up at her house with my tools and some lumber, she didn't even bat an eye. I'm not sure if Ben warned her I would be coming or not, but she didn't ask any questions. She showed me the board she tripped on like it was the only problem with her porch. It's not. The whole deck needs to come down. If I had to guess, the wood is original to the house, probably built in the thirties. The fact that it's still standing is a miracle, but just replacing the worst boards is not going to be worth it. I'm rebuilding this thing.

I'm going to need way more lumber than I had originally

thought, so today is more of a meet and greet, I guess. I've made friends with the guy at the lumber yard, so I should be able to start on this thing on Wednesday. I would say tomorrow, but there's no way I'm postponing my cooking date with Lillian. Even for a sweet old lady.

I had hoped to stop by to see Lillian tonight, but Mrs. Langley pulled out her photo albums and has started what seems to be a family history lesson. My grandparents on both my mother's and father's sides were dead before I was born, so honestly, this is kind of nice. I'm not sure why Ben is looking out for this old lady, but I don't blame him. I wouldn't mind if she adopted me. And her cookies, my god. Lillian warned me that any and all cookies I received must be shared, but how would she know there were two cookie tins to start?

I have a theory that the unknown text I received earlier was from Ben, also laying claim to these cookies. And if I had to guess how he got my number, suspect number one is Aspen. The more time I spend with Lillian, the more I know that just saying 'Aspen' is enough of an explanation in a lot of cases.

Around 8 pm, Mrs. Langley says it's her bedtime, so I help her put away the photo albums, grab my cookies, and head for my truck. It's parked around the corner since Mrs. Langley's driveway only has enough space for one car.

As I walk around the bend, I stop dead in my tracks. There is a red liquid that looks a lot like blood smeared all over my grey truck. Looking around the street, I don't see anyone outside.

This is a quiet street with small bungalows. From what Mrs. Langley told me, almost everyone on the street is retired, so I imagine the dark houses are filled with sleeping seniors. I slowly approach my truck, making sure I don't see anyone hiding around the side, and pull my phone from my pocket, immediately calling Constable Peters.

"Constable Peters," he greets after two rings.

"Hey, man, it's Jackson. I've got a problem."

"I'm just on Main Street. Are you at Lillian's?"

"Do you know where Mrs. Langley lives? 'Cause that's where I need you to head."

"Sure do." I can hear the sound of his car starting. "I'll be there in two minutes." He hangs up before I can thank him and true to his word, he pulls up behind my truck about two minutes later.

"Oh, that's pretty gross," Peters says, as he steps towards my truck to get a closer look.

"Is that your professional opinion?" I ask, mostly joking, but I want to make sure he's taking this seriously.

He gives me a look that has me closing my mouth. Peters can be an intimidating man when he wants to be.

He grabs some stuff from his car to take a sample of the blood and then takes photos.

"Unfortunately for us, this happened on one of the quietest streets in town, so odds are no one saw anything. The blood is still wet, so this most likely happened in the last thirty minutes. I am hoping when I send my samples to the lab, it will come back as animal blood, but I will let you know either way. Have you had any trouble or seen anything suspicious since Lillian's tires were slashed?"

"I haven't, no. Lillian thought she might have heard something late at night a couple of weeks ago, but assumed it was an animal. We both figured whoever it was had left town or was done. This doesn't look done."

"I'm afraid not." Constable Peters loads everything back into his vehicle and hands me some wipes to use on my door handle.

"There is a car wash in this town, right?" I ask.

He shakes his head. "No, but we have a power washer at the station. If you follow me back, you're free to use it."

"Lead the way."

I was only able to spray my truck with water; they didn't have any soap lying around. As gross as it is, the blood being mostly wet still worked to my advantage and my truck looks basically clean.

I will be driving to the nearest car wash in the morning, regardless, and putting my truck through it multiple times for peace of mind.

Constable Peters agrees that someone is messing with me. They haven't had any other vandalism in town. It seems as though I am the only target of whoever is doing this. Well, me and Lillian, by association.

It's for that reason that I find myself at her door after leaving the police station. I raise my hand to knock, but the door opens before I make contact.

"Oh, Jackson." Lillian startles, holding a bag of garbage in her hand while the other clutches her chest. I take the bag from her hand and quickly dispose of it in the bin at the end of her driveway. The second I'm back in front of her, I haul her into my body and crush her into a hug. I didn't know how much this evening affected me until this moment, but all I want is to hold Lillian for the rest of the night.

Lillian returns the hug, but slowly walks us backwards into the cottage without letting go. Once we are through the doorway, I flick the door closed with my foot and urge Lillian to keep walking us until we reach the couch, where I pull her down with me, forcing her to straddle my lap. Lillian pushes the stray hair from my forehead, reminding me I need a haircut, and strokes my cheek.

"Are you okay?"

"Kind of," I answer truthfully. "I'm glad to see you, but my truck was vandalized tonight."

Lillian looks over my shoulder, like she is trying to see my truck through the wall. "It's dark out, but I didn't notice anything wrong with it."

"I had to power wash it."

Lillian looks straight into my eyes, wearing concern all over her face. "What did you have to wash off, Jackson?"

"Blood."

"Blood?!" she shrieks. "Whose blood?"

"Probably a small animal, but Peters is running tests to confirm."

"That is so disturbing. Are you okay? Did anyone see anything?"

I pull her closer, resting my forehead against hers and just breathing her scent for a moment. I'm not sure if it's all the time she spends around books, but she smells a bit like weathered paper. There is also a lingering scent of flowers and citrus. It could be her shampoo, but I would like to bathe in it if I could. Just to be surrounded by her at all times.

"I'm better now. With you," I say, because it's the truth. Being around Lillian makes everything better. Suddenly an idea comes to mind and it may be stupid, but I've got to go for it. "How would you feel about a roommate?"

"What do you mean?" she asks skeptically.

"Someone is clearly out to get me. And possibly you by association. It's up to you, but I would feel a lot better if you weren't staying in this cottage alone." She doesn't look completely put out by this idea, so I continue. "Whoever is out to get me either followed me to Mrs. Langley's or recognized my truck and saw an opportunity. Regardless, they're watching. What do you think?"

She takes a moment, looking like she's putting serious thought into it.

"I can sleep on the couch or on the floor. In any of the bedrooms. Whatever makes you most comfortable..."

A sassy smile appears on her face. "Is this your way of getting more home-cooked meals?"

A laugh bursts out of my mouth. If you told me an hour ago I would be laughing tonight, I wouldn't have believed you, but Lillian has me laughing and feeling lighter already.

"It certainly is a perk." I chuckle. "What do you say, roommate? If you ever want me to leave, I will. You choose my move-out date."

With a mischievous look in her eyes, she holds out her hand to shake and says, "Roommates."

I take her extended hand and kiss each of her fingers, then her palm before taking it in my hand and shaking it. She giggles and pulls me into a hug, hiding her face in my neck.

Suddenly, her body stills, and she pulls away from me slowly. "You smell like cookies. Where are they?"

Hesitantly, I say, "There's a tin in the truck." Before I have the final word out of my mouth, Lillian is up and out the door. I pull my keys out of my pocket to unlock it for her, relocking when she returns to the cottage, cookie tin in hand.

"First things first," she says, putting the tin on the counter and shoving a cookie in her mouth. Mumbling around the cookie, she continues, "We put half of these in an airtight Tupperware container for my brother."

"Is he that serious about these cookies?"

Lillian looks at me like I have zero brain cells.

"Jackson, he would beat you up over these cookies." I laugh, but she doesn't. "I'm serious. He takes his cookies very seriously."

"Okay, got it," I say, raising my hands in defence as I join her in the kitchen. "I don't want him to hate me before he's even met me. His cookies are safe."

Now the text from him makes more sense.

"If she gives me any more when I go back on Wednesday, I will make sure to save them."

"Thank you," she says, as another cookie enters her mouth, crumbs falling down her chin. "Do you need to go pack a bag or something?" I can hardly understand what she's saying because she hasn't finished chewing yet.

Before Lillian can grab another cookie, I snatch the tin from her and put it in a cupboard out of her reach. She grumbles something I can't quite hear and sticks her lower lip out in the cutest pout ever.

"Cookies," she whines.

I grab her around the waist and lift her onto the butcher block counter.

"You're going to have nightmares if you have too much sugar before bed."

"Nu-uh." She continues to pout. "You'll be here to chase away all the bad guys and bad dreams."

I step between her legs and run my hands up her thighs, watching the goosebumps scatter across her bare arms and legs. With everything going on tonight, I hadn't taken in her outfit until now. Lillian is wearing what looks like a pair of men's striped boxer shorts, rolled up at the waist a couple of times, and a tank top, seemingly without a bra.

Remembering her question, I say, "I'll be fine for tonight, but I'll grab some stuff from The Inn tomorrow." I wait a few moments for Lillian to respond, but she doesn't. When I look up at her, she's just staring back at me with a look I haven't seen from her but can recognize. Lust. Testing the waters, I lean forward and run my nose along the nape of her neck, breathing in that uniquely Lillian smell. She lets out a quiet moan that goes straight to my cock. I will it to stay where it is, but it's no use.

"Lil," I choke out. "I know you said you aren't ready for this yet. And I completely respect that. We can take this as slow as you need, but I'm getting some mixed signals here."

She arches towards me, whispering, "Maybe not so slow."

That is all the permission I need.

I pull her as close as I can, so we are lined up in all the places I want her most. I weave my fingers through her hair and plant a kiss on her lips. This kiss isn't like the others we've shared; it's intense and full of need.

Lillian's hands are everywhere, in my hair, roving over my back, and squeezing my ass, pulling me closer. My cock is rock hard as it presses against Lillian's centre, causing her to whimper into our kiss. I trail my lips down her neck, nibbling on the delicate skin as I go.

"Jackson," she moans, as I continue my path down her throat to her collarbone. I slide the right strap of her tank top off her shoulder and leave an open-mouthed kiss there. Lillian's head falls back as she continues to rock against my aching cock. If she keeps this up, I'm going to finish in my pants.

I'd like to say I have stamina, but it's been a couple of months of just me and my hand, and I have definitely fantasized about us in this exact position in the shower a couple of times.

"Lil," I whisper, making my way toward her hard nipple that has fallen out of her shirt. "We either need way less clothes on or we need to stop."

She's completely lost in the moment and doesn't respond. I swirl my tongue around her perky pink nipple, while I hold her other breast in my hand, massaging it.

Lillian's hand travels down my chest until it reaches the hem of my shirt.

She slides her hand under my shirt and scratches her nails across my abs, sending another jolt to my dick. I am about to burst.

Reluctantly, I let Lillian's nipple out of my mouth with a pop and slide her shirt back into place. Lillian looks into my eyes, dazed and confused. "Why are we stopping?"

"I don't want to stop. Trust me, I don't want to." I press my erection into her once more before taking a step back to prove my point. "A lot has happened tonight and I don't want either of us making an emotional decision. I also don't want our first time together to be on the kitchen counter."

She gives her head a shake. "Right, you are so right. Let's go to bed." I chuckle at her eagerness and she growls at me, her cheeks blushing bright. "Not like that, just to sleep. And cuddle?"

Like I could ever turn her down. "Yes, all of the cuddles, please."

Considering I was prepared to sleep on the couch, floor, or even my truck, being invited into Lillian's bed is better than I could have expected. Either she's more scared than she's telling me, or she might like me as much as I like her.

Based on the scene in the kitchen, the chemistry is certainly there, but I'm in this for more than just her body, no matter how good it feels pressed against me.

This day went from bad, to better. I may need multiple car washes in the morning, but I am choosing to not think about tomorrow just yet. We make quick work of getting ready for bed. I borrow the same pair of her brother's sweats as the last time I stayed over. I may have been in Lillian's bed that time, too, but she wasn't in there with me, and we don't have Aspen as an audience this time either.

Lillian pulls the floral quilt back and gestures for me to get in beside her. I do so quickly and with less grace than I could have.

Lillian can tell I'm eager, but she only laughs, not making too much fun of me.

Someone is out to get me. I need to sit down and seriously think through my next steps tomorrow. But right now, I'm cuddled up in Lillian's bed, her body pressed against mine, head resting on my chest and all I can think of is, this is how I want to finish every day from now on.

Chapter 19
Lillian

This morning, I wake up with Jackson's rather large erection nestled between my ass cheeks. Good morning to me.

What happened in the kitchen last night? That was hot. There is no other way to describe it.

I am glad Jackson stopped us before we went too far. I don't regret any of it, and I don't think he will either, but it was the right thing at the time.

My bladder screams in pain, telling me it's time to get up. The sun is peeking through the curtains, so I know we've slept through the night.

I try to unwrap myself from Jackson's strong arms, but he pulls me closer into his chest instead.

I turn over in his arms and plant a light kiss on his nose, because of morning breath, then try to extract myself from his hold.

He is having none of that.

Crushing me in his arms, he takes my mouth in a slow and sensual kiss. The frenzy from last night is gone, but this feels just as passionate. We kiss for what could have been minutes, or hours until my bladder really can't take it anymore.

I pull away slowly and whisper, "Morning." Jackson is attractive at all times of day, but Jackson disheveled and sleepy. Panty melting.

He gives me a lopsided smile, dimple and all, and nestles his head into my chest while grumbling, "Good morning," back to me.

"You're very cute right now, but I need to pee. Please let me go." He grumbles some more and then finally releases me from his tight hold. I jump up and run to the bathroom before he can change his mind.

I breeze through my morning routine and get dressed while Jackson lies in bed, arm resting behind his head as he watches me.

"Enjoying the show?" I ask, making eye contact with him

through the mirror over the dresser. He smirks at me.

"I could watch you do just about anything and be entertained." I crinkle my nose because that's a bit cheesy. Cute, but cheesy.

"You know, you aren't anything how I thought you would be?" I say because it's true. I definitely judged a book by its cover with him.

This gets his attention. He sits up and leans against the headboard. "What do you mean?" The blankets fall around his waist and I completely forget what we are talking about for a moment. Jackson clears his throat, a small smile on his face, bringing me back to my thoughts.

"Well, after we met, I told Aspen about you and she quickly figured out that she knew you, or of you, from some high school parties. I was convinced you were some party playboy who would never be interested in talking to me, let alone anything more."

Jackson swings his legs over to the side and stands from the bed, slowly approaching me. He pulls me into his arms once I'm within reach. "And what do you think now?"

"I think you are kind, thoughtful and hardworking. You are also a big softy."

He looks into my eyes. "Only soft for you."

I look down between us, because there is a very not soft body part pressing against me.

"It's the morning," he grumbles, dropping his face into my neck, and I can't help but laugh. I kiss each of his cheeks and then his nose. Now that we are kissing each other, I can't help but want to do it all the time. Everything he does and says makes me want to kiss him. I guess I'm a little obsessed with him.

We reluctantly untwine our body parts from each other. We both have work to do today and for Jackson, he has people waiting on him.

The sun is warm and truly feels like a summer day for the first time this year, so I set up shop on the deck overlooking the lake and tell Jackson to use whatever he wants inside if he wants to work from here. He heads out to get the things done that he needs to.

I can't tell you exactly what he does in a day. It seems to be different every day, but he promises he will hit up the grocery store at some point for dinner ingredients.

Tonight, we are making Sopa De Pollo, a Colombian chicken soup that serves as one of my comfort foods.

I thought Jackson staying here would be weirder than it is. I know it hasn't even been twenty-four hours, but even getting ready, and making breakfast and coffee together felt completely normal.

I have been trying not to compare my relationship with Christopher to what I have with Jackson, but since it's my only point of reference, it's hard not to.

When Christopher and I first moved in together, I felt like I was tripping over my feet to constantly stay out of his way. We actually had our own bedrooms at first, because we were so young and our parents insisted. It was a smart choice. Sometimes I would hide in my room if I needed time alone or didn't want to talk. I obviously got over that eventually, but I just assumed that would always be how I felt when I first lived with someone new.

I know Jackson has never been in a real relationship, and we are going to have to learn how to communicate better and just about each other in general, but this man was made to be in a relationship. Like, he screams golden retriever boyfriend without even trying.

If I wasn't the one he was interested in, I would be very jealous of the person he chose to give all his affection and attention to.

I get a decent amount of work done. I explained the concept to Jackson this morning and he thought it was great, so I sent off the outline to my editor and graphic artist for approval. I also sent an email to Christopher, because I always have. I don't necessarily need his approval, but he's been a part of every project I have worked on since graduation, and even if we aren't dating, I still want our working relationship to be maintained. It's now been six months since we broke up and although our interactions have been greatly reduced, they've been pleasant. He responds right away not saying much, but asking if we can meet in person sometime.

Nerves are officially on edge.

With me working remotely, we plan for a time at the end of the next month when he plans to be in the area, giving me enough time to hopefully have all the storylines complete and with the editing team.

I've been so engrossed in my work that I'm startled when the screen door opens and closes behind me. Jackson appears in front of me, shirtless, in a pair of light blue swim trunks. I remember running my fingers over his abs last night, and I wouldn't mind another touch. I know he mentioned going for a run most days, but this is not a runner's body. He either secretly lifts weights or has ridiculous genetics.

"Hello?" He snaps his fingers in front of my face and jokingly wipes the nonexistent drool from my chin. I've been caught ogling him and I don't even care.

"You said something?" I asked, openly checking him out now, exaggerating my perusal.

"You want to go for a swim? I got a bit sweaty today and the lake is calling me."

"That sounds like a good idea!"

I quickly change into my go-to black one-piece. It's certainly more modest than some of the suits Jackson has seen me in, but still cuts high enough on my hips and low enough on my chest that it makes me feel sexy.

Jackson seems to appreciate it just the same as my skimpy two-piece. His eyes linger longer than is decent on my chest as I jog towards him on the beach.

I cock my hip, giving him the same look he gave me when I was checking him out earlier, but he says nothing.

We drop our towels on a log and dip our toes in the lake. On warm days like today, the lake feels a lot colder than you would expect. Come August, it will feel like bath water.

I hesitantly take a step and stop. Jackson isn't one to wait, so he grabs my hand and all but drags me behind him into the lake until we are waist deep, and I dive under.

When I emerge from the water, Jackson is nowhere to be seen. I know he is lurking under the water, ready to grab me, but that doesn't stop me from shrieking when he grabs my ankle and pulls me under the water. I feel him grab my hips and pull me up with him. Once I'm able to take a full breath of air, I smack his chest lightly. "Not nice."

"I think I'm very nice." Jackson lifts me slightly, prompting me to wrap my legs around his waist and arms around his neck. He keeps his hold under my ass while I run my fingers through his wet hair, basically giving him a head massage.

We stay like that, just enjoying the quiet together. My eyes travel up the bank to my cottage and then over to the one next door.

"Can you walk me through the Waldens' place? I want to see all your progress."

"I mean, it's a construction site, but sure. We can go tomorrow morning before any of the crew get there."

"Are you hiding me from your crew?" I joke.

"Is it so wrong I want you all to myself?"

"I guess not. Honestly, if you asked me to walk on site and meet your full crew, I would hide instead. Regardless, I want to see your work. Please." Batting my eyelashes, I know I've got him.

"Fine," he mumbles. "But it's a work in progress. I don't want you to think I'm some chump who builds messy houses."

Oh, so it's the perfectionist in him that's keeping me away. Cute.

"I promise to take it in as a work in progress."

He kisses my lips lightly to seal the deal.

"So this is what all the noise has resulted in. Was it worth it?"

Jackson's eyes go wide. Clearly, my sarcasm is not appreciated right now. "Jackson, this place looks great. I know you had to tear down the original cottage, but this is miles better than what I would have imagined. Look at these windows."

Floor to ceiling windows cover the two stories overlooking the lake. There is a loft along the back of the cottage, so the kitchen and living room are completely open to the ceiling twelve feet above us.

"This is amazing." I twirl around, taking it all in. I don't know much about design, but this is phenomenal. Aspen would go nuts in here.

Jackson looks a bit bashful at the compliments, but it's all the truth. Not that I would openly tear this place apart if it was ugly, but I wouldn't be throwing the compliments around either. We continue our tour. The main floor consists of the kitchen, living room, and dining room, all open concept, with a full bathroom off the mudroom. There are five large bedrooms framed up upstairs with two bathrooms. He has also included a full-sized basement, something most cottages don't include. I know the one at my cottage is more of a cellar that you have to access from outside.

We take a couple of steps down the stairs toward the main floor before Jackson stops in front of me. I hear the sound of rushed footsteps and then the back door slamming shut.

"Stay up here," Jackson says, which I promptly ignore. I may not want to be running towards danger, but I don't want to be left behind either.

I follow him down the stairs where we see...nothing. Everything looks just the way it did five minutes ago. Jackson pulls out his phone, most likely calling Constable Peters, while I look around for signs someone has been here. When I get to the mudroom, I notice the door to the basement is open. We haven't been down there yet, so it jumps out at me.

"Hey, Jackson," I call to him. I hear him say goodbye on the phone and then he comes up behind me.

"That was not open before," he says, reading my mind.

"I didn't think so."

"There's probably no one down there anymore, considering we heard the outside door close, but I think we should wait for Peters. Come on."

He guides me out of the house and to the end of the driveway where we wait until Peters' SUV pulls in beside us.

"Did you find anything?" he asks instead of a greeting. I'm sure this isn't a normal thing you have to deal with being a small town police constable, so I'm not offended at his bristliness. I note that he has another constable with him. That fact that he thought to bring backup heightens my nerves even more.

"Maybe?" It comes out as a question, because we really don't know.

"Lead the way." Constable Peters directs his hand towards the Waldens' cottage. Jackson wraps my hand in his as we make our way back inside.

We run through what happened and what we heard before showing Peters and his partner the open basement door. They head down there to clear the area while we wait. Jackson strokes my hair gently. I'm not sure if he's trying to calm himself or me, but it's not working.

We hear Peters' voice call from below, "It's all clear, but you should come see this."

Jackson and I share a worried look before I follow him down the stairs. What we are greeted with is horrible.

There is spray paint everywhere. I'm surprised we couldn't smell it from upstairs. Pulling my shirt over my nose, I take in the words littered on the walls. There is almost every swear word I've ever heard, painted several times, along with what looks like a completed game of Hangman.

I drop my eyes to the phrase spelt out to complete the game and freeze.

meet your fate

I got out of that basement as quickly as I could.

I've never been a fan of scary movies or thriller novels, and now it feels like we're living in one.

We reconvened in my cottage, after Constable Peters called in crime scene techs and Jackson called around so his crew would be dispersed to other sites today. Gathering around my dining room table, Jackson pulls up the feed for the cameras next door.

I notice there are a couple of camera angles aiming straight at my cottage, but honestly, I'm not going to get mad about it. If Jackson wants the entire place bugged and armed, I won't stop him.

He rewinds the footage to a couple of hours before we got there and we see nothing. We watch all the way through until you can see us exiting and waiting for the police.

We are the only people on the feed.

"I didn't vandalize my own property," Jackson states, a mixture of confusion and anger in his tone.

"Blind spots," Peters mumbles under his breath. "Shit."

We both look up at him as he stands behind us, looking over our shoulders toward the computer screen and then toward the Waldens'.

"You've got blind spots. And whoever did this knows exactly where they are."

Jackson and I look at Peters, at each other, and then back to the screen. Running through the footage again, you can see different areas where we go in and out of the footage.

When Jackson installed the cameras, he was focusing on protecting the equipment outside. The cottage hadn't even been fully framed at the time, so none of the doors were covered.

Most of the perimeter of the property has a camera aimed towards it.

Jackson drops his head and shakes it. "Shit. I should have prepared for this. I'm moving those cameras around today."

"Don't beat yourself up. Our suspect went from petty vandalism to breaking and entering. None of us could have predicted this." Peters puts a hand on Jackson's shoulder and gives him an encouraging squeeze. Based on the resigned look on Jackson's face, it missed its mark.

"I'm increasing patrols on your street. You're going to see a lot of my constables from now on. We don't have trained criminals in town. Odds are we will find DNA in the basement and have this dealt with soon." Peters hesitates a moment, seeming to struggle with whether he wants to continue or not.

"Just say it." I grab Jackson's hand, hoping my touch is more reassuring. He laces our fingers together and holds me tightly, nodding at Peters to continue.

"It may have been someone on your crew. I know we originally thought it might be a disgruntled local, but whoever it was knew exactly where the cameras were. The only way to get the information without being seen beforehand would be by working around them and knowing where they were pointed these last couple of weeks."

"So what do I do?" Jackson asks. "Fire everyone? Bring them all in for questioning? Pack up and leave?"

His last question makes me flinch a little. I know we live in the same city, but I'm not ready for my summer with Jackson to end.

Constable Peters cuts in, stopping my thoughts from spiraling too much further. "You're going to adjust your cameras and continue on, business as usual. If you start acting weird, it could send our suspect into hiding. We have a better chance at catching them if they think they're getting away with it."

That makes sense. Not that I doubt Constable Peters' ability to do his job, but I honestly was heading towards worst case scenarios right along with Jackson. We certainly need him to be the rational one for us right now.

Chapter 20
Jackson

I was able to get all the lumber needed for Mrs. Langley's porch on Thursday morning. I spent my Wednesday evening demolishing the existing wreckage with Lillian's help. Considering she has no experience, I was pleasantly surprised with her willingness to get her hands dirty. I'm choosing to believe it was because she wanted to hang out with me and not because Mrs. Langley seems to have an endless supply of cookies for us.

She came back to help me again today, which is certainly making the work go faster, even though she's insisting she's "the muscle" and won't touch any of the power tools. I won't call her out for it, but she's avoiding being alone right now.

The last two days, she's chosen to either work at the library in town, a café, or my truck.

I've been dropping her off around town in whatever location she chooses for the day so she isn't biking alone either. I think she's also afraid for me, which I hate. Someone all but threatened my life with their Hangman message. I'm choosing to push that to the back of my mind. Living in fear isn't going to solve anything.

We are doing what we can to get through this. And if spending all our free and working time together puts us both at ease, what's the harm in it? Lillian is certainly cuter than anyone on my crew. If she wants to spend her evenings building porches with me, all the old ladies in town will be lining up for our services.

Just as I finish up the last section of the porch railing, I hear commotion from across the street. A car door slams and then someone yells, "Spotted. Jackson Mane helping old ladies cross the street."

Simon.

"Oh! And is that the elusive wildflower I've heard so much about?"

Lillian looks over at me with wide eyes, then looks around the area she's been working in for something. Probably her phone considering Simon, a stranger to her, is yelling in the street.

"Hey, buddy, I've missed you." Simon wraps me into a hug and grunts, lifting me off my feet.

He spots Lillian hiding behind me and grabs her into an equally aggressive hug. "Wildflower!" he exclaims, shaking her from side to side. When he puts her down, she immediately reaches for me, so I pull her under my arm.

"Wildflower?" she whispers to me.

"It's better if you don't ask him."

I turn back to Simon, who has a shit-eating grin on his face, looking from Lillian, to me, to my arm wrapped around her. I've been a bit preoccupied since moving in, temporarily, to Lillian's cottage and dealing with the aftermath of the break-in/basement vandalism and haven't had a chance to give Simon any sort of update on our not relationship.

He was also apparently too busy to warn me that he was coming into town.

"Hey, Sim, this is a surprise," I say, because it is. Not that I'm complaining. Simon is the closest person to me I have in my life. Since I've been in Bluefield, this is probably the least amount of time we have spent together since we were born. Not only do I miss hanging out with him, but I am also excited for him to meet Lillian. She is shy and he is the exact opposite. Hopefully, he doesn't scare her away. It's important that the two most important people in my life get along.

We get pleasantries out of the way. Apparently, Simon stopped at The Inn looking for me and the lady at the desk said I would be here. I'm not sure if it's the benefit or the curse of a small town, but everyone is certainly in everyone's business here.

For the most part, the locals avoid the tourists. Somehow it seems Lillian and I have moved into the local category very quickly.

Simon is a very successful real estate agent. He's all suits and business deals now, but he spent a summer or two on my dad's job sites and isn't afraid to get his hands dirty. That's why I'm not surprised when he removes his jacket, rolls up his sleeves and helps me mount the new planter boxes to the railing of the porch.

I may have taken some artistic liberties on this project.

Instead of a standard wood platform, Mrs. Langley now has a wraparound porch, built-in bench seats with storage below, a porch swing and planter boxes that can hold flowers or herbs.

Mrs. Langley is one of the nicest people I've ever met, so I just couldn't help myself. She deserves to have a nice space. The brownie points I'll get towards Lillian's brother are a bonus, and so are the cookies.

With everything done and the finished project looking amazing, Lillian snaps some pictures to send to her brother and promises to come back this weekend to take Mrs. Langley to the garden centre and get her planters all set up. This part is the small-town blessing. Looking out for a neighbour or even a stranger is not common in the neighbourhood I grew up in in Toronto. It was everyone for themselves and you didn't get involved in anyone else's business.

Simon helps me pack up my tools and the extra lumber scraps into the back of my very clean truck. I've been taking it through the carwash a town over every morning. If my paint starts melting off, I won't be surprised. I swear I find a new drop of red every time the sunlight hits the vehicle from a different direction.

Lillian and I are both too tired to cook, and Simon can't. We decide to order a pizza to be delivered to Lillian's cottage and tell Simon to follow us there.

Lillian decides to shower and change once we get inside, leaving Simon and me to catch up on the deck overlooking the lake. Before he can even start snooping for information about my relationship status, I update him on the crime spree that is centred around me.

"Shit, man."

"Yeah," I say, because what else can I do? It's wild and annoying and out of my control.

Taking a sip of his beer, Simon turns to look me right in the eyes. "Are you okay, though? Like mentally, physically, how are you doing?"

I take a moment to think about his questions. To anyone else, I would brush them off, say I was fine, but not Simon. We've always been honest with each other. I think because we are best friends and cousins, we have a unique relationship. We've never felt the need to soften or guard our words or feelings with each other. I know family doesn't have to love each other. But we've both made an effort to actively love each other throughout our lives. Simon had a lot more love at home than I did, but he's always been more than willing to share it with me.

Truthfully, I don't know how I am with everything going on. "I'm not great. I'm not terrible either. There's good and bad going on right now. Some are really bad. Some are really good. I'm just trying to remember to breathe through it all. I guess."

"That's a good way to look at it, I think. There's no rule book on how to cope when some deranged person is out to get you. The fact that you aren't hiding in a panic room right now is impressive to me."

I know that's Simon's way of lightening the conversation and not making me talk more about it if I don't want to. I appreciate that, a lot.

I drain the rest of my beer, staring out at the water. Regardless of what's going on, I can say I'm lucky to be sitting here with Simon, on a beautiful night, with a beautiful view.

That beautiful view gets even better when Lillian emerges from the sliding door, three beers in one hand, a box of pizza in the other, and her curls still damp, but bouncy, with her face fresh from the shower.

She places the pizza box and some napkins on the table between the two lounge chairs Simon and I are occupying. After a moment of hesitation, she hands Simon his beer, giving him a small smile and a nod when he thanks her.

It reminds me of the first couple of times we met and how I struggled to get her to talk to me. Lillian is, I hope, one hundred percent comfortable with me now. Even her interactions with Peters aren't awkward anymore. She's never the life of the party, that's not who she is, even around Aspen, but she does open up to people when she's ready.

We dig into the pizza, and Lillian sits on the end of my lounge chair, keeping a respectable distance. I don't want that distance. I pull her back to me, settling her so she's able to lean on my shoulder and arm that I'm not using to eat. Simon and I fill most of the silence, catching up on anything and everything we think the other person has missed since our last conversation. Lillian follows along, mostly nodding or humming when a response is needed, until Simon decides to tell her every embarrassing story about me he knows. That has her laughing and cuddling closer to me.

After he finishes explaining that I peed my pants in high school when he scared me one night in his backyard, he lets silence surround us.

I know Simon is dying to ask me about my relationship with Lillian. His eyes are constantly travelling from me to her and then back to me again. He's made eye contact a couple of times, raising his eyebrow in question. Thankfully, I know he won't ask while she's around.

Not only does Simon have a lot of experience with relationships, even if they are typically short-lived, he also has a sister.

I'm grateful he understands the social etiquette for this situation. Lillian would probably crawl into my sweater and hide if he said anything.

Simon excuses himself inside to clean up what little mess we made from dinner. Lillian has her head resting on my shoulder and I can tell she's fighting sleep.

"Hey, you should head to bed. I'll give Simon my key for my room at The Inn. He can stay there for the weekend."

"You still have your room at The Inn?" she asks, suddenly seeming a lot more awake.

"Yeah..." I feel like that's the wrong answer, but it's the truth. "I didn't want to give it up in case I overstay my welcome."

"It's just... I don't know, maybe I'm being silly."

"It's not silly," I prompt. "Tell me. Please."

"I know it's taking longer for me to get on the same page as you. And you having a room at The Inn still, I know is smart, considering we don't know each other that well. It's just that it makes me feel like you have an exit plan or something. Like, at any point you could decide I'm not worth the wait and go back to your life. Without me." She drops her eyes from mine, feeling exposed and vulnerable. I wish I could climb into her brain and tell it she has nothing to worry about, but I know that's not how anxiety works. This has more to do with Lillian and her own mental health journey than it does with our relationship.

If something goes wrong and Lillian doesn't want me around anymore, because I can guarantee it won't be me ending things, I'll sleep in my truck or camp if I can't find a place to stay. I want to ease Lillian's worries in any way I can.

"I'm in this with you, Lil. No timelines or expectations. After Simon leaves, I can check out of the room."

"He should be staying here. He's important to you, which makes him important to me. He's staying here. And so are you." Is it too soon to love her? Because I could get there very quickly with some of the things she says.

Lillian tips her head up to me and seals the deal with a kiss. It's not gentle, but it's also not as full of passion as some of the ones we share before we fall asleep at night. It's comforting. Like we have all the time in the world and a lifetime ahead of us to fill with all sorts of kisses.

Simon clears his throat from the doorway, causing Lillian to pull away. She doesn't hide her face like she normally would, but her cheeks still turn a pretty shade of pink at being caught kissing me.

"Grab your stuff, you're stuck with us here," I say. Redirecting the conversation before Simon can comment.

"Are you sure?" He looks to Lillian instead of me, gauging her comfort level.

"We're sure," Lillian says with confidence. Simon nods, accepting that as the truth.

"You can have my brother's room. Aspen stays in my parents' room normally, so I doubt you want to be surrounded by the stuff she manages to leave behind every time."

I hear Simon mumble under his breath something that sounds an awful lot like, "You have no idea how wrong you are on that one, wildflower."

When I try to catch his eye, he breezes past me, following Lillian up the stairs and towards Ben's room.

Chapter 21
Lillian

Simon is great.

Not that I thought he wouldn't be. He is Jackson's family and best friend and he doesn't seem like the kind of guy who would be friends with anyone who isn't great. But Aspen has something about not liking him. She's never told me why or straight up said she doesn't like him, but the signs are there. A small grumble when Jackson mentions him or just changes the subject to avoid anything to do with him. Aspen and I don't keep many secrets from each other.

If it was something important or terrible, she would tell me. I have to assume she's being petty and form my own opinion. Unlucky for Aspen, I think Simon is great.

He and Jackson are so similar but also so different. They are about the same height and size, both with brown hair. Jackson's has a bit of a wave to it and has been lightened by the sun in the last month or so. Simon's is darker and he keeps it longer on the top.

Even their mannerisms are similar. The way they form a sentence, gesture while they talk, and even move about the cottage. It goes to show how much time they spent together growing up and the amount of influence they had on each other. Their personalities are where things separate. Jackson is friendly and helpful to everyone, mostly just being polite, but still sociable. Simon is beyond outgoing. He went into town this morning to grab coffee and breakfast for everyone and came back an hour later with the names and life stories of half the locals.

I don't think the man can meet a person and not become their friend.

Simon decided he would work on the deck with me today while Jackson is next door cleaning up the basement. He didn't want everyone to see what was down there, deciding to take on the job by himself. I offered to help, but he declined. I'm not sure if this is his way of working through everything that's happening, but truthfully, I'm relieved. I don't want to be anywhere that someone has written such vile things.

The whole thing gives me the creeps.

Simon and I both set up our laptops on the picnic table and got to work. He put his headphones in when he needed to make a call, but otherwise, we chatted casually.

I'm not sure how Simon did it, but by the end of the day, I couldn't stop talking. Considering I could hardly string a sentence together in front of him last night, this was a miracle.

I've shared almost as many details about my life with him as I have with Jackson and I know just as many about him, too. If I didn't trust Simon, by proxy through Jackson, I would be seriously concerned that I have been manipulated in some way.

When Jackson joined us at the end of his work day, he didn't seem surprised by my new friendship with his cousin. This must just be what Simon does. No wonder he's so successful with his real estate career.

Simon picked up groceries based on my list this morning, so I offered to make dinner for us. I know I have monopolized most of Jackson's time this summer, by his choosing, but I want to make space for him to spend time with the important people in his life. The most important seems to be Simon.

The boys leave to head to the beach for a swim as I pull out my grandparents' million-year-old deep fryer. I'm not one hundred percent sure it's the safest appliance to be using in a cottage this old that's built of mostly wood, so I take it outside and set it up on the deck. We have fresh fish from the market in town, and potatoes to fry for fish and chips, along with a side salad to keep this meal a bit more cholesterol friendly.

While everything cooks, I look down towards the water to watch Jackson and Simon. They look like children. They're fighting in the water, trying to drown each other, splashing, having handstand competitions and practising their dives. I have a feeling this is normal behaviour for them when they are with each other.

I haven't seen Jackson this carefree in the last couple of weeks. The stress of everything is getting to him more than I originally thought.

As much as I would like to be the one to put a smile on Jackson's face, the one with the dimple that likes to pop out, I think Simon's visit came at the right time.

We are still on alert and know the danger could come back at any time, but Simon has created a distraction bubble for us. Our lives have become so centred around Bluefield, that it's hard to see outside of it sometimes, without actually leaving. Simon is a connection to the city that we haven't had.

I am so relieved that Simon seems to want to spend time with me, and not just whisk Jackson away. In my entire relationship with Christopher, I almost never hung out with his friends. They were all about boys' weekends. I never even met most of their significant others. I'm not saying we needed to be one big happy family, but when I think about my friendship with Aspen, I want to be able to have her be a part of my life with whomever I'm in a relationship with. I want her to hang out with us, hang out with his friends and vice versa. Isn't it strange to not want to know the people your significant other chooses to spend their time with?

But like I said, Simon is great, so no worries there. Aspen will get over her issues, for my sake, and I kind of love this potential family we could form together. I love my family, but I've never been one to have a lot of friends. I don't need a lot of people surrounding me, but I do want a couple of good ones.

The more I think about it, the more I'm sure there's no need to drag my feet around Jackson anymore.

Our conversation last night solidified that for me. We were able to have an open conversation about my fears; he heard them and tried to ease them the best he could. And I know that's not his job, but his reaction was perfect. I just needed him to hear me.

I knew the insecurity was about me and not him, but I needed to voice it to work through it. I don't see any reason why I can't continue to grow while dating Jackson.

My healing isn't going to follow a timeline, and my anxiety is never going to be cured, only managed. Why am I waiting around and torturing both of us in the meantime?

The way we've been acting since I told him I'm not ready for a relationship is basically a relationship. I mean, he's living with me. But I have a feeling being all in with Jackson, it's going to feel like flying. Finally letting go, and knowing he'll catch me if I want him to, but also fall when I need to grow. As long as he's there to wipe my scraped knee, I'll be okay.

Of course, I won't be telling Jackson any of this while Simon is still here. And of course, I have to head into the city next week, so that will delay things even further.

The walls are thin here, but maybe I can still show Jackson how I feel before we sit down for a proper conversation.

After dinner, we set up a bonfire on the beach. Simon ran into Julia from the bookstore today, got her number and invited her to hang out tonight. That man works fast. Jackson also sent Constable Peters an invitation. He said as long as it was only going to be the five of us, he would join. I guess he is super strict about what he does in his time off and with whom.

I wish Aspen could be here, too. I'm not sure how that would work with Simon, but if I'm having fun, I want her there having fun, too.

And I am having fun. Simon found an old guitar of Ben's that is terribly out of tune. He created a game out of us guessing the song he's strumming.

I've learned a lot about Julia and Dylan, too.

Julia has lived here all her life, aside from when she left for school, but Dylan hasn't.

He's from a town outside of Toronto, but was placed in Bluefield soon after Police College and never left. Learning that he doesn't have family here, and probably not many friends, I want to include him in all our plans. I think Jackson's golden retriever behaviour is rubbing off on me because I am never one to want to initiate friendships. With everything going on, I don't want to force Dylan to spend more time with us, considering how much we require of him while he's on the clock. But once all of this is cleared up, hopefully, I think I would like him as a friend.

Julia asked me to go to the bathroom with her at one point and then told me she needed the scoop on Jackson and me. I guess the last time she saw us was in the bookstore and I was so awkward. I'm not surprised she wants an update considering he's had at least one body part touching me at all times tonight.

I would like to be friends with Julia, too. We bonded over our favourite books and authors, and she asked me to do a reading at the bookstore sometime. Sounds like the last thing I want to do, but she doesn't need to know that. Simon has been shamelessly flirting with her all night. I can't tell if she's reciprocating or not. Half of what comes out of her mouth is sarcastic, so I can't always keep up. Aspen is going to love her.

As the night winds down and the fire becomes nothing but embers, Dylan offers to give Julia a ride home. He only had one beer, and she and I split a bottle of wine, so it's probably for the best. Simon doesn't seem disappointed when she leaves, further proving that he's just like this with everyone.

It's Jackson's charm on steroids.

Jackson grabs the bucket we brought down and fills it with water from the lake. After five trips back and forth, the fire is completely out and it's safe for us to return to the cottage. Simon immediately retreats to the room he's staying in, only giving us a wave over his head as he climbs the stairs.

Although it's later than I normally stay up, I had a lot of fun tonight and I don't want to go to bed just yet.

I make myself cozy, curling into the corner of the couch and wrapping a wool blanket around myself. Jackson returns from the back door where he was putting the empty beer cans in the recycling and starts to head towards the stairs before he sees me sitting on the couch and reroutes his path.

"Look at you all cozy," he says. "Not ready for bed yet?"

"Nope." I pop the P at the end of the word and give him a shy smile. I've been thinking all night about how I want to take our relationship to the next level, both in name and physically, and now it's all I can think about. With Simon upstairs, we can't get too out of control, but we can still have some fun.

I crook my index finger towards him and back to me, signaling that I want him to join me on the couch. Jackson smirks at me, but then quickly rounds the couch and sits down beside me, pulling me to sit on his lap. I rotate so my knees are planted on the sides of both of his thighs and I'm straddling his lap.

"Hi," I whisper, leaning in to drop a light kiss on his lips.

"What did I do to get this sort of attention?"

"Nothing."

"Nothing?"

"Nothing," I repeat. "You're just you." I kiss his lips again, the corner of his mouth, his cheek, and then trail them down his jaw and neck. Jackson lets me continue my descent, allowing me to dictate what we do. When I reach the sensitive spot behind his ear, he groans, the vibration of the noise tickling my lips. I can't help but giggle.

"Oh, you think that's funny?" His voice is deeper than normal, my seduction affecting him. I try to subtly push my hips forward to feel him between my legs. He catches me in the act, grabbing my ass with both of his hands and pulling me impossibly closer. "You're trouble, you know that?" He drags my hips back and then towards him again.

I continue kissing down his neck until I'm stopped by the knit sweater he's wearing. I drop my hands to the hem and look to him for permission. "Please." He nods. I pull the sweater and shirt underneath up his body and over his head. I fling it to the floor somewhere behind me.

"Not so fast." He stops me as I try to wiggle my way off the couch and down to my knees. "You first." I look at him, not understanding, but before I can ask, he pulls my body back to level with his. I'm about to settle on his lap when he flips us around so my back is on the couch and Jackson is hovering over me.

He works his way down my body. I pull my shirt over my head before he even has a chance to ask.

"Beautiful," he whispers, more to himself than me, but I can still feel my cheeks heat. He kisses down my chest, paying attention to each of my breasts as he makes his way to my belly button and then my hips, making sure every inch of me has been kissed.

When he reaches the band of my leggings, I know what's coming next, so I wiggle and nod before he can even ask for permission.

He grabs the waistband, taking my underwear down with my leggings, leaving me naked except for my simple black bra. Before I can really think about what's about to happen, Jackson drops his face and dives in with his hands, tongue and teeth. He hooks my right leg over his shoulder, giving him more access. I grip the top of his hair, keeping him in place as he circles my clit with his tongue while his fingers pump in and out of me.

"Fuck, you taste so good." I'm delirious. There are words coming out of my mouth, but I'm not sure they make any sense. As his tongue slips inside of me, I go off.

"Ahhh," I cry just before his hand clamps over my mouth, reminding me we aren't alone in this cottage. The only response I can get out is a giggle. This guy just orgasmed me stupid.

Jackson slides my bottoms back on me and then settles his body on top of mine, planting a soul-crushing kiss on my lips. I can taste myself on his tongue and it's intoxicating. Even though I just came, I'm already ready for round two. I could kiss him forever and never tire of it.

I reach my hand between us, rubbing the very large bulge under Jackson's jeans. He raises his hips away from my touch. "Why?" I pout, bottom lip out and all. I don't want to stop.

"It's late and we're in the living room. We both need sleep after the week we've had." He grabs my hand to pull me up off the couch and hands me my shirt. I don't bother putting it on but do hold it over my chest in case Simon is awake upstairs and sees me.

If it wasn't for Jackson's lazy, dimpled smile, I would be a bit annoyed.

I know I don't have to reciprocate, but I want to.

Chapter 22
Jackson

This is the best dream I've ever had.

Lillian is between my legs, naked, with my cock in her mouth.

One of her hands is stroking the part of my shaft she can't fit in her mouth, while the other is squeezing my balls. I groan. God, that feels good.

She pops her mouth off my cock and licks it from base to tip and then swirls her tongue around the head, licking up the drop of cum that's leaking out. She takes me back into her mouth, bobbing her head up and down, increasing her pace. I want her to hold it at the back of her throat a bit longer, so I reach down to grab the hair at the back of her head.

When I feel her soft curls beneath my fingertips, it feels so real. Too real.

My eyes snap open and Lillian is deep-throating my cock. This is not a dream.

When I turned her down last night, I died a little inside, but I also wanted to make sure we weren't moving too fast. It took all my self-control to keep my clothes on when we got into bed, but it seems I'm being rewarded for my efforts now.

This is the best wake-up call I've ever had. This is also the best blow job I've ever had. I almost pinch myself.

Lillian looks up at me, seeing that I'm awake, and smirks. Little minx. She maintains eye contact as she treats my cock like it's her favourite flavour of ice cream, slurping and licking it all over. I know I'm not going to last much longer. "Lil, that is so good. I'm close."

She hums around me and raises one eyebrow. I'm ready for her to release me so I can come on my stomach, but it seems she has other ideas. She covers my cock with her mouth until I can feel her throat swallowing around me and then bobs her head there. That does it, and I explode in her mouth. She swallows every drop, then pops her mouth off my cock and gives me a breathtaking smile.

"Good morning, handsome."

"Yes," I cough out, my voice suddenly hoarse. "Good morning to me." Lillian giggles and then pounces on me, planting kisses all over my face. I pin her arms to her body to stop her from wiggling and bring her lips to mine. I kiss her slowly, lazily, like we've got all the time in the world. When we break apart, I can't help but smile. Lillian does, too, and we just stare at each other for a moment. I don't know if it's the orgasm I just had or just being here with Lillian, but I can't remember a time I felt this happy.

"Race you to the shower." She laughs and jumps from the bed. I throw the sheets to the floor and chase after her.

We stay in the shower until the hot water runs out—sorry, Simon—both of us ending up on our knees a couple more times before we actually get clean.

Simon left on Monday night, and all I wanted was my hands all over Lillian. We only had one night together before she had to head out of town and we didn't waste it. All weekend, she seemed a bit distracted, like she had something on her mind, but then at night she spoke with her body.

I'm not complaining; I love the physical side to our relationship. I had assumed Lillian's shyness would transfer into the bedroom, and it certainly doesn't. But it's not enough. I want her to be my girlfriend. I want the commitment with her. I want to start planning our future together.

Boy, if fifteen-, twenty-, or even twenty-five-year-old me could hear me now, they would laugh in my face and call me whipped.

I am whipped. Happily whipped.

I can also admit that I have both mommy and daddy issues. When your mom takes off and basically forgets about you, abandonment becomes a bit of a fear, and as much as I am trying to work through that, being one hundred percent committed to each other would ease it.

Of course, that is not the only reason I want Lillian as my girl. I've been trying not to think too much about it because I may blurt it out by accident, but I am fully falling in love with her. I've probably already fallen, but considering I haven't told anyone I loved them since I was probably ten, I'm keeping this close to my chest

I'm just heading to my car when I see that teenage boy, Sam, who works at The General Store approaching with what looks like his grandmother trailing behind him.

I haven't been to The General Store in weeks, so I kind of forgot about him.

"Hey, man, what's up?" he greets me. I'm still getting used to everyone being so friendly here.

"Just running some errands. Is there something I can help you with?" I respond.

"Nah, nah, just out with my Grams. Thought I would say hi and ask how Lily's doing. I haven't seen her around in a couple of days."

Should he know where she is?

"Oh, she had a work thing, and probably won't be around for a couple more days if I had to guess." She will be back from the city tonight, but I have no reason to offer that information to this kid.

"Oh, cool. She has seemed busy lately. Our chats are always

cut short, but I respect her prioritizing her work," he says. I don't think she has mentioned going to The General Store since we were there with Aspen a month ago, but maybe I'm mistaken. I guess he could be running into her at the library or café, too.

We both stand there staring at each other. This conversation is over, but he's currently blocking the path to my truck and his grandma is rifling through her giant purse, so he must not be in a hurry.

Desperate to have this situation behind me, I point to my truck and give a tight-lipped smile, hoping that conveys my message. The kid gives me an equally awkward smile in return and finally moves out of my way. I get into my truck as quickly as possible and head to the grocery store on the other side of town, trying to put as much space between myself and whatever just happened. What a weird kid.

I promised Lillian I would make dinner for us tonight.

When we spoke on the phone last night, she said she had been eating takeout the last four nights to avoid having anything in her fridge go bad once she's back in Bluefield, so I'm hoping to win some points with a home-cooked meal for her tonight.

Lillian had to go into the office for a quarterly department meeting. While she was in the city, she chose to stay for a couple of days, meeting with anyone who would prefer face-to-face for her project. I've watched her on a couple of virtual meetings and I can't believe the person she turns into. Her voice holds unmatched confidence as she leads the discussion. When I brought it up to her, she just laughed and said, "Yeah, that's not me, I'm acting." When I was confused by that, she clarified that she knows what she's doing at work. She has confidence in her abilities, so she is able to put on a bit of a show. I guess working for the same company for so long also affords her more comfort in her situation, but I was still shocked. I must say, I prefer my quiet but comfortable Lillian over corporate Lillian any day.

With the lessons Lillian has been giving me, I've improved, but I'm still not the best cook if she's not standing right beside me. Luckily, the grocery store sells fresh pasta, and pesto is within my culinary range, so I plan to pair it with a French loaf, spring salad and, of course, a nice bottle of red wine.

I finish setting the picnic table on the porch, candles and all, when I hear Lillian's car pull into the driveway. I could play it cool and wait for her to find me, but at this point, I'm not even going to pretend I'm cool. I jump off the side of the porch and jog my way to the driveway. Just as Lillian shuts her door, she spots me, and her entire being lights up. I pick up my pace to a run as she starts for me. Once she's within five feet of me, she launches her whole body at me, which I catch with ease.

This is my kind of hello.

"I missed you," I whisper into her hair. It may have only been four days, but it sucked. We called each other each night, falling asleep mid-conversation, but it's not the same. I just want her around all the time and when she isn't, I feel off-kilter.

She adjusts her body in my arms, wrapping her legs around my waist and arms around my neck. She speaks against my lips. "I." Kiss. "Missed." Kiss "You." Kiss "Too." Kiss.

On the last kiss, I hold the back of her head to me, drawing it out. If Lillian were a drug, I'd happily be addicted.

"Hi," she says, her lips still touching mine.

"I have a surprise for you." Bypassing the cottage, I take her back to the deck, still carrying her in my arms, and sit her down on the bench facing the water. "You wait here. Dinner will be served in a moment." She claps her hands together excitedly. I drop one last kiss on the top of her head before heading back inside. If I don't get into the kitchen now, I'm just going to take her upstairs instead.

Everything in the kitchen is waiting, mostly ready. The final step is to drop the fresh pasta into the boiling water for a couple of minutes.

I swear it takes longer than it should. I just want to get back out there and soak in this evening with Lillian. Once everything is ready, I bring it outside, serving Lillian first, and then taking my seat across from her.

We both dig in right away. Lillian catches me up on her day and anything she hadn't told me during our nightly phone calls. I do the same, even mentioning my encounter with Sam, which she also thinks was weird.

By the time we are done, we are both happily full, drinking our second glass of wine. It's crazy to see the difference in how she talks about work now compared to when we first met. I can tell she's still not the most passionate about her current project, but she seems to be in a good flow now.

Before, the stress was practically seeping off her body and she always looked defeated. The Lillian sitting in front of me is bright and cheerful.

"This was so nice. Thank you for cooking for me. You did good."

"I didn't choose anything too complicated. But thank you."

I take her hand across the table and hold it in mine. The sun is setting behind me, but I think I have the better view in front of me.

"Um. There's something I want to talk to you about."

I'm immediately on edge. I don't think anything good comes after a sentence like that, and Lillian looks nervous. I slide out of my seat to sit next to her.

She takes a deep breath, fiddling with her hands in her lap before meeting my eyes. I must look like I'm ready to combust because Lillian practically shouts, "It's not bad!"

I only feel a small amount of relief. I try to school my face, giving her the silence to continue. She finally says, "I think I'm ready." She thinks she's ready. Ready for what?

"I'm going to need more context than that, Lil."

"Right, sorry." She laces her fingers through mine on both hands. "Ready for us?"

I'm not sure if she meant for it to come out as a question, but it takes me a moment to comprehend. Ready for us? Like "us" us?

Shit.

Yes!

To make sure I'm not getting ahead of myself, especially since I've never had a conversation like this before, I ask, "Like a relationship? Us?"

"Yes," she says on an exhale. "I'm not sure why I couldn't figure out how to say it. I'm glad you understand my brain." She laughs and then looks at me expectantly.

Right. I need to say something. I let go of her hands and she looks upset for a moment, but then I hold her cheeks, bringing her face closer to me, and she smiles. I lean my forehead against hers. For some reason, this feels more intimate than if we were kissing.

"Lillian Shaw, will you be my girlfriend?"

She kisses me hard. "Okay. Yay! Yes. I'm your girlfriend?"

"You're my girlfriend," I confirm.

Her eyes widen, and then she states, "Your first girlfriend."

"And my last," I say this more to myself than her, but if she hears it, she's been warned. She's it for me.

We sit there just smiling at each other for far longer than is probably acceptable. I drop what is meant to be a quick kiss on her lips, but she deepens it before I can pull away. When our lips meet again, I almost sigh against hers.

The stress of the week and everything happening in my life evaporates against her lips. My tongue slips into her mouth as I pull her closer to me. Her arms wrap around my neck, her fingers gliding through the hair at the back of my head. One of my hands spans over Lillian's lower back as the other makes its way south. I palm her ass with one hand before swooping under her thighs and lifting her, off the bench and into the air.

A small yelp escapes her lips in surprise.

"Jackson," she practically moans. I'm not sure if she's trying to scold me for lifting her or ask me to keep kissing her.

I pull at her ponytail, opening her neck to me. My teeth graze the sensitive skin before I nip at it. There is only one place this is headed, so I make quick work of blowing out the candles and running inside, and up the stairs, all while still holding Lillian.

The second I get into our bedroom, I throw Lillian on the bed. She bounces and squeals with shock and excitement. I would love to take this slow, but I don't think I'm capable of slow at this point. I make quick work of removing my clothing. Lillian follows my lead, removing her own. I would love to be the one to undress her, but we've got plenty of time for that. This won't be the last time I have her in bed, naked.

I crawl over top of her until my face is just above hers. Lillian's hand finds my hard cock, and she begins stroking it up and down.

"Oh, there's no time for that right now. I need to be inside you. Now." I'm practically panting. I try to keep my voice even, but there is no way she can't tell how much I want, no, need her right now.

I grab a condom from the nightstand drawer. I hid a box in there a couple of days ago. I didn't want Lillian to find it and feel pressured, but I also wanted to be prepared. I'm really glad I thought ahead.

I fit the condom over my erection and line myself up to her entrance. As I drop my head to her, capturing her lips in a blistering kiss, I feel her hand wrap around my cock and drag it through her wetness.

If she doesn't stop, I'm going to embarrass myself and end this before we even start. I take both her hands and place them over her head.

"Keep those there or else I'm going to have to tie you up." Lillian gasps, but then licks her lips. I think she may want to be tied up. I'll try to remember that for next time.

"Jackson," she moans. "Please."

Yeah, I can't wait either. I slowly push my cock inside her, stopping halfway to let her adjust to my size before I push all the way in.

"Shit, you feel so good."

"Move," she demands. I like that she isn't afraid to ask for what she wants. Luckily, it's what I want, too. I slowly begin to rock in and out of her, setting a slow pace to make sure she's comfortable. "Harder. Please," she chokes out. "You aren't going to break me." I don't increase my pace, but I do thrust into her with more force. The headboard begins banging against the wall, and I'm thankful we are alone in the cottage. Lillian hooks her legs behind my back, bracing against me and meeting my thrusts. I can already feel myself getting close to coming, but I don't want to until she does.

Without warning, I flip us over so my back is against the headboard and Lillian is seated on my cock. "Ride me, Lil."

She looks at me nervously, and I'm suddenly worried I've pushed her out of her comfort zone. I'm about to say something stupid, like "Never mind," when she leans forward and begins grinding her clit against me.

"That's it. Use me, Lil. I want to see your pussy dripping all over me."

"Ahh, Jackson," she cries. She slowly rises to her knees until only my tip is left in her, then suddenly drops back all the way.

"Shit, that feels good," I grunt out. I grab her hip with one of my hands to help guide her up and down, while my other one finds her clit and rubs.

"Oh, oh. Don't stop. Fuck, I'm gonna come. Jackson!" I feel Lillian convulse around me as she comes, chanting my name as she goes. I slow our pace and she comes down from her high.

"Wow." She practically giggles. I can't help but smile at her beautiful face. Cheeks flushed, eyes bright, there isn't anything prettier.

I pull her face down to mine and ravish her lips. She kisses me back with just as much passion as I increase the stretch and pace of my thrusts. As much as I want this to last forever, I know I'm not going to be able to hold this off any longer.

"Fuck." With one final pump, I come, filling the condom inside her. Our kisses slow until we are just staring at each other, smiling.

"That was..." I start, not knowing how to finish.

"Amazing?" Lillian asks.

"Everything," I conclude. I flip us around so I'm back on top and then ease out of her. I make quick work of disposing of the condom before settling on the bed beside her. I move until there isn't any space between us. I grab her leg and hitch it over my hip, tangling us together, and lift her head so it's resting on my bicep.

"Getting comfy?" she asks with a giggle. "Orgasms, then cuddles. Is there anything better?"

I hum in agreement. We pull the covers over our bodies and settle into a more comfortable position. I'm pretty sure we left our dinner dishes outside, but I guess the animals will have a nice snack because there is nothing that could move me from this spot. A cozy bed, my freshly fucked girlfriend in my arms. Yeah, I'm not going anywhere.

Chapter 23
Lillian

I got a call from my brother this morning. He and Noah will be coming up for the weekend!

I wasn't able to see either of them when I was in the city this week, so I'm beyond excited. My nephew typically spends the majority of his summers at various camps and summer programs, so I'm not sure that he misses me as much as I miss him, but I do miss him a lot. I guess I miss my brother, too.

I have not mentioned to Ben that Jackson is staying at the

cottage with me. He tends to pick and choose when he wants to be Mr. Protective Big Brother, so I don't know where he will sit with it all. I'm sure if I told him it was for my safety, he would understand, but he would also be mad that Jackson has me in some sort of danger to begin with.

I have decided it's best that I not worry him with it.

I would rather he be grossed out that I'm sharing a bed with my boyfriend than have him trying to convince me to move back to the city where I'm safe.

One of the largest cities in Canada not having more crime than the little beach town that is Bluefield seems crazy, but that's just my opinion.

I had every intention to get lots of work done today. Even though I spent the week in the city for work, it wasn't my work, it was everyone else's. All the meetings were to get others up to speed or to collaborate, no writing is happening for me.

Now that Ben and Noah will be arriving just after dinner; I want to make sure everything is perfect for them. That means I needed to fill the cottage with food for meals, but also all the snacks and junk food. I'm going to pick up some new beach toys that we definitely don't need, water guns and a sprinkler toy. This weekend is going to be all about fun.

My hope is that Ben can relax and not feel like a parent this weekend because Noah will be too busy having fun with me. I take my role as fun, childless aunt very seriously.

As much as I missed working alongside Jackson while I was in the city, we will have to put it off until next week. There is so much I want to do, and I can't expect Jackson to ditch work and follow me around all day. Based off everything I was able to accomplish this morning alone, it is probably for the best.

We decided to meet in the park, bringing leftovers from dinner last night for an impromptu picnic. When I get to the park, Jackson is already there, sitting on a blanket under the same tree where I spent my first couple of days here trying to write. We have come so far since that day.

I plop down beside him and give him a peck on the cheek.

"Nice try," he says, before hauling me to him and kissing me slowly with passion.

"Jackson," I scold while pulling away. "We're in public and that was a bit indecent."

"What? I just want to greet my girlfriend."

I can't help but laugh. The man is acting like a twelve-year-old girl, calling me his girlfriend every chance he gets. Part of me hopes it wears off because we're adults and boyfriend/girlfriend not only seems a bit juvenile, but also not strong enough words for what I feel for him.

Jackson is so much more, and I feel like the relationship we are building is more. I don't know how to define that "more" right now, but it's something. The other part of me hopes he never stops wanting to call me his girlfriend because he always looks so damn happy and proud of himself. Like he can't believe I'm with him, when I feel like I can't believe he's with me.

I plant a light, and appropriate, kiss on his lips, lingering there a moment before smiling against them. I don't want him to be discouraged because I am just as happy for our new relationship status.

"What have you been up to this morning?"

"I've been shopping!" I can't wait for Jackson to see all the fun things I got for us to do this weekend, but first I should tell him about our guests. "Ben and Noah are coming for the weekend!"

Jackson chokes on the sip of water he had just taken. "I'm meeting your brother this weekend? Like tonight? In a couple of hours?"

"Yes! They should be here just after dinner."

"Okay. Okay, I can handle that. I just need to shave and iron my shirt or something." Jackson stares off into space, lost in thought.

"Are you planning on dating my brother?" I ask, because what? Why would he need to do either of those things? I hold his chin in my hand and turn his face to me.

I can see the pure panic in his eyes. "Jackson, it's going to be okay. Ben is not very scary. He might pretend he is for, like, two seconds and then he'll forget and act like a normal guy. He is coming for a relaxing weekend. We'll keep Noah busy and he will be napping in a beach chair all weekend. It's going to be okay."

"It's going to be okay," he repeats. I motion for him to breathe in and out in time with me a couple of times, until his shoulders drop. "Okay, freak out over. I'm good."

"Good, because I bought so much stuff. We are going to be so busy this weekend, you won't have time to freak out."

"Okay, I am a bit worried about your brother, but your nephew? Him, I can handle."

"Have you spent much time with kids?" I don't think he's mentioned any of his friends or family having children yet.

"Not at all." He laughs to himself. "We would get paired up

with younger kids at camp sometimes, so that was kind of like babysitting. But I was a five-year-old boy once. It'll be fun." He pauses a moment. "If you had a five-year-old niece I would be more worried, but I can do princesses if needed. I mean, if Noah likes princesses, I can also handle that, but I may need to watch some of their movies or google them or something. Does he like princesses?"

Mr. I'm Not Worried seems pretty nervous and worried.

"Noah is a roll-in-the-dirt, superheroes kind of kid. He's not opposed to a tea party every once in a while, but that's his and Aspen's thing."

He really likes anything as long as he's having fun. I'm probably biased, but he's such an easy-going kid. It's probably because my brother is so even-keeled at home.

He has enough stress at the law firm he works at that when he goes home, they just do whatever.

"Superheroes, tea parties, got it. Got it."

Yeah, he's freaking out again. I take both his hands in mine and make sure he's holding eye contact. "Jackson, you aren't going to be left alone with him, expected to entertain and care for him all weekend. I will be there. Ben, his father, will be there. It's not on you. I only have all these ideas because I love my nephew and I like taking the parental load off my brother sometimes."

He shakes his head, giving me an embarrassed smile. "Yeah, you're right. Sorry, my freak out is actually over now. I am not normally like this. Why am I like this now?"

"Because you care?" It comes out like a question, but I know it's a fact. Jackson has floated through life making connections that are beneficial, but not always long-term. He's out of his comfort zone here, which is okay. I like that he gets nervous. It's cute and, again, it shows that he cares.

"I do care," he agrees. "A lot actually. But if I'm a total dweeb in front of your brother, you can't give me shit about it."

"I won't give you shit about it." I'm totally going to give him shit about it.

He kisses my nose and then grabs the cooler with our food in it. "Let's dig in."

Just as we finish washing our dinner dishes, three bodies come piling through the cottage door.

We were only expecting two, so Aspen's presence is a surprise. Noah barrels his way through Ben and Aspen and launches himself at me.

"AUNTY! I MISSED YOU!"

I squeeze his tiny body against me and bury my face in his neck, blowing raspberries against his skin. He breaks out in a fit of giggles and squirms in my arms, but I don't let him go. I've spent too long away from him this summer. I swear he's grown ten inches and ten pounds since I last saw him. Video calls just aren't the same as in person when they grow this fast. He's starting to not look like our little baby and more like a kid. I swear he's going to be a clone of Ben in a couple of years. They have the exact same shade of blue eyes. Noah's hair is a lighter shade of blonde than Ben's, but I'm sure it will darken as he ages.

"I missed you, too, baby."

"I'm not a baby, Aunty." His little voice filled with so much sass makes me laugh. I love this kid so much. Noah suddenly turns still and looks over my shoulder to where I know Jackson is standing. Noah leans in, not breaking eye contact with Jackson and asks, "Is that your boyfriend?"

I whisper back, "Yes. That's Jackson. Can you say hello to him?"

He nods and wiggles at me to put him down. He slowly approaches Jackson, looking back to me and Ben for reassurance. Once he is practically toe to toe with him, Jackson drops down to one knee so they are the same height.

"Hi, Noah. My name is Jackson." He sticks out his hand, expecting a handshake in return. I can hear my brother chuckling because he knows his kid is not going to shake his hand.

Noah stares at the hand, then looks back to Jackson's face. "Hi, Jackson. My name is Noah."

Noah looks back down to Jackson's outstretched hand before looking back to his dad who nods at him. Noah turns back to Jackson and throws his body onto him for a hug.

The Shaw's like hugging. Noah is no different. He hasn't completely grasped the concept that you don't hug everyone. It's a work in progress.

Jackson looks startled for half a second before wrapping his arms around Noah and returning the hug. Jackson looks up at me over Noah's shoulder, and his face melts my heart. He looks like he's in awe and already in love with the little boy. Noah has that effect on most people. The whole family is wrapped around his finger. When Noah pulls away, he runs and grabs his bag from his dad before disappearing upstairs with Aspen to unpack. I guess that cute moment is over.

Jackson raises to his full height and steps towards my brother. I can tell he's not as confident sticking his hand out to shake Ben's after what just happened with Noah. I hold back my laughter because I know he's nervous right now.

"Hey, Ben. It's nice to meet you." They shake hands, then release. "Your son is something. I think I already love the kid." He laughs a bit but sounds sincere.

Ben chuckles, too. "Yeah, he has that effect on most people. It's nice to meet you. I've heard a lot about you." He pauses a moment and looks straight at me. "From Aspen. Lillian has stayed tight-lipped about you." I flick his ear, but he just dodges me. He turns back to Jackson. "Can you help me unload my car?"

"Of course," Jackson responds with just a tiny bit too much enthusiasm. I think his voice may have even cracked, but I am not going to be the one to point that out.

As they head out the door, I hear Ben ask, "Do you happen to have one of those big radios you always see on construction sites? I want to listen to the baseball game tonight."

"Yeah. I'm sure I can find one next door. Not a problem," Jackson responds.

I wasn't worried, but I can already tell that Ben accepts him. They are going to be fine.

We spent all day outside. I have reapplied sunscreen a hundred times and my hair is a mess. I couldn't be happier. Ben lounged on the beach while Aspen, Jackson and I built sandcastles. Then Aspen and I made lunch while the boys had a water gun fight. We then inflated way too many floaties and played shark attack in the lake. It was such a great day. As soon as we ate dinner, Noah passed out. We had planned to have a bonfire tonight, but I think the adults were just as tired as Noah was. We didn't make it through more than one game of cards before we all agreed we should sleep so we are ready for more sun tomorrow.

It feels like my head has just hit the pillow when I hear a scream from downstairs. Jackson whips out of bed and flies out the door before I even have a chance to open my eyes.

Once I come to my senses, I follow after him.

When I get downstairs, Jackson is standing over Ben as Ben consoles Noah. I feel warmth behind me and see Aspen standing one step above me with her sleep mask halfway off her face.

"What happened?"

Noah looks up at me, tears streaming down his splotchy red face. "The boogie man was outside."

All the adults in the room look to Ben for more clarity, but he only shrugs at us. Rubbing his son's back, he asks, "What were you doing down here, buddy?"

Noah stops shaking, but his tears continue to fall down his small face.

"I woke up and needed a drink, but my bottle was already empty. When I came down here, I saw someone at the window at the bottom of the stairs. It was the boogie man!" he cries, dropping his head back into his dad's chest.

Ben shakes his head, mumbling something to Noah.

"The camp he went to last week had older kids mixed into his group. He came home one day worried the boogie man could get into our house. I think they were telling the younger kids ghost stories. He didn't seem too bothered after the first night, but I'm going to have a word with the camp leaders when I drop him off on Monday." Ben's face is in full Papa Bear mode. Outside of work, you don't often see him so serious, but no one messes with his kid.

He stands up and pulls Noah into his arms. "Come on, buddy, let's get you back to bed." Jackson quickly grabs a glass of water from the tap and hands it to Ben before he reaches the stairs where Aspen and I still are standing. We both drop a kiss on Noah's head as he passes us, but he's already almost asleep in my brother's arms.

Jackson takes my hand as we follow Aspen up the stairs and head back to bed. We cuddle in under the covers before Jackson speaks.

"That scared the crap out of me. I heard the scream and knew it was Noah. I was so scared that whoever is after me had come after him."

I hug him closer, feeling his heartbeat against my chest.

"Do you think there was actually someone out there?" No one said anything while we were down there with Noah, but it's something we need to be conscious of.

"I doubt it. Like Ben said, some kids got into Noah's head. Simon and I watched a scary movie we weren't supposed to when we were, like, seven. I thought I saw the scary killer guy everywhere I went for weeks. Anyway, the doors and windows are locked and with the amount of noise we all made stomping down the stairs, I'm sure every human and animal within a hundred yards was scared away."

I don't know if I'm convinced, but I think I'm too tired to care right now. It's got to be at least three in the morning at this point. I want to get something special for breakfast to make Noah feel better, so I'll need to get up early and beat the morning rush at the café.

I kiss the edge of Jackson's jaw and then stuff my face in his neck. I breathe him in as I fall into dreams of the beach, boogiemen and donuts.

Chapter 24
Jackson

"NOAH!"

I pull my pillow over my head, trying to drown out the sound of Ben calling for his son. After everything last night, I had trouble getting back to sleep. I'm going to have to function on only a couple of hours of sleep today.

"NOAH!" Ben's voice sounds more frantic than normal. I peek my eye to Lillian's side of the bed, seeing it empty. That's weird. My phone flashes from the nightstand, showing I have a missed text. Looking over, I see it is from Lillian. She's gone into town to get treats for breakfast. Noah is going to be excited when he sees her.

I now understand why she was so excited for this weekend. Noah is great. I haven't spent a lot of time with kids as an adult, but I'm already attached to him.

If we didn't have to work during the day, I would ask Ben to leave him with us. This place will be quiet when they leave this evening. Thankfully, we have a boat day planned for him today that we get to enjoy before then.

"NOAH!"

Okay, I don't know what's going on, but I am not getting any more sleep and I want to make sure both Ben and Noah are okay.

Rolling out of bed, I throw on a pair of shorts, skipping a shirt and head for the bathroom. The second I open the bedroom door, Ben is in my face.

"Have you seen Noah?"

"No...not since last night. I just woke up. What's going on?"

"Where's my sister?" Ben pushes past me, trying to see into our room. She's not in there, but if she was, I'm glad she told me to make sure I wore clothes to bed. Her family has some boundary issues.

"She went into town for breakfast. She sent me a text about fifteen minutes ago. What's going on? You can't find Noah?"

"No." He shakes his head, absolute panic in his eyes. "He

wasn't in his bed when I got up and he's not in the cottage. He would never go outside by himself."

"Okay, breathe, I'm sure he's okay. I'll call Lillian and make sure he's not with her. Where's Aspen?"

"I don't know. Her bedroom door is locked and her phone is on Do-Not-Disturb. I think she's still sleeping."

"You go outside and look for him. I'll call Lillian and figure out what's going on with Aspen."

He nods his head once before running down the stairs. I go back to the nightstand for my phone and call Lillian.

"Is Noah with you?" I ask, getting straight to the point.

"No, why? Did something happen?" Shit.

"Is Aspen with you?"

"No, I'm alone. I'm, like, two seconds away from the cottage. What's going on? You're scaring me."

"Don't panic, please. You're driving. Just get home and I'll explain."

"Jackson! You can't tell me not to panic. I'm panicking! I'm pulling into the driveway now. I see Ben. Why is he running around out here?"

"He can't find Noah."

"What?!" she shrieks. "What do you mean you can't find him? Like he's hiding or like someone took him?"

"Like we can't find him. We also aren't positive where Aspen is, so everything could be fine. Her door is locked and she's not answering her phone or when we knock."

Lillian doesn't respond, so I assume she's in shock. "Lil?"

No answer. Looking down at my phone, I see she hung up on me. She's probably talking to her brother outside. Suddenly, I hear yelling coming from downstairs. As I reach the top of the stairs, Ben and Lillian come barrelling up towards me. Ben is yelling in her ear, but she's ignoring him and speaking into her phone. She brushes past me to Aspen's door which opens just as she's about to turn the handle.

Aspen stands in the door frame holding her finger to her mouth in a "shhh" motion. She then points over her shoulder. Lillian takes a step back, allowing me and Ben to crowd the door. Just over Aspen's shoulder lies a sleeping Noah with headphones over his ears. Aspen has a matching pair around her neck.

Ben pushes past Aspen and gently lies down in her bed next to his son, pulling him towards his body and burying his face in the boy's hair.

I am utterly confused as to what has happened in the last ten minutes, but this feels like a personal moment, so I step back, grab Lillian's hand and pull her into the bathroom with me. In all the chaos, I haven't even brushed my teeth yet.

"What is going on?" I ask around a mouth full of toothpaste. Lillian wipes a dribble off my chin.

"We'll have to ask Aspen, but I'm assuming after Noah was scared last night, he climbed into bed with her. She likes to sleep with white noise, so I'm guessing neither of them heard you guys shouting for Noah this morning."

I guess that makes sense. I'm glad Noah is okay, but I can't imagine the panic Ben must have been feeling.

I finish up in the bathroom and we both head downstairs. Noah is sitting on the couch, staring at the box of treats Lillian must have bought. Aspen and Ben are arguing in a whisper in the kitchen. When they see us, they both stop talking, but hold each other in a stare-off.

Ben breaks first, dropping his gaze to the ground before giving Aspen a half-hearted hug. We watch him walk through the living room and out the sliding door to the porch. Without a word, Lillian follows him outside.

Noah looks around and shrugs his shoulders before opening the box and stuffing a chocolate donut in his mouth. I choose to join Aspen in the kitchen to make sure she's doing okay.

"Everything okay?"

"It's fine." She looks out the window towards Ben and Lillian. Lillian is rubbing his back while they both sit facing towards the water.

"It was a misunderstanding; emotions were running high. Everything will be okay."

She looks back to me as I give her shoulder a squeeze in support. Aspen's eyes fill with moisture. She doesn't let the tears fall, but this is the closest I've ever seen her to crying.

"He came into my room shortly after we all went back to bed. He claimed he needed to stay with me so I wasn't scared. I think he was trying to be brave for his dad, so he came to my room. I offered to lock the door to make him feel better, but then he wouldn't stop chatting. I put on my headphones with white noise. He was asleep within minutes and I didn't think about setting an alarm before putting headphones on myself and passing out. Noah normally wakes up at 6 am. I didn't even think about telling Ben he was with me. It was 3 am, I thought we would be awake before him! Ben's upset that Noah went to me instead of him for comfort, I think. He's also made me change my phone settings so his calls always go through. I've apologized and he said he forgives me, but he's still processing his emotions. He'll be fine soon, especially with Billy out there." She pauses for a moment and looks down at her hands. "I just hate feeling like I overstepped. The Shaw's are like my family, and I just want to help Ben out in any way I can. I didn't mean to cause all this emotional distress."

Aspen turns to face the fridge and drops her head against it, looking defeated. I place a hand on her back, rubbing lightly, to hopefully offer her comfort like Lillian is to Ben.

"You didn't do anything with bad intentions. I'm sure Ben understands that." I don't have kids, so I can't imagine how he felt when he thought Noah was missing.

We both turn at the sound of the screen door opening. Ben looks towards his chocolate-covered son. He shakes his head, but a tender smile appears on his face.

"Alright, Noah, get cleaned up and change. We're going on Jackson's boat today." Noah looks towards his dad in shock and then to me. I nod my head, causing him to pump his little fist in the air in celebration.

Aspen quickly grabs a wet cloth and goes to where Noah is still sitting to clean his face.

I walk to where Lillian still stands by the door.

"Aspen seems to be kind of obsessed with Noah."

"Oh, he's equally as obsessed with her."

"I can tell. I just mean, like, I wasn't expecting it. Not that I thought she wouldn't be good with kids, but she's really good with kids." Directing my question to Aspen, I ask, "Aspen, why weren't you a teacher or something? You are amazing with children.”

She gives me an uncharacteristically shy smile before clearing her face and putting on her normal cool and confident look. “Too much politics. Listening to the principal, dealing with annoying parents and all the problems with the school boards. No, thank you. I can't wait to have my own little monsters, but I'm not down to deal with all the rest.”

“Well, I think you'll be a great mom, Asp,” Lillian's brother says, overhearing the conversation as he makes lunch.

“Thanks, Ben.” She walks past him and drops a kiss on his cheek before grabbing us all drinks from the fridge. I guess all is forgiven.

“Has anything ever happened between the two of them?” I ask Lillian, quiet enough that neither of them can hear. Lillian snorts out a laugh. I guess not. “She called him hot yesterday,” I add.

“God, no. She says that to mess with me and make him un-comfortable. Aspen is like a little sister to him. She got noogied just as much as I did growing up, and Aspen would never be with a guy like Ben. He's too go-with-the-flow for her. She needs someone to match her energy or else she'll walk all over them.”

I think about her answer for a moment before I reply. I can see that, but they do seem compatible, and Aspen loves Noah like they are related.

I swear what we witnessed this morning was a lover's quarrel, but what do I know? I don't want to push it more because I don't know that Lillian would be okay with them getting together. Maybe she isn't seeing what I'm seeing. I'm probably wrong. In the case that I'm not, I will bring up this moment.

I've never seen anyone as excited about going on a boat as Noah is. The kid was vibrating in my truck the whole way to the marina. I don't think I understood how much more preparation goes into doing anything, even leaving the house, when you have kids. Ben looks like a pack mule.

He and I unload everything into the boat as the girls get Noah settled. My slip neighbour Rick is once again cleaning his boat. I'm not sure if we operate at different times, but I've yet to see his wife and kids. They must come on Saturdays, while we are always here on Sundays.

"Oh no!"

I look behind me to Lillian who is in the bench seat grabbing life jackets.

"What's the problem?" Aspen asks.

Lillian riffles through the jackets again. "We don't have one that fits Noah's weight requirement. Ben, is there one at the cottage?"

"Shit." Ben thinks for a moment. "No, I think he's outgrown his last one. They sell them in town, right?"

I hold my hands up, trying to stop everyone's panic. "Wait, I've got one." I reach into the small cabin door beside the wheel. We mostly use it for storage, but I've got a surprise in there. I pull out a life jacket that is the right size for Noah, and a white and navy child-sized boat captain's hat.

Handing both to Noah, I say, "These are for you. Are you

ready to set sail?" Figuratively speaking. There aren't any sails on my boat.

He squeezes his small arm around my waist before grabbing both the life jacket and hat and turning to his dad for help getting them on. "Let's go!" he yells.

I smile at the little boy and turn to see both Lillian and Aspen staring at me. Aspen with a coy smile on her lips, and Lillian with a look of shock.

"Where did you get those?" Lillian grabs my hand and pulls me aside. I don't think I did anything wrong, but her wanting this conversation to be private does worry me a little bit.

"I ordered them online?" I don't know why it comes out like a question. I did order them online.

"When?"

I hesitate a moment. I'm wondering if I overstepped and the truth may make things worse. I've never lied to Lillian before and I don't want to start now. "As soon as you told me you had a nephew..." My answer makes me feel a bit like a creep, but the look on Lillian's face washes all the worry away.

Her smile could give the sun a run for its money. Her entire being is bright and warm, and I would make it my home if I could. I want to make her smile like that every day for the rest of my life.

She throws her arms around me, knocking me enough that the whole boat rocks from side to side. "I did good?"

"So good," she says against my neck. She gives me one more squeeze before letting go.

"You are something special, Jackson Mane."

I hear a snicker from behind us and look to see Aspen and

Ben whispering to each other while they look at us. Noah is oblivious, pretending to steer the boat. I clear my throat, trying to remove the attention from us. Lillian and I have only been dating for, like, three hours. If I'm not careful, I'll be in love with her by the end of the week.

Chapter 25
Lillian

The weekend with Ben, Noah, Aspen and Jackson couldn't have gone better. Everyone got along well, Ben didn't try weird brother intimidation tactics on Jackson, and Noah was obsessed with the boat. The minor mishap of Ben losing Noah, only for him to be in Aspen's room, was quickly forgotten. Ben wasn't really mad at Aspen. He was terrified. Noah is his entire world. When I sat with him outside, he didn't say much. He just needed a chance to breathe and process his emotions without his son seeing him break down. Once we were on the boat, everything was behind us.

When Jackson pulled the lifejacket and captain's hat out, I nearly swooned myself off the boat. He had ordered them both long before he knew Ben and Noah were visiting. Hell, he ordered them long before we were even dating. I'm not sure why Jackson has never wanted to be in a relationship before—he's great at it.

The last two weeks have been a dream. Our relationship isn't much different now that we have labelled it. We still cook together, try to work near each other, spend days on the boat, nights on the beach and a weekly visit to Ron's, but it still feels different.

I've never felt this secure in my life.

Jackson is so strong and steady; he seems confident in everything he does that it makes me feel brave. We haven't had any trouble on any of his job sites since the vandalism, so I've started to branch out a bit more on my own. I like to stop in and visit Julia at the bookstore at least once a week. I wouldn't say we are friends yet, but she doesn't seem to mind my company. I've also volunteered at the library a bit. With my connections in publishing, I've helped them set up some events with local authors to help bring more tourists in their doors.

Once a week, I meet with Mrs. Langley. We either spend time in her garden and she sends me home with fresh produce for dinner, or we enjoy tea and treats on her porch swing. Jackson has been running any errands she has that would require her to leave town. Every time he claims he needs to go wherever it is, too, but I know he's doing it for the cookies.

We have completely immersed ourselves into the town of Bluefield. I've spent more summers here than I could count, yet I've never felt like a part of the community until now. If we aren't careful, Jackson and I are going to be grey-haired with grandchildren running around before we know it.

Although that doesn't sound entirely bad. I would live anywhere as long as I got to keep spending most of my time with Jackson. And a life here with him sounds like a dream.

I always assumed Christopher and I would be getting married in the next couple of years.

Not because I was dying to marry him, but because that was the natural next step, all part of the plan I had for myself. It's sad, the more I think about it. We weren't the best versions of ourselves together, certainly not the happiest, but we were successful, so we let it continue, until he didn't. I'm grateful that Christopher saw what was happening and ended it. At the time, I thought he just wanted to sleep around. It was an ugly thought to have, but I found it easier to swallow than the truth. Because I didn't want the plan in my head to have gone wrong. I didn't want to start over. I didn't want to put the work in to improve myself and heal. I wanted blissful ignorance. It was easier.

Now that I am on the other side of things, the hard work and pain is so worth it to get to the happy. Because that's what I am.

Six months ago, if you asked me to describe myself, I would have listed off either physical or professional qualities.

Late twenties, blonde, short, shy.

Career-oriented, driven, organized, creative.

I wouldn't have mentioned anything mental or emotional. Now if you asked me the same thing, the first thing to pop into my head would be happy.

Happy, optimistic, excited, content.

I am still in my late twenties, blonde, short, shy, career-oriented, driven, organized, and creative. But those things feel less important. And Bluefield has a lot to do with that. I can breathe here, I can try and fail, I have support like I've never felt before. I love my family, and I am grateful for the childhood I was provided, but this place feels more like home than my parents' house or my condo. The only thing that would make it better is if everyone I loved wanted to stay here with me, too.

I know that isn't realistic and I'm choosing to be happy with whatever reality I have. And right now, that reality is popping the Bluefield bubble we live in, for forty hours.

Jackson has a meeting in Toronto, and I'm going to go with him. The meeting will only take a couple of hours on Thursday, so we've decided to leave Bluefield on Wednesday and come back on Friday. We could stay in the city for the weekend, but neither of us wanted that. We like our slow weekends in Bluefield.

It feels surreal driving into Toronto with Jackson. We both spent the majority of our lives living in this city, but never together. Aspen likes to remind me that if I had gone to a couple of parties with her in high school, Jackson and I would have at least been in the same room. I don't like to think about it. Who we were in high school is not who we are now, and chances are we wouldn't have even spoken. Things needed to happen how they did.

I know without a shadow of a doubt if Jackson tried to talk to me when I was a teenager, I would have said nothing and then ran away. Not so different to our first interaction after he dumped my dinner on me, but our proximity in Bluefield helped force another chance on us.

Tonight, we are staying at Jackson's and tomorrow at my condo. We are both eager to show each other our lives outside of Bluefield. Jackson wanted to just lounge at his place tonight, but Simon just showed up insisting we go to a pub around the corner to play pool. I pretended to be surprised by his idea, but really, Simon and I have been plotting for weeks.

It seems as though Jackson thought he could get away with not telling me that it's his birthday this weekend. Thankfully, Simon told me about it when he visited a couple of weeks ago, so we were able to plan a little surprise party for him.

He's turning twenty-eight, so it isn't a milestone birthday, but I can tell he doesn't usually have anyone to make a fuss over him on his special day. I just so happen to love fussing over birthdays. Aspen is the type of girl who thinks the whole month of April is her birthday, so one little party for Jackson is the least we can do. I made sure to spend a little extra time on my hair and makeup this morning so I would already be good to go. I have no idea how many people will be there tonight. Simon was in charge of the guest list, so if I end up in a room with every girl Jackson has ever slept with, I want to at least have a layer of makeup as armour.

Of course, that's not what Simon has done. The pub is warm and inviting, with booths lining the windows and dark wood tables filling the space in front of the bar. In the back, there are a couple of pool tables, more booths and high-top tables. Because it's only a Wednesday and most people work tomorrow, the place isn't very busy. Almost everyone here is in the back waiting for Jackson.

Simon walks in first, then Jackson and then me. I squeeze Jackson's hand to draw his attention behind him to me for a moment so he doesn't see what's coming.

"Everything okay?"

I pull him in for a quick kiss, mostly to calm my own nerves but also to act as a distraction.

"All good. Just wanted a kiss."

"Well, in that case..." Jackson gets a mischievous look in his eyes before pulling me close and then dipping me low. Our kiss is slow and passionate. His tongue swipes across my lips and I can't help but open them so he can deepen the kiss. Our tongues duel for control. This kiss is quickly becoming one that is not appropriate for our public setting.

Right as he grabs my ass to pull me even closer, whistles and cheers break out in the bar. I pull away and try to right myself as quickly as possible, turning my back to everyone.

When I look up to Jackson, who's still got his hand around me, he's looking over my shoulder, shocked.

"Surprise!" Simon yells, before everyone echoes him.

"I just groped you in front of all my friends," Jackson whispers to just me.

"Uh-huh." I can feel the heat reaching my entire face, but Jackson just chuckles. He plants a quick kiss on my lips mumbling, "Worth it," against them.

He doesn't give me a chance to cool down my face as he grabs my hand and pulls me towards his party guests. Multiple people engulf him in handshakes and hugs. I try to pull my hand away, trying to give him his space to catch up with his friends, but Jackson has other plans. He pulls out a seat at one of the high-top tables, sits down and pulls me onto his lap.

And that's where I stay for the rest of the night. Jackson's friends cycle through with introductions and casual conversation. I mostly smile and nod, listening to the conversation but not overly participating. This night is about Jackson, not me, although he does tell everyone all the fun things we've been doing this summer, keeping me included without forcing me. Both Aspen and Ben make an appearance, which really makes Jackson smile. I don't think I could ever take my family for granted after seeing how much it means to Jackson when my people show up for him. Jackson has his own group of friends, but he's not very close with any of them. Before me, I'm confident Simon is the only person Jackson has ever opened up with.

Ben doesn't stay long. Noah is with a sitter, but they both need to be up early, so after one beer, Ben leaves.

I watch with fascination as Aspen works the room. She may know some of these people casually, but you would think it was her party the way she's interacting with everyone. Simon, who actually planned the party, is similarly catching up with everyone. His eyes find Aspen every couple of minutes, while hers look everywhere but at him. It's quite entertaining how she skillfully avoids any conversation Simon is a part of. I am ninety-nine percent sure Simon has a crush on Aspen. I am also ninety-nine percent sure Aspen wants nothing to do with Simon. It would be funny if Aspen's boyfriend, John, wasn't watching the same thing as me and shooting death glares at the back of Simon's head.

Jackson is shocked when he meets John, but he tries to play it cool.

Aspen grabs John's hand, dragging him over to us and then dropping it to give Jackson a hug.

"Happy birthday," she coos like he is a baby, and she squeezes him harder than necessary. "This is John, my boyfriend." John gives Jackson a head nod and then heads to the bar to get a drink. He isn't a big talker, which I don't fault him for, but he's not always very friendly either.

I give Aspen a hug, too, before she takes off to find herself a drink and mingle.

"Aspen has a boyfriend?" Jackson whispers into my ear. I nod, hoping no one around us can hear this conversation. "Since when?"

"John's been around on and off for a couple of years, maybe?" I try to think of when they first met. I think it was shortly after we graduated from university. I kiss the shocked look off Jackson's face.

"Why didn't I know this? I was convinced she and Ben were secretly an item!"

I can't help but laugh. Sometimes Aspen jokingly hits on my brother. She tries to make both of us feel uncomfortable, but I know it's not serious. They truthfully are like siblings. From the outside, it's hard for others to see, but there's no way.

"Aspen keeps her private life private. I honestly kind of forgot about John. As long as things are going well, I don't hear much. And when they aren't doing well, she cuts the cord."

I used to envy the way Aspen was in relationships. No bull-shit. If she's happy, she continues on; when she isn't, it's over.

She makes it seem so simple. I know when she meets the right guy, things will change for her, but she's told me her career is her priority, and once it's at a point where she's settled, she'll settle down. I trust that she knows what she's doing, so I can't do anything but support her. Even if John is a bit blah. Maybe his jealousy towards Simon will put a bit of spunk into him.

By 9 pm, most people have already left or are closing their tabs, getting ready to leave. I don't think we would normally be in bed by this time if we were in Bluefield, but it sure feels way too late. When we leave the pub with Simon, the air has a chill to it. Jackson throws his arm over my shoulder when he sees the goosebumps covering my bare arms. My sundress seemed a lot more practical when the sun was still in the sky.

"Is there a reason you weren't going to tell me about your birthday?"

Jackson looks a bit sheepish. He gives me a shrug and then tries to change the subject.

"It was nice of your brother to stop by. I understand why he didn't bring Noah, but I wish he could have brought Noah."

"Yeah, yeah, they're both great. Why didn't you tell me about your birthday?"

Jackson rolls his eyes playfully, and I hear Simon chuckle from behind me. I look over my shoulder at him, trying to give my best death glare, but I don't think it hits its mark.

"Hey, don't look at me." Simon raises his hands in the air in surrender. "I told you about it because I knew he wouldn't, but I'm staying out of this."

Jackson huffs beside me and tries to swat at Simon behind him.

"Jackson..." I know he wants me to drop it, but I need to know. "If there is some sort of trauma I'm unknowingly pushing on you, then we never have to celebrate again. But I won't know if you don't communicate with me."

"OOOO, you're in trouble," Simon chirps from behind.

"Hey, Simon...What's your deal with Aspen?" I don't look back, but I hear his feet against the sidewalk stutter and then stop.

"Oh, I'm thirsty actually. I'm going to buy a drink from the convenience store we just passed." He quickly scurries away. I knew that would shut him up. I guess I should have waited until we got back to Jackson's to have this conversation, but Simon knows him better than anyone else. I thought he would be more helpful than he was.

Jackson stops and guides me towards the small alleyway between the buildings we are passing. He pushes me against the brick wall and drops his forehead to mine. Jackson doesn't often look this vulnerable. I'm worried I pushed at something I shouldn't have.

"My dad hasn't acknowledged my birthday since I was in high school."

What?

"On purpose?" I have so many questions, but that's the first one that fights its way out of my mouth.

"I don't think so." He pauses. "I don't know. I think he genuinely forgot a couple of times. I would get a present a couple of days later when he remembered. After a couple of years, he just stopped saying anything. Like he eased his way out of the obligation."

"And your mom?" I ask, because I think I know the answer and it's worse than his dad.

"She sent me a birthday card the first year she was gone and then nothing since."

"Oh, Jackson." He stops me by putting a finger against my lips.

"I don't need your sympathy or your pity. I'm used to it by now. Simon's parents always took me out for dinner, and he and I would do something fun to celebrate. I'm an adult now, so we don't do that anymore. It's fine."

I take his finger and place it against my heart, then take his cheeks in both of my hands, forcing him to look into my eyes. "I don't pity you. I never will. But your parents are assholes. If you don't want to celebrate your birthday, then that's okay with me. But I want to celebrate you. Any day, every day. You do so much to take care of everyone around you, let me take care of you. You deserve to feel special. To be thought of. To be celebrated. You have made my life so much better than I ever could have imagined. Let me give some of that back to you. Please."

I see the glassy edge to Jackson's eyes. He blinks away the excess moisture before it can fall and clears his throat. His voice still comes out a bit gravelly and full of emotion.

"Okay."

"Okay," I agree. "Now that that's cleared up, that bag of trash smells really bad. Let's go home."

I look down at our feet. I don't know if garbage day is tomorrow, but it looks like the raccoons have already had their pick of snacks.

"Home, eh?" He cocks his eyebrow at me playfully, the

somber mood all gone now.

"You know what I mean." I try to smack his chest, but he grabs my hand before I can make contact and kisses my knuckles.

"Yeah, I know exactly what you mean."

Chapter 26
Jackson

I feel like I'm running on fumes today. This weekend was a blast, but I could use twenty more hours of sleep.

I haven't done anything for my birthday in years and I think Lillian's goal was to make up for lost time.

After we spent the night at my place, I had a quick meeting on Thursday and then we headed to Lillian's place. She ordered in for dinner from her favourite restaurant, and Noah joined us for both dinner and dessert.

Lillian and Noah made a cake from scratch and he looked so proud when I blew out the candles.

Her parents insisted on video calling when they heard about my birthday and then apologized for not being around to celebrate.

I know most families celebrate each other's birthdays. I know my parents forgetting is not great and not the norm, but I can't believe how much effort everyone in Lillian's life is putting into this for me. My childhood was different, I know that. But this has put a lot into perspective.

Our time in the city together was great. We took turns showing each other our favourite spots from cafés to pubs, bookstores, and parks. Experiencing a place you've lived forever through someone else's eyes is fun. It made me appreciate the city more, but I was so excited to get back to Bluefield.

Both Lillian and I agree Bluefield feels like home. We haven't talked too much about what will happen at the end of the summer. The relationship is new and I don't want to pressure her to make those decisions right now, but I wouldn't mind staying here a bit more permanently.

When we got back to Bluefield, Lillian surprised me with a

new little outfit. She claimed she was my present. I had a lot of fun unwrapping her all weekend.

A part of me is scared to anticipate this again for next year. It's easier to expect less than to be let down by high expectations.

I am trying to remain hopeful. Lillian has set the bar high, though. I already know I'll need Aspen's help in February to make her birthday just as special.

Even though we hardly left the cottage over the weekend, I'm exhausted. I want this week to hurry up so I can relax over the weekend.

I used to live for work. Crazy how priorities change so quickly. I still love what I do, and I'm glad I have the opportunities I do at my dad's company. But it's not the most important thing in my day anymore.

So many of our projects are hitting the critical stage, so when Peters texted asking to meet at the station, I was a little annoyed. I shouldn't be, but more often than not, he has bad news for me. If he's calling me in to tell me he's found nothing, I don't even know what I'll say to him.

Just as I pull out of my parking spot in front of the café, a familiar truck pulls out in front of me. There's only one person who would be driving a sparkling new truck with the Mane Construction logo on it.

Gord. My father.

When he's in the city, he drives a sports car, typically. He probably thinks he's more relatable to the crew in this area by driving the truck. So, fake. Yes, the man started the company from the ground up and was once doing grunt work. Gone are the days of Gord Mane getting his hands dirty.

I checked my phone before getting in the car. I know I don't have any missed messages or calls from him. Why would he come into town without telling me? Either there's an issue or he's being nosey.

Anytime we've had an issue this summer, he seems to know about it before I've had a chance to tell him, so I am well aware someone is feeding him information. I would be annoyed, except for the fact all the information is one hundred percent true. We kept the basement graffiti and threats to ourselves, so I was able to gently tell him about that one to avoid a blow-up if he found out from someone else. Either the suspect isn't my father's mole or I just got lucky and told him first.

I really wish I could follow him to wherever he's going, but Peters is expecting me, and I need to keep the man on my side.

If I know my dad, and I think I do, he'll stop by every project to get an update. Seeing as it's almost lunchtime, there is a chance he will run into Lillian at the Waldens'.

We give the guys an hour for lunch now. The summer heat has really set in, so this gives them the opportunity to properly cool off midday. Lillian has discovered she enjoys painting walls. She may be the first person to ever say that, but she's been help-ing speed things along. I told her it wasn't allowed to interfere with her own work, but she insisted it was a calming midday break. I'm not going to argue with her if she thinks painting is calming, to each their own, and I appreciate the help.

I send off a quick text to Lillian, giving her the heads up that Gord is here and to avoid him if she can. I'm not trying to hide her from him. I just don't want her to have to meet and deal with him for the first time when I'm not there to make sure he plays nice.

Since I've never had a girlfriend, I've never had to introduce him to anyone. I don't think he'll make a big deal of it, but it's still uncharted territory for both of us.

I haven't met Lillian's parents in person yet, but I did crash a couple of her parents' weekly calls. I was nervous for half a second before realizing that Lillian was the perfect combination of both her parents and they are, therefore, great people.

They were very cute during our birthday call. Her mom is warm and cheerful, and her dad has the same sneaky sense of humour as Lillian. They've been nothing but nice to me, and I'm so glad that I'm getting to build a relationship with them.

Lillian surrounds herself with awesome people and I'm just the fool hoping she'll keep me around.

When I walk into the station, Peters is waiting for me at the desk. I follow him back to his office.

He takes a seat behind his large oak desk, while I sit in one of the two chairs across from him.

"Thanks for coming in. Oh, and happy belated birthday." He chuckles at the look on my face. Almost every person I've seen today has wished me a happy birthday. I swear Lillian and Simon must have rented a billboard; the whole town knows. "Lillian told me when I ran into her last week."

"She's been doing a lot of that," I reply with a chuckle. She's one of a kind.

"Okay, I don't want to waste any of your time today. I'm going to be honest with you. We have no leads with your case." Basically, what I thought he was going to say.

It's almost been a month since we found the spray paint in the basement. I don't want to believe nothing is going to happen again and it's over because I'll feel like I'll jinx it, but I'm secretly leaning that way.

Peters continues, "There seems to be an incident or two and then nothing for a couple of weeks. We had a theory that it was someone working for you since they knew where the cameras were, but the random timeline has been bothering me."

This piques my interest a bit. "What do you mean?"

"It's almost like our suspect isn't permanently in town. They come, execute an attack or two, and then go ghost for a couple of weeks. Then return and do it again. Do you have anyone on your site that would be working out of town sometimes?"

"No, it was a requirement for everyone assigned to the job to be in town until we're done. They can do as they wish on weekends, but they are all here all week."

"Hmm, that's what I thought, but I wanted to confirm. I can't figure out why a tourist would be doing this, but the behaviour pattern matches. I wish I had more for you, but we're still working on it. You and Lillian stay safe."

I don't know why a tourist would be doing this either. Aside from Lillian and my employees, I only interact with locals at this point. I don't know of anyone from my past that's come into town. Nor do I know anyone with a grudge they would be acting on. Peters' theory that it's someone coming and going from town does make sense, but it also doesn't. I'm not surprised that this has stumped him. I feel the same way.

"I appreciate your effort." I can tell this is getting to Peters. I can't imagine this sort of case is normal for a small town like this.

We both stand and Peters walks me out to my truck. The second I get inside; I rip out of the parking lot and head towards Lillian's cottage. My conversation with Peters was a distraction, and while I want whoever is terrorizing us to be caught, my dad talking to Lillian is more of a pressing matter right now.

When I get to the Waldens' I see my dad's truck exactly where I thought it would be.

I hope that either Gord missed Lillian and they never even interacted or that he hasn't scared Lillian off yet.

Chapter 27
Lillian

Jackson's father is standing in front of me.

How can I tell? He is Jackson's clone.

Handsome, lean, but muscular, tall, brown hair, brown eyes. But the eyes are where things take a turn. Gord, Jackson's father, has hard, calculating eyes. They are emotionless and cold like the depths of December; Jackson's are warm and inviting, like a crackling wood fire driving the chill away. It feels like Gord isn't looking at me but through me. It's very unnerving.

Did I expect to meet my boyfriend's dad today? Nope.

Did I expect to meet my boyfriend's dad without said boyfriend present? Very much nope.

Am I panicked? Yes.

Am I letting him see that I'm panicked? Only a little. I hope.

I've told Jackson before that when I'm at work, I channel a different person. I'm acting. In all honesty, I sometimes pretend I'm Aspen because she is a boss, and no one ever messes with her.

I think she's the perfect person to emulate in this situation. I can be witty and charming like her. Sure, I can. Maybe.

Gord approaches me and I can tell he's analyzing my movements, so I stay still. Probably weirdly still, but his lack of emotion gives nothing away. I have a feeling I'll end this interaction without knowing if he hates me, tolerates me, or is indifferent. I'm not even going to pretend like he'll like me. I don't think Gord likes many people.

Jackson doesn't talk a lot about his family, and I don't really blame him. His mother abandoned him and he has no relationship with her, his dad only sees him as a useful piece of Mane Construction, not an ounce of fatherly warmth to be had, and he has no siblings. After our chat this weekend about no one celebrating his birthday, I'm not a fan of either of his parents.

I am, however, forever grateful he was able to spend so much time with Simon's family growing up. If not for them, I don't know how Jackson would have made it this far as a functioning, friendly, and loving adult.

"Do you work for me?" Gord asks. No greeting; we've skipped all pleasantries. Got it.

"Um, no." I try to sound confident, but I can tell the hesitation in my voice carries out more than I wanted.

"Then you're on my property...because?"

I try to gather my thoughts before I continue. I don't think he knows or cares that Jackson has a girlfriend. Do I say I'm a friend? A neighbour? A nosey local?

No, I'm not going to do any of that. If this man wants to intimidate me, I'm not letting it happen. I don't think Jackson ever had anyone stand up for him with his father. And I'm not going to start yelling at this man for all the ways he went wrong as a parent, but I also won't let him push me around.

I don't want to be a weakness he can use against Jackson. I can be strong for him. This is a game I plan on winning.

I stick out my hand to initiate a handshake. "I'm Lillian Shaw. My family owns the cottage next door. I'm your son's girlfriend."

Gord seems to be taken aback by my sudden burst of assertiveness. He recovers quickly, taking my hand in a firm handshake that I reciprocate.

"Gordon Mane. But you already knew that."

I smile because, yes, I did, and he knows nothing about me.

"So what is my son's girlfriend doing on my job site?" He's asserting dominance. That's fine. It won't make me stumble.

"I'm providing free labour." His eyes widen the slightest bit. Yeah, I thought that would get him. "I don't like to sit all day. I've been helping paint on my lunch breaks. Keeps the brain creative and eases Jackson's stress. Win-win." I lean my hip against the counter, trying to look relaxed when I am anything but. Gord chuckles under his breath, and I just know somehow

I slipped up.

"What does Jackson have to be stressed about? Having a job?"

Shit. Think, Lillian, think.

I put my hands in the back pocket of my jean shorts. I don't want him to see my hands shake or accidently fidget my fingers in front of him.

"He's in a new position. This project is out of the norm for him. If he didn't feel at least a little bit of stress as he learns the ropes, then he would be overqualified for his role and in need of a promotion."

I have no idea where that came from.

I feel pretty freaking smart for pulling that out of my ass. Gord knows what I'm insinuating. The only person above Jackson is him. And I know Gord loves hanging the future of the company over Jackson's head. As much as he may not get along with the man, he wants to be the one to run Mane Construction when his dad retires. This company may have taken up the majority of his dad's time when he was a child, and still today, but it was a constant for him. And I know a tiny part of him is vying for his father's approval, even if he doesn't need it.

Gord clears his throat and simply answers with, "Fair enough."

There isn't much more he can say on the topic, as I'm sure he doesn't want to talk about business or family issues with me. I may be his son's girlfriend, but he has no idea how to handle me.

"Have you had a tour of the place recently?" I ask, knowing he hasn't. I don't want the guy to hate me, maybe respect me, so I think switching gears to the charming aspect of this whole charade is probably best at this point.

"Not recently, no."

"Well, I'm no expert, but I would be happy to show you around. I don't think he knows it, but Jackson mumbles to himself task lists and things he needs to check on while we cook. So I should be able to tell you what they still have to do in each room."

Gord looks at me like he wants to ask a question, but then shakes his head, thinking better of it, and gestures towards the living room.

I proceed to walk him from room to room on all three floors, explaining to the best of my ability what the plan is.

For the most part, everything has been dry-walled and all electrical and plumbing completed. They are almost to the home stretch, waiting on fixtures, appliances, furniture and paint.

Gord doesn't say much, just nods along, but I think that's a good thing. If he was unhappy, he would express it. I'm taking his silence as acceptance—of me or the project, I'm not sure.

As my tour wraps up, I'm not sure what I should do next. If he leaves or dismisses me, fine, I'll go. But if we're both lingering, I know I'm going to start to be awkward. I've done so well to this point and I know it won't last. My energy is starting to fade. I don't know how Aspen does it. Entertaining people is exhausting.

I'm about to offer to get him something to drink from my cottage, which I don't want to do, when the back door bursts open and Jackson comes flying in. I don't know what he was expecting, but he looks relieved to see us both standing in front of him, content and unharmed. He was probably worried his dad would reduce me to tears. I don't blame him, but he will be proud of how I handled things.

"Gord." He nods to his dad as he passes him. Jackson seems to vacillate between dad, Gord, or father, depending on the situation or his mood. When he reaches me, he pulls me into a quick hug and kisses the top of my head. He releases me, but I keep one arm wrapped around his middle back, and I lean into his body just enough that he knows I'm here and I'm okay. For the brief moment that my head was on his chest during our hug, I could feel his heart beating faster than normal. I know he's on edge. Anything I can do to help, I will.

I feel him relax a fraction next to me. Goal accomplished. I rub my hand up and down his back, out of Gord's view, hoping to soothe him even more.

"So what have you two been up to?" Jackson asks, looking only towards his dad. I'm not sure if there's an accusation in his eyes, but it's laced in his tone.

I answer before Gord can. "We had a little chat and then I gave Gord a tour." I smile up at Jackson so he knows our interactions were pleasant enough. He looks down at me, returning my smile.

"A tour?"

I nod my head, my smile turning cheeky. "I should be on the payroll."

This makes Jackson laugh, and I feel the remaining tension leave his body. He looks back towards his father, who hasn't said anything.

"Jackson, can I have a word with you outside?" Shit. That was said like a question, but I think it was a demand. Without waiting for a response or saying goodbye, Gord heads out the door, assuming Jackson will follow.

Why does it feel like he's being sent to the principal's office for something I did? If I somehow got Jackson in trouble, I don't even know what I'll do. I look up at Jackson, wide-eyed and worried.

"Are you okay?" Am I okay?

"I think so," I answer. "He was mostly indifferent with me, but I don't think I did anything to get you in trouble. Why does he want to talk alone?"

He rubs his hands up and down my arms in a comforting motion. "He just does that. Don't worry. I can handle him."

"Don't worry?" I'm always worrying. You can't tell me not to worry.

"Okay, you can worry if you want. But I will be fine. Trust me. Why don't you head into town and I'll meet you for dinner after I finish up?"

He kisses both my cheeks and then my mouth as he waits for my answer.

I know he wants me to go distract myself while he talks to his dad. It's a smart move and just shows that Jackson knows me well. He's the one who has to have this ominous conversation, so the best thing I can do is listen to his suggestion.

"Okay, yeah. I'll hang out at the bookstore until you're ready." This appeases him. He drops another quick kiss to my mouth, but I pull him in for more. I try to put everything I'm feeling into the kiss. The stress and anxiety from the last hour, but also the strength that he might need for whatever is to come.

When we pull away, we're both breathless. "I wouldn't mind some more of that later," Jackson jokes.

"Count on it." With one last kiss, I grab my bag and head out the front of the cottage to the porch, conveniently avoiding Gord, who is most likely waiting in the driveway.

If I didn't live in a house, I would live in a bookstore. Julia basically does. Since her grandparents own the store, she lives in the small apartment above it. I think that sounds like a dream. She says all her clothes permanently smell like old books. I'm not sure what the problem with that is.

I've been wandering around for ten minutes now, browsing shelves but not really reading anything.

I don't need anything new to read right now. I have a stack of physical books at the cottage and in my condo waiting for me, as well as way too many downloaded on my e-reader. But do you ever need a new book?

It's always a want, not a need.

Julia finishes checking out the only other person in here and then flips the sign on the front door to closed.

"Oh, do you need me to leave?" I ask Julia.

"No, not at all. I'm not supposed to close for another thirty minutes, but I'm all peopled out."

"So do you want me to leave?" I ask again, because I am also people.

"No, I'm just tired of tourist season. Every year it gets harder."

I can see that. I love the hustle and bustle of the town when it's full. But some of the peacefulness leaves at the same time. I can't complain, because I am basically a tourist, too. A long-term tourist, I guess. Maybe cottagers get their own category in all of this.

"I don't know," she continues. "I think I just need something more. This bookstore has become my whole life." I shuffle through some of the magnets at the front counter, thinking about Julia's problem. I can relate.

At the beginning of summer, I was so lost. I feel a lot more sure of myself now, but it's still a work in progress. I found Jackson, but I also found some of the missing self-confidence I needed.

"Do you need something more professionally or personally?" I immediately think of Simon. While I'm not sure they are the perfect match, I'm sure he would be fun to go on a couple of dates with. I would also suggest my brother, but he doesn't date anymore.

"Both, maybe. I don't know." She huffs out a breath, typing on the touchscreen in front of her, probably closing the till. "Can I tell you a secret?"

"Yes!" I think I'm a bit too excited. I don't want to weird Julia out, but sharing secrets is something friends do. I think we might be friends now. We haven't hung out a lot, but I run into her a couple of times a week in town, typically, and we'll grab a drink at the café. When I first met her, I thought she was way too cool to want to hang out with me, but I guess not. We look like complete opposites.

She's not at all put off by my enthusiasm. "I want to hold a secret yoga night here."

That was not what I was expecting. I look around the store, trying to figure out where there would be space for that. "I would move stuff around."

"Okay... Why would it be a secret?"

"My grandma said no. She's so old school. I've been trying to add more book club options, but she won't let me host one for anything that isn't historical fiction. I run the place, but she has me on the shortest leash. I have so many ideas and they all get shot down. How can we expect anyone our age to want to live here year-round when there isn't a social scene? It's not like we need a nightclub or something. Just things to do. This place is so boring. Ugh. Rant over. Sorry."

"No, don't apologize. I can't say I relate, but I can empathize. You clearly love this store and this town. Wanting to improve it isn't a bad thing. Rant all you want."

Maybe I can relate to her a bit, considering I have no say over the projects I'm assigned at work, but this isn't about me. I want Julia to get all the feelings out that she needs to.

"So, secret yoga?" I prompt.

"Yeah, wouldn't that be fun? We could lower the lights, light a fire in the fireplace, do some yoga and then drink wine. It's just an idea right now, but it's an idea I can't get out of my head."

"I like it!"

"So you would come?" she asks. Shit.

"Can I just come for the wine afterwards? I'm not very good at yoga... Aspen would love it, though. She became a certified instructor on a trip to Peru one summer!"

Julia pins me with a look. She can look scary when she wants to be, so I relent. "Okay, yes, I would come. I could even force Jackson to come if you wanted."

"Yay!" She jumps in the air and claps her hands, scary look completely gone from her face. "It's just an idea right now, but I'll let you know if—no, when it comes to be. I'm going to need to talk to Aspen about this."

"What other ideas do you have?"

"So many!" I can feel her excitement rubbing off on me. If there's anything I can do to help her, I know I will. "More book clubs, obviously. Or audiobook clubs. We could have group listens, with booze. Or audiobook walking clubs. Like the running clubs you see in cities. I wouldn't mind being able to serve drinks and snacks here, too. We have so much space, but no one ever sits to read for a bit. That could be fun. If I could get licensing, we could be a wine bar at night. I know there's a book and alcohol theme going on, but this town needs some fun, and the alcohol will draw people in. Then they will stay for the great company and good books. There is so much we could do for children's programs, too. The library does its best, but I think they tend to have funding issues. Obviously, I'm going to convince you to do a reading. But we could also have craft time or dress up days. The possibilities are endless. Wow, I am on a ranting spree today. I'm so glad you are a willing listener."

"You have so many great ideas, I could listen to you all day." I laugh a little, but it's true. Julia could really transform this place. Maybe not with every idea, but the right combination and this could be very cool.

A knock sounds at the window and we both jump. Not only was coming here a distraction from everything with Jackson's dad but also the person out to get him. Normally I am way more conscious of my surroundings, but Julia and I really got lost in conversation.

"Shit, that's the plumber. My sink is leaking upstairs."

"I'll get out of your way. Next time, text me and we'll put Jackson to work. He's very handy."

"I bet he is," she says with a mischievous smile. I shake my head as she walks me to the door. I give her a hug goodbye; she gives me an extra squeeze.

I survived meeting Jackson's dad and definitely have a new friend. Today was good.

Chapter 28

Jackson

When I exit the cottage, I see my dad standing by his truck. He was definitely able to see Lillian sneak back to her cottage, but I doubt he'll say anything. He starts walking toward the lake, so I follow.

"She said you two cook together?" he asks me randomly as we both look out at the sun glistening on the lake.

"Yeah." I'm a bit confused by his curiosity. "Every night we try to. She's great, so I'm learning a lot. I like it."

He hums to himself, lost in thought. I don't often see my dad like this. He's always straightforward and to the point. My father being introspective like this isn't something he ever does in public.

"Your mother and I never did anything like that."

I stop in my tracks.

Not only does my dad almost never talk about my mom, but when he does, it is never positive. I know almost nothing about my parents' relationship that didn't come straight from my own memory and experiences, and even then, I was young, so I don't remember much.

He doesn't seem put off by my reaction as he continues, "We weren't good for each other. I think you and Lillian are good for each other."

Woah. Who is this man and what has he done with my father?

We don't talk about this stuff. It's business or nothing. I have no idea how I'm supposed to react right now, so I stay silent.

"She was strong for you. I know she put on an act for me. Her voice was confident, but her hands were shaking. I know you were worried when you found us together, but you were calm with her. Hold onto that. Not everyone gets a chance at it."

Wow, that's nice. He's being thoughtful and nice. "I don't plan on letting her go," I tell him. I really don't. I'm proud of how Lillian handled herself with my father. And I will be telling her that the second I can.

Back to business, he says, "The buyers of this property aren't happy. Fix it." With a slap on the back, he heads to his truck.

Conversation over.

When I make it into town, I spot Lillian hugging Julia goodbye on the sidewalk.

"Did you have a nice time catching up with Julia?" I ask as I sneak up behind her, pulling her back to my front. She squeals out a noise that's a mixture of startled and happy.

"I did," she says, turning in my arms, her smile growing.

"What did you two talk about that's got you smiling?"

"Oh." She blushes, gathering her thoughts. "Just random stuff. Girl talk, I guess. I'm just excited because I think we're friends now."

"Of course you're friends, you hang out and talk often." Why would she think they weren't friends? Did Julia say something to make her think that?

"Okay, easy for you to say, cocky." She hits my stomach playfully. "I'm not a natural at making friends like some people." She gives me a pointed look. "We probably have been friends for longer than I think, but now I feel confident in the friendship. Less worried and awkward."

Oh, my sweet, sweet Lillian. It's so easy to forget that things that come naturally to some are so foreign to others. Before I met Lillian, I don't think I ever struggled to form a connection with a person that I wanted to be friends with. And the only reason it was harder with Lillian was because I was so interested in her, I put too much pressure on myself.

I pull her into a hug, resting my cheek on the top of her head. "I'm glad you found a friend in Julia."

"Me, too," she whispers into my chest. When she looks up at me, she asks, "Ron's?"

"Ron's," I agree.

Ron's truck is pretty busy for a weeknight, but I guess that's normal for this time of year. He gives us a nod from behind the register and points towards the tables. We take that as confirmation he's got our orders, so we find a seat.

"So," Lillian says the second we sit down, "what did your dad say?"

"He likes you," I state. As weird as he was acting, that's the most supportive he's ever been towards me.

"No, he doesn't." Lillian laughs like she's the least likable person there is. I'm not sure how she doesn't realize that she's more like the sun, with everyone rotating around her.

"He does. I swear. He thinks we're good together"

"I know I don't know him very well, but I can't imagine him saying that."

She's not wrong. "Trust me, I was shocked. He even talked about his relationship with my mother." That reminds me. "Did you tell him we cook together?"

She thinks for a moment. "Honestly, it was such a blur, but I could have. Why?"

"He mentioned it. All in all, it was a weird conversation. He showed more emotion in five minutes than he has in the last five years." I shake my head. I still can't wrap my head around all of it. If he had hugged me, I would have assumed he was dying or something. "Anyway, everything's fine. I think he likes you. Not that you needed his approval, but yeah. I'm proud of how you handled the situation."

Ron drops off our food and I hand him some cash with a hefty tip. I'm not sure what I'm going to do when it gets too cold for his truck to stay open. If I can convince him to come over and cook for us, I will. Maybe that would be a good cooking lesson. Ron could probably teach both of us something.

"Question."

"Answer."

Lillian giggles before continuing. "Julia was talking about how there aren't a lot of activities or events drawing young professionals to live here. You mentioned wanting to approach the town council about a housing development. Have you started working on that yet?"

The short answer is no.

"I haven't," I say. "Honestly, I've put it on the backburner. Since someone is clearly unhappy I'm here, I don't want to make any big moves. I don't know what could set them off, so I've put a pause on it for now."

"That's too bad." Lillian gives me a sad smile. It does suck. I really like this town, but we need to keep the project scale large enough to keep me here.

This summer we lined up multiple cottages, but I can't guarantee there will be that many available next year to make it worth it.

"I agree. Not only could we have places for people to buy as vacation homes, but also starter homes for families. Or rental units for locals. I think it would make a positive difference here, but I don't want to take any risks."

"I get that. Promise me that once Peters catches this person, you will be on the mayor's doorstep the next morning."

"I promise to make a meeting with the town council when it's safe to. I'm not going to stalk them."

"Fair." She giggles.

"What's got you so giggly tonight?"

Lillian drops her head to the table, almost getting her hair in her leftover poutine. "I think I'm delirious. The time I spent with your dad really took it out of me. I feel like I rode a roller-coaster of emotions today."

"Let's get you home." I raise from my seat and offer my hand to pull Lillian up. We dispose of our garbage and walk to my truck. I have already stowed her bike in the back. If she isn't riding the thing, it seems to be in the bed of my truck more than anywhere else.

I startle awake while it's still dark outside. I look to my right and Lillian is still sleeping peacefully. Rolling towards my nightstand, the clock reads just after 3 am. Groaning, I pull the covers over my head and will myself to go back to sleep.

I've survived on less sleep, but I hate being tired when I finish work. I want to be awake and engaged since that is my time with Lillian, and I don't take a second of it for granted.

After fifteen minutes, I'm still awake and mostly annoyed. I remember Lillian mentioning a tea she had that was good for sleeping. Maybe that will help. I quietly creep out of bed, careful not to disturb Lillian, and climb down the stairs. After a couple of minutes of searching the cupboards, I find lavender and chamomile tea. I can't say I've ever had either of those things before, but the box says it's caffeine-free, so it at least won't hurt. Just as I'm finished filling the kettle with water, something catches my eye out the window.

Normally I would just ignore it. But considering all the issues we've been having, especially at the Waldens' next door, I'm not taking any chances.

I send a text to Peters as a heads-up. I might be waking him for no reason, but it's his job and I will buy him a beer if nothing comes of this. I wouldn't mind being friends with the guy, but I don't think that's a real possibility until he's able to hang out with me and not also respond to all my calls for help.

I grab the sweater that I left on the couch and slide it over my head, then slip on my sneakers. The Waldens' still has motion-sensored lights and cameras, so I don't worry about a flashlight.

The second I am outside, I smell it. Smoke. As I run towards the cottage, I pull out my phone and call 911, requesting the fire department. I know we keep fire extinguishers around job sites, but I want to make sure everything is by the book. We do have a client that plans on owning this cottage in the near future and a misstep at this point in the process would have my dad revoking my job title pretty quick.

I walk around the corner and spot the fire. So far, it's still small. A bush next to the framing for a platform off the front deck is engulfed. It hasn't made its way to the structure yet; I'm not sure how long it will take.

Not wanting to waste time searching, I run back to Lillian's, get my truck keys and find an extinguisher in my back seat. Just as I'm running back towards the fire, I hear Lillian calling for me and Constable Peters' voice telling her to stay back. I pull the pin and aim towards the bush. I haven't had to use one of these since high school chemistry class, but within seconds, most of the flames are gone. Peters is beside me, kicking the dirt. I look at his feet and see some sort of liquid on the ground, leading from the bush to the deck. I would assume it's gasoline, and this fire was meant to take the whole building down.

Shit.

Sirens wail in the distance as the fire trucks approach. The fire is mostly out now, but I assume they will know how to investigate this best.

I stumble back from the bush and drop the fire extinguisher from my hand. I feel a small arm wrap around my waist, pulling me towards them. Lillian holds me in front of her, burying her face in my back while first responders flit around us like flies.

A few moments pass and the shock wears off. I turn in Lillian's hold and wrap my arms around her shoulders, holding her to me.

This could have been way worse. If I hadn't woken up when I did, this entire place would have burned to the ground. With how dry it's been this summer and the trees surrounding us, the fire could have taken out multiple cottages on the lake, including Lillian's.

I feel a hand tap me gently on the back. Lillian looks up over my shoulder at whoever it is.

"Do you know what happened?" she asks.

I hear Peters clear his throat. "There's no sign of anyone still lurking around. I'd like to look at the cameras."

I pull out of my hold on Lillian slightly and look back to where the fire was set. There are at least two cameras pointing in that direction. They are hidden in the eaves, so if you didn't know where to look, you probably wouldn't know they were there. Which is exactly why I chose their locations.

I keep one arm wrapped around Lillian's shoulder as I guide her back to her cottage, Constable Peters following close behind. My laptop is sitting on the dining room table. I've been using it as a desk since we eat most of our meals on the couch or outside.

Settling into a chair, I pull Lillian into my lap to keep her as close as possible, while gesturing for Peters to sit next to me. I open the camera software and rewind back to thirty minutes before I was awake and skim through the footage from the cameras closest to the blaze.

A dark figure appears in one camera frame. It looks like a man wearing a dark hood over his head. The view is only from behind, his face out of frame. Switching to another angle, I bring the feed to the same time frame and freeze it as the man's face is caught directly in front of the camera.

"Shit."

Lillian stills. She must have seen Frank around at the Waldens', working, when she has been helping me during the day.

"Do you know who that is?" Peters prompts as Lillian and I sit there, silently staring at the face of the person who has been tormenting us.

Lillian speaks up first.

"I don't remember his name. But he works for Jackson."

That he does. I don't know the guy well, truthfully. I think he is in his late thirties or early forties. He was a local hire, living a town over.

I hardly interact with him, but for the most part, he's been working on the Waldens' all summer. Right under my nose.

"You have any problems with him?"

"Frank Johnston. I'm not his direct supervisor, so I wouldn't know if there were any petty issues. He's the foreman on the Walden project, but he's very self-sufficient. I've hardly interacted with the guy, aside from having him move the crews when they couldn't work there. And apparently, they couldn't work there because of him."

Why would he do this? If he was a disgruntled employee, I could see him messing with me. But he isn't. He's on payroll, and we pay well. He has job security. I have no idea why he would do this.

"I'm going to need a copy of all the footage you have. We'll have our techs comb through the footage from when the cameras went up until tonight to see if we catch anything else. Now that we know who we're looking for, I need to get my team searching for this guy. Excuse me."

Constable Peters leaves us alone in the cottage. As the silence stretches between us, I can see Lillian looking at me from the corner of my eye, but I refuse to meet her stare.

Looking out the window into the dark lake, my thoughts run wild.

I must have done something to piss this guy off. Did he take this job because he was pissed off about the company being here like some locals were? Did I forget to say hi to him when I was rushing through the site on his first day? He already lived here, so he couldn't be pissed about the living accommodations I offered.

Whatever it was, it was obviously my fault. Not only did I bring danger to this town, but I also brought danger to Lillian's safe place.

If she's mad at me, I don't blame her. She was enjoying a quiet summer before I came along and now look. Her cottage could have been burned down.

I look back to the computer and replay the footage all the way through.

Frank douses the bush in a liquid and creates a trail from the bush to the Waldens'. From there, he continues to pour the liquid, heading in the direction of Lillian's cottage.

Lillian gasps from her spot on my lap, clearly watching the feed, too. I switch to the cameras that are pointing at her cottage and watch as Frank continues to pour liquid on the ground until the jug he is holding empties, just beside the deck. Then he turns back to the bush, lights a match and takes off into the forest.

Not even three minutes later, I appear on screen, running towards the fire. He was out there while I was in the kitchen making tea.

That fucker wanted this place to burn down with us inside. This isn't just arson. It is attempted murder.

He wanted to kill me.

He could have killed Lillian. Fuck!

I finally look at Lillian, tears clouding her beautiful blue eyes. Eyes far too perfect and warm to look so sad.

I pull her face to my chest, letting her silently cry into my shirt. I stroke her head, mumbling comforting words I'm not even comprehending into her hair.

When Peters comes back inside, I don't stop.

With my free hand, I wordlessly rewind the feed so Peters can see Frank's intention of burning Lillian's cottage, too.

He mutters, "Shit," under his breath before typing something out on his phone.

"I'm going to keep someone stationed outside until we have him in custody. Constables are on the way to his house now. His face will be all over the internet and TV by morning if we don't find him there. But we will find him. I promise you that. It's going to take a while to have both properties processed for evidence. Do you feel comfortable staying here tonight?"

I drop my head so my mouth is right beside Lillian's ear.

"Do you want to see if we can stay at The Inn? Or even go back to the city, even just for the night?"

Lillian shakes her head no. "That's exactly what he wanted. Whatever his reasons were, he wanted to scare us, and when that didn't work, he wanted us gone." She steels her spine and removes her face from my chest, gaining confidence as she continues. "He doesn't get to win. He doesn't get to tarnish this place. I'm not going anywhere and I hope you aren't either."

I drop my forehead to rest against hers.

"I'm wherever you are. You stay, then I stay, too." Those three little words that I know to be true are on the tip of my tongue. I hesitate and hold them in. Now isn't the time. When I finally say them after all these years of keeping them to myself, keeping them from family and friends, I want it to be perfect. That's what Lillian deserves. Not some heat of the moment, adrenaline-induced admission. I mean them, and I don't want her to doubt that.

Also, Constable Peters is still standing behind us, and he doesn't need to be present for that intimate moment.

"Here's an external hard drive for the footage." Peters hands me the device. "Once I have that, I can leave you guys alone for the night. I'll take statements tomorrow."

I get everything loaded, and Peters excuses himself. I don't want Lillian out of my sight or arms anytime soon, so I cradle her against my body and pick her up as I stand. She doesn't make any effort to move, understanding my need to hold her and wanting the same thing. I leave all the lights on downstairs, not caring that the crime scene techs will be able to see inside all night, and carry Lillian back to bed.

Neither of us sleep at all. We just hold each other close.

Chapter 29
Lillian

Things have been quiet around here for the last two weeks. Frank is in jail, awaiting trial, and I guess we are meant to carry on with our lives. He admitted to the basement graffiti and the fire, but nothing else.

I don't know why he is drawing the line at admitting to

slashing our tires or the bloody truck.

I guess he figures there's nothing linking him to them, so maybe he'll get a reduced sentence. He also won't explain why he did it, so I'm assuming some sort of jealousy with Jackson's position of power over him. His lawyer is trying to make a deal with the crown attorney, so we are all left in the dark, outside of our own speculation.

Whatever the reason, I'm choosing to ignore it. Jackson and I are happy and moving on.

After making our statements the next morning, Peters said we were free to carry on with our lives. It feels weird. We've both been on edge for so long, it's hard to turn it off.

Aspen is going to come into town like a tornado tonight. At least that's my guess based on the texts she sent me. Jackson and I had plans. They will now be readjusted for Aspen, but I know Jackson won't mind too much. Aspen is such a great friend and she doesn't ask for much, so if she needs to let loose tonight, I'm her girl. She would do the same for me.

It has been all hands on deck at the Waldens' the last couple of days. Once the crime scene was cleared, Jackson was able to get the crew back in to not only clean up the mess, but also get everything back on the planned timeline. Jackson said some of the crew had questions about the obvious fire remnants and a couple noticed Frank's absence, but he kept tight-lipped. He told them simply that there had been an incident and it was dealt with. Any further information they could get from town gossip. There hadn't been a lot, but there was some.

I know that buyers on the project have not been happy with their new cottage being the scene of multiple crimes at this point. Jackson has been hoping that if they can deliver the project completed ahead of schedule, that will keep the deal moving forward. I'm not entirely sure of the logistics of everything, but Jackson and I spent the last couple of nights doing paint touch-ups on the main floor.

With the amount of new skills I've learned this summer, I could update my resume as an amateur DIY'er. Aspen would be horrified, of course. But it would make Jackson and Simon laugh, I'm sure.

Simon stopped in for lunch, needing to drop some documents off for Jackson, thankfully leaving before Aspen's arrival. I still don't know what her deal is, but if she's as stressed as she seemed during the quick call I had with her before lunch, I'm not going to bother her about it now.

I've decided forgiveness brownies are on the menu tonight. Jackson won't be upset that our date night is not happening if he's eating brownies. No one can be mad while eating brownies. And even if he is, he deserves a treat. I know everything that has happened, especially the fire, has been weighing heavily on him. He has tried to blame himself, and no matter how much I try to reassure him, I don't think he's fully letting it sit.

I had a call with Miranda this week, checking in and having her listen while I talk through the events that happened over the last month. To say she was shocked was an understatement, but she was also proud of how I've been handling things. She said the Lillian I was a year ago, or even three months ago, would have struggled a lot more than I have. I like to think that was all me, and a lot of it was, but also knowing I have Jackson's unwavering support has helped a lot.

Yes, we could have died and that is terrifying. But we didn't. And I don't want to live in the what if. I've lived a lot of my life filled with worry and if I add potentially dying to my list of anxieties, I'll be frozen.

After our chat, Jackson could tell how much lighter I seemed and within an hour, he had an appointment with a therapist that works with Miranda. Jackson has never been to therapy. Him just taking the step to book and go through with the first appointment made me immensely proud. I don't know if he is going to be a therapy lifetime member like myself, but he has a couple more appointments booked at least.

While in town, I pick up some paint Jackson needed and my brownie ingredients, plus a bottle of tequila. When I get home, I pop the brownies into the oven and quickly run next door to leave the paint for whoever needs it. It will probably be us this weekend.

I leave the paint in the mudroom and then continue into the cottage. I just love this place. Not much has changed since I was here last, but it looks like some furniture has been delivered for staging. I know Jackson has been having issues with his design team, so maybe we can get Aspen to help a bit this weekend.

Just as I'm about to head back for my brownies—the timer will be going off in two minutes—I see a pile of papers on the counter. They must be what Simon had dropped off today. I know I don't need to look, but if Jackson wants to see these tonight, I could bring them with me now. Save him from needing to re-enter work mode for a couple of hours at least.

I shuffle through the pages, realizing they're real estate listings for properties in town that aren't for sale, as well as some renderings of brand-new cottages that could replace them. None of this is of much interest to me until I get to the last one.

My family's cottage.

Is Jackson trying to buy the cottage and tear it down? As much as I love what he's done with all his current projects, my family's cottage is still in good shape. It doesn't need to be torn down.

Would my parents sell? They don't spend much time up here anymore, and my grandparents are content in their retirement home now. I guess they could sell?

Have they already been sent this? Would Jackson let Simon approach my parents without telling me? They obviously know we are dating. If he approached them, they would think I was on board with this.

I am not on board with this.

The cottage is my safe place; I'm not ready to let go of it. Maybe if I sell my condo, I could finance this place. Ben doesn't spend much time up here, but he would want to keep it for Noah. Right? At the very least, Aspen would buy it with me. She loves this place as much as I do.

How could Jackson do this to me?

The timer on my phone goes off and I realize I've been standing here for too long. My brownies might be overcooked.

I sprint out of the back door and back to my cottage. I think I see Mr. Flannigan, an elderly man who has a cottage down the road, out for a walk, but I can't stop. If I start a fire in that oven, we will never get the smell out of the wood.

Once inside, I rip open the oven and grab the oven mitts to pull my brownies out, and sure enough, they're...raw? What?

I check the timer on my phone. It was set for twenty-five minutes, that's correct. I put the pan on the stovetop, checking the old dials for the stove, and there's the problem.

The oven wasn't even turned on.

Whoops. I preheat the oven correctly this time and return the pan back inside for another twenty-five minutes. Hopefully more successful this time around.

While they bake, I grab a glass of water and take a seat on the couch, allowing the adrenaline to fade from my body.

Okay, so the listing.

I am ninety-nine percent sure all my previous reactions were overreactions.

I have known Jackson for three months, and he's been living here with me for over a month. He has never done anything close to going behind my back. If anything, he overshares. On any given night, I've sat listening to him talk through a problem out loud, not needing my input, but he likes to work through his thoughts by speaking them out loud. There is no way he would have plans to buy and tear this place down.

I must be missing something. I know I am missing something. I will not let my anxiety spiral. I trust Jackson. More importantly, I trust myself. I trust that I have invested my time in an honest and good man. I trust that he cares about me, and wouldn't do something to jeopardize that. I trust that he would talk to me if something like this was a real possibility.

I trust that all of these things are true because I have thought about them and I feel good about them.

I trust that I love Jackson; that I've loved him for a while. And I trust that I can trust my heart.

By the time I've finished my glass of water and the timer goes off again for the brownies, I feel so much better than when I left the Waldens'.

I set the brownies on a cooling rack and head upstairs. We've been so busy this week that the cleaning has taken a back seat. Aspen's suitcase always explodes, so the least I can do is make sure there isn't a layer of dust under her clothing that will be scattered.

I spend the next hour or so cleaning the cottage from top to bottom. It isn't until 5 pm that I look at the clock and see that Jackson should be home soon. Somewhere during my cleaning spree, I misplaced my phone. I have a couple of missed texts from Jackson, but I'm sure I'll see him soon for dinner. I also have ten voice notes from Aspen, letting me know she's on her way.

Chapter 30

Jackson

I texted Lillian to meet me at the Waldens', but she's not here.

The paint I asked her to pick up is sitting in the laundry room, ready for the loft touch-ups, and there is packaged furniture everywhere. I would have loved to have this stuff already put together, but I've had so much manpower dedicated to this job, some of the others are slipping a bit. I know if I spend a couple of hours here this weekend, I can put us in a good place for Monday morning, when the potential owners have a virtual walk-through. The place won't be completely done, but I can't see them having an issue with about a week's worth of work to be done.

We wouldn't normally do a virtual walk-through for an unfinished house, but these clients aren't happy. Not only has there been the crime, obviously, but we've had to reorder and install some hardware because it wasn't what the clients wanted in the first place.

Most of our other projects are done deals.

The client has signed a purchase agreement, buying a finished cottage from us, so we let them work with our design team to have the cottage furnished, and with all the finishes they want.

Unfortunately, the Waldens' hasn't worked out that way.

The buyers are friends of my dad's and with that, they've been allowed to wait on signing the deal. This is something I would never want to do and will never do again. My dad made an exception, but it's been biting us in the butt all along.

Now, I'm stuck kissing up to these people. We have a waitlist a mile long of clients that would be more than happy to take it off their hands, but for as difficult and distrusting as they've been, they also won't fully back out of the deal.

At this point, I want the job done, to not deal with them anymore. The worst part about this is these cranky clients are more than likely going to be Lillian's neighbours for years to come.

And since I plan on being around Lillian for all those years, I need to wrap this up on a pleasant note.

I see a stack of papers on the counter, left in a bit of a mess, but I know Simon needed to get back to the city after his lunch with Lillian, so he must have left in a hurry.

The documents were the reason I wanted to have Lillian meet me here.

When we first started the project, my dad asked Simon to put together a list of properties that fit our parameters. Older cottages, lakefront, private, decent-sized lots. Simon would then put together listings that we could potentially present to the owners. If they were interested, we would have the information ready for them to make a decision to move forward, and if not, we would move on.

I was so excited about this project, that I even sent him some rough drawings of what I would want to build in their place. In all honesty, if the owners didn't want to sell, I would still offer to renovate their place if that was something they were interested in.

The listing sitting on the top of the pile stops me in my tracks.

It's Lillian's family cottage.

It makes sense. It fits our ideal property. But I know it is very much not an option. I should get rid of this before Lillian sees it…

She's already seen it. In this moment, I know she has. The papers were a mess; it was sitting on top. She was in here to drop off the paint.

This is not good.

I decide to leave the documents where they are. I can deal with them tomorrow. Or in ten minutes when Lillian kicks me to the curb. No time like the present to get my heart broken. I head outside and in the direction of Lillian's. When I'm twenty feet from the door, I hear a voice call out from behind me.

"Hey, Jackson, is everything alright?"

Turning around, I see Mr. Flannigan. I've met him a couple of times. He has a place down the road and spends most of his days fishing now that he's retired. He's a nice enough guy, but I'm not in the mood to chat.

"Hey, Mr. Flannigan." I muster up every ounce of kindness in my body not to brush him off right now.

"Everything's okay. Why do you ask?"

"Oh, well, you seem to be rushing around with a scared look on your face, and earlier I saw Miss Lillian run from the Waldens' back to her cottage looking frantic."

My stomach drops.

She saw, and she's mad. I do have an explanation for this; I would never try to buy her cottage. I just really hope she gives me a chance to explain. If not, well... I don't know what I'll do.

"I need to handle something. But don't worry about us, Mr. Flannigan." He nods his head, his greying ponytail bobbing up and down, and thankfully retreats to the road, leaving me to face Lillian.

When I enter the cottage, Lillian is standing in the kitchen cutting up some vegetables. She looks over her shoulder at the sound of the front door closing and graces me with a soft smile.

Okay, maybe this isn't as bad as I thought.

"Hey, baby, are you getting started on dinner?" I ask, the unease in my tone noticeable. The use of a pet name I've never called her before makes me question if my frontal lobe is, in fact, fully developed at this point in my life.

"Yeah, I thought we could put some roasted vegetables in pasta tonight. Nothing fancy." She looks up at me when I don't respond. Confusion marks her face as I stand in front of her, not answering.

"Did you want something else?" she asks.

"No. Ah, no, that sounds great," I say, giving her an awkward smile.

"Are you sure?" she pauses. "Is something wrong? You're being weird." She steps away from the counter, towards me, and wraps her hands around my waist, looking up into my eyes. She must not have seen the documents like I thought.

I know what it looks like and it isn't good. I need to at least tell her about it. If she found out later, it would hurt her feelings that I kept this from her.

"Were you next door at all today?" I ask, even though I know the answer is yes.

"Yeah, I dropped off the paint cans like I said I would. Was there an issue or something?"

Okay, I'm so confused.

I know I'm a smart guy, but what?

"No, no issue, just there were some documents on the counter..." I trail off. I don't know how to say this. I don't want to make a problem out of nothing. Realization replaces the confused look on her face and that smile I love so much returns.

"I saw the documents," she states, her emotions unchanging.

"And you aren't mad? Because they aren't what they look like. Simon was asked to put that all together months ago and he just dropped it off. I know this place was in there and I'm not trying to do anything with it. We won't even approach your family. I would never do that to you. And the price? Not enough obviously. Okay, that's a lie, it's actually decent. Simon knows what he's doing, but still. You can't put a price on a place like this, right? On the family memories? On us, on our story? At least, I hope we still have a story considering you're smiling at me. Why are you smiling at me?"

I take the first breath in what feels like ten minutes and wait for the blowup.

And then she laughs.

She laughs. At me?

How is she laughing?

What is going on right now?

Why is she laughing?

"Why are you laughing?"

"Oh, you sweet, sweet man. It's okay. I saw the listings, yes. I saw the listing for this place and the probably accurate price. Was I taken aback for a moment? Yes. Did I want to call and yell at my parents for not telling me? Initially, I thought about it. Was I worried you went behind my back? For a brief moment. But I know you. I know us. You had listings there for most of the town. There is no way those were all about to go on the market. I wasn't mad. I'm not mad."

I take a deep breath.

"But— But Mr. Flannigan said he saw you run out of there and you looked upset, and then you weren't there, and I had texted you to meet me there, and I was so worried and I'm just a bit confused," I say, feeling some relief but not enough to fully untie the knot around my chest. Her hands move from my chest, gliding up to the nape of my neck where she lightly scratches at the hair on my scalp.

"I went to call you when I saw that the timer on my phone had been silenced and the brownies I was making for you were going to burn to a crisp. I ran over here hoping and praying the kitchen wasn't on fire or something. Turns out the oven wasn't even turned on."

She laughs at her mistake. And there's the relief.

I pull her in close, resting my forehead against hers, and breathe her in. How did I get so lucky?

After a moment she pulls away slightly, looking into my eyes. I could get lost in them and never want to be found.

"Hey, we communicate, remember? We don't jump to conclusions. We don't expect the worst in each other. We trust." She pauses as something passes through her eyes for a moment before they soften even more.

"We... We love each other. Because I love you."Before I have a moment to respond, her lips are on mine in a soul-crushing kiss. This isn't timid or light; it's all consuming, it's everything. Because she is everything. We break apart, but I hold her close for another moment, breathing her in, and I utter three words I haven't said in years but have never felt so right.

"I love you. I love you, Lillian Shaw."

"Yay," she squeaks, laughing a bit. "Whoops, that was supposed to stay in my head."

That's not exactly what I was expecting, but cute nonetheless.

"Yeah, I love you," I say again, because now that it's out, I can't stop. "I love you, I love you, I love you." I kiss a part of her face with each word until she's a mess of giggles.

"I love you, too, but stop." She keeps laughing. "That tickles."

She wants me to stop? Not going to happen. In the span of ten minutes, I went from the worst-case scenario to the best moment of my life, and we are going to celebrate. I throw Lillian over my shoulder and run up the stairs. She doesn't even protest or fight me as I throw her onto the bed. Our bed. She bounces a couple of times before crawling her way backwards towards the headboard.

I stalk towards her, pulling my shirt over my head in one motion. I remove my belt, then let my pants and boxers drop to the floor. I stand there naked as I watch Lillian's eyes roam all over my body, with a hungry look on her face.

"Strip." I'm not messing around. I want her, and I want her now.

She nods her head, not breaking eye contact, and she quickly rids herself of her cute light blue sundress. When only her panties are left, I tell her to stop.

"Those are mine." Crawling towards her, I drag my nose up her tanned legs. Tanned legs I want wrapped around my waist, or my shoulders. I nip and lick the skin as I reach her hip. Lillian is squirming below me, trying to get friction where there is none. I grab the corner of her panties with my teeth, dragging them down her body. With the wet spot that was left on the fabric, I'm not surprised to see she's soaked.

"Is this all for me?" I ask, my voice huskier than I intended.

"Yes. Jackson, please." I know what she wants, and I'm not one to deny her.

I drop my face between her thighs and make a meal out of her. Licking, sucking and teasing. She grinds her pelvis against me, constantly seeking more.

"Please," she whines again, her back arched and head thrown back in the pillows.

"Do you want to come?" I smirk up at her, and she tries to

shove my head back down. I swat her hand away. "Don't make me tie you up." I slowly kiss up her body until we are face to face.

"Don't worry, Lil. I'm going to make you come. But it's going to be on my cock." I quickly grab a condom from the nightstand, roll it on and align myself between her legs. Right before I push myself into her warmth, I hold both her cheeks in my hand.

"I love you, Lillian."

"I love you, Jackson."

I thrust into her in one steady stroke until my hips meet hers. Lillian mews, linking her ankles behind my back, trying to push me into her even further. The room fills with the sound of skin slapping and moaning. I can feel Lillian begin to tense around me, so I slow my pace, not wanting this to end yet.

"No." She tries to increase our rhythm again. "You feel so good. Don't stop."

"I'll make you feel good. Don't worry, Lil." I maintain the slower pace, grinding my pubic bone against her clit until she is on the edge again. She hums into my neck, sending a vibration through my body. As I start to feel her clench, I increase my pace again and drop my mouth to hers. She finds her release a moment before I do.

"That was good." She giggles, clenching around my half-hard shaft that's still inside her. Post orgasm Lillian is always giggly.

I pull out gently and quickly dispose of the condom before climbing under the covers and pulling Lillian into my arms.

"I love you," she whispers into the skin on my chest, her head resting on my heart.

"I love you, too, Lillian." And I have a feeling I will forever.

Chapter 31
Lillian

"Well, I'm glad you love me, because we have a change of plans for tonight." We are currently lying in bed after making love, but I know we need to get up soon. I can't help but internally squeal a little. Jackson loves me!

I'm not surprised. The connection we have is too strong for it to ever be one-sided. I've sat on those three little words for weeks, waiting and hoping for an opportunity for a big declaration. I'm happy it wasn't, though. We don't need elaborate or grand. We need us. Our love is quiet love. It's evenings cooking together. It's Sundays on his boat. It's reading beside each other on the couch. It's watching sunsets curled up in a blanket. Our love is a lot of small quiet loves.

Jackson's face drops. "If those plans aren't still taking the boat out for a sunset ride, butt naked, then I don't want to hear them."

"Unfortunately, clothing is required for this. Aspen is on her way. She broke up with John and wants to go get drunk tonight. Something about city boys wearing tiaras. I don't know, but she's set her mind to this, so I don't think we can stop it."

John is now Aspen's ex for the fifth time? She has only dated five guys since high school, but she seems to have them on a rotation, continuing to get back together with one for a couple of months before everything goes wrong again. A month or two later, she's back with a different one. It's a lather, rinse, repeat situation.

"I'm texting Peters," Jackson says in a serious tone, pulling out his phone.

I grab the phone out of his hand. "You can't have her arrested for ruining your plans."

He takes his phone back from me. "I'm asking him to meet up with us. I saw him in town earlier and he's off duty tonight. If Aspen wants to go hard tonight, I need backup. I won't be able to carry you both over my shoulder and out of the bar."

I mean, I wasn't planning on drinking that much, but it's not a bad idea.

We decide on a bar the next town over. Dylan doesn't like

drinking around people he may have to arrest one day. I can't imagine having to think about that in your everyday life, so I'm not complaining. This also means we get to go to a real bar with a dance floor, not the tiny pub in Bluefield filled with tourists.

When Aspen shows up at the cottage, she comes in like a tornado. She flips between complaining about boys, demanding Jackson mix her a drink, and letting her suitcase explode into every bedroom upstairs while she tries on every item she brought and everything in my closet, too.

Once she settles on a very small skirt and tube top and approves my light yellow sundress, we are out the door. Jackson offers to drive and not drink, so we pick Dylan up on the way and make our way to Saintrich, a town forty-five minutes away. Aspen claims Jackson is her favourite person ever for inviting "Constable Dreamboat." She says this in front of Dylan. She has no shame.

We got some drinks for our table before Aspen grabbed Dylan's hand, leading him straight to the dance floor, where they spent most of the night. Dylan can be so serious; I am pleasantly surprised he's such a great dancer.

"I wonder what it feels like to feel as free as she does?" I wonder out loud. Jackson gives me a quizzical look, clearly wanting me to elaborate.

"I would say that Aspen is unapologetically herself. She always has been," I say.

"I could see that," he responds, so I continue, my voice a bit quieter now.

"I think I am apologetically myself instead." I don't look up at him, but I can tell by his body language he's a bit shocked and probably confused, so I give him a small shrug of my shoulder and muster up all the confidence to continue. "I overthink everything. I've never once claimed to be cool, but sometimes I look back and cringe at the things I say and do. But then I also feel like I miss out on having careless fun because I'm already overthinking the things I haven't said and done yet. So where Aspen is unapologetically herself ninety-five percent of the time, I feel like I should apologize for who I am."

I don't even realize I'm crying until Jackson wipes a tear from my cheek and grabs my face with both of his hands, turning me so we are eye to eye.

"Lillian Shaw," he begins, "you are smart, talented, thoughtful, beautiful, generous and so kind. I know your anxiety sometimes feels like it's fighting against you, and that doesn't seem fair, but I don't want you to ever feel like you need to apologize for who you are. You are one of the best people I know, and if you ever need a reminder or someone to lean on when you have doubts, lean on me. Talk to me. I want you to love yourself, but when that's hard, let me love you enough for the both of us."

Letting out a noise that is somewhere between a snotty gurgle and a sob, I press my lips to Jackson's with as much force as I can, which he reciprocates eagerly. When we break apart, I rest my forehead against his.

"I love you, Jackson. Thank you."

"I love you, too, Lil."

We sit there in the loud bar, just staring at each other, until we hear a throat clear. Looking up, I notice Aspen and Dylan are back from the dance floor. Dylan looks amused, while Aspen looks like she could kill.

"Tell me you did not make my little Billy cry, Jackson William Mane," she says, venom on each letter of his name.

"That's not my middle name," Jackson says, but I interrupt him before she blows a gasket.

"It's okay, Asp, just having a moment. I love you, but put the claws away. Please."

"Are you sure?" she asks. "Men don't make women cry, only boys do. Even if they look like Jackson does, we can still downgrade him to a boy, if needed."

"I'm sure, Aspen. Everything is okay." I give her my most reassuring smile. Though I'm sure it looks crazy because I probably have mascara running down my face at this point.

Aspen catches the cocky smirk Dylan is giving Jackson, probably loving that Jackson is the one getting a talking to from Aspen.

"Hey, don't look so smug over there, Constable Muscles."

Dylan isn't at all put off by Aspen's sass. He puts his arm around her, leans in and I hear him whisper, "I would never make you cry."

She gives him a shy smile, but then says, "No, you wouldn't. Because I don't cry. Ever." Dylan's eyes widen slightly. I shake my head at him, hoping he drops it, just as the band switches to a slow country song.

I hesitantly look towards Jackson, who is already sliding out of the booth, hand held out to me.

"Lil, would you like to dance with me?"

I don't answer with words, but I take his hand and he guides me onto the dance floor. I spend the rest of the night either in Jackson's arms as we slow dance or with my hands around Aspen's waist as she grinds into me while Jackson and Dylan shake their heads. I know this wasn't what we originally had planned for tonight, but I think it's what we all needed. A night to be free with the people we love. A night to be unapologetically ourselves, even if we won't feel that way in the morning.

Chapter 32
Jackson

Why is it that as soon as a project really gets going, you hit every roadblock imaginable? I've been saying this for months, but we need a new designer for this project. Not just that. We need to fire our current firm and never work with them again. Every week, I swear I'm stuck between the client and the design team, playing peacemaker. We've had budget issues, differences of opinion, and supply chain breakdowns all on one cottage.

The light at the end of every day is knowing I'll end up in bed with Lillian.

Who knew being in love was so great? I can't even put into words the amount of joy I feel just looking at her. She is my queen, my sun, my moon, my everything, and I wouldn't want it any other way. Everything in life that I have and everything that I am is made better with her at my side.

It's Friday and all I wanted to do was finish up early, send the crew home, and hit the lake with Lillian.

We've both been putting our heads down these last couple of weeks, aiming to meet our individual timelines and deadlines, and I want to relax. A cold beer, the sun on my face, and Lillian in a swimsuit? Sounds like heaven to me.

I know when I get to the boat, I will find Lillian sitting in the sun reading a book, happy as ever. But that doesn't stop me from going a bit faster than I should be through town to get to her as soon as possible. I was already delayed fifteen minutes. Any time I can save, I'm going to.

I park my truck in a spot as close to my slip as possible and see Lillian's bike resting against a tree. It's not locked, so I toss it into the back of my truck, assuming that's why she left it there. No reason for her to be biking home when we are headed to the same place.

I know her family cottage isn't technically my, or our, home, but it sure does feel that way. There is only a month left of the typical summer season, but I will be here until Thanksgiving in October most likely. Lillian and I haven't discussed when she plans to go back to Toronto, or what we will do when that time comes, but I'm not worried.

Whether we end up in my condo or hers, I will make sure she's curled up in my arms at the end of every day. I hope that we both end up back here next summer, though. I'll be the first to admit, I thought this town was a bit strange when I first arrived, but the kooky old people here have really grown on me.

It feels like I am with family everywhere I go, something I didn't have growing up. And now that Frank is behind bars, and the stress of our safety is no longer there, there isn't any other place I can see myself living long-term.

A bold statement for the born and bred city boy.

I make my way to the slip, stopping to do a double-take.

My boat isn't there.

I see Rick's boat, and mine belongs next to it, so I am in the right spot. Not only would Lillian not take the boat out without telling me, but she doesn't have her licence yet, and I have the only set of keys with me.

Something is wrong.

I pull my phone out of my pocket, dialling Constable Peters, and tell him to get here right away. I'm not going to waste my time explaining a situation when we need to be looking for her. Frank is definitely still locked up. We would have been told otherwise, so I have no idea what could have happened, but I can feel it in my gut that something is very wrong.

I hear the sound of gravel flying as multiple police cruisers come ripping into the parking lot. Constable Peters flies out of his SUV without closing the door, running straight to me.

"There's no way she took the boat?" he asks as soon as he reaches me.

I hold up the keys. "The only set in town. She wouldn't take it anyway. She's reading up to get her boating licence, but she takes this kind of thing seriously. I was running late and now she's gone, and I don't know where she is, but it's bad. It must be bad. Her bike is here. She's supposed to be here."

"Take a deep breath, Jackson. We're pulling boats out now. I've got all hands on deck looking for her."

"And Frank is still locked up? He didn't escape and come after her?" I ask, because I need to be sure.

"I called the holding cells on my way here. He is firmly locked up."

Two police boats come to a roaring stop at the end of the dock with their sirens already blaring and bow waves sending the docked boats all around us clattering. Peters looks to his right a moment and then pauses. "How much do you know about your slip neighbour?"

I follow his line of sight and see what looks like a sleeping bag and food garbage in Rick's boat. Considering the man cleans it obsessively, this is very strange. There's a to-go cup of coffee from the café in town sitting just on the ledge. I grab it without thinking. It's still hot. I have no idea why Rick would want to take or hurt Lillian, but the bad feeling in my stomach just got worse.

Constable Peters must be filling in the same blanks that I am as he boards the waiting boat. I don't wait for an invitation as I get on behind him.

"Jackson, this is against protocol. You shouldn't be out here," he says in a stern voice.

"And if the woman you loved was missing? Would you sit at home like a good boy, or would you get out there and look for her? Please, you can't make me sit and wait. I promise I will stay out of the way, but I need to help. Please." The desperation oozes out of my voice. "Please."

"Fine," he says, throwing me a lifejacket. "Put this on and sit down. We're heading south, the other boat will head north. I have a message going out to all boaters in the area and we've called in the helicopter as well. We'll find her."

I give a description of my boat to Peters so he can send it out to all active Constables and boaters. We leave the marina, eyes wide, and I pray we find Lillian unharmed.

Chapter 33
Lillian

My head throbs.

I feel like I've been on a three-day bender and haven't had water in weeks. Did Aspen come into town and convince me to drink a whole bottle of tequila? No, that didn't happen. Think, Lillian. I should open my eyes, but I can tell it's going to be bright, and just the thought of sunlight makes my stomach sway.

Except that's not my stomach swaying, it's my whole body. I'm floating. I'm on the water.

How did I get here?

Jackson and I were going to spend the afternoon on his boat. Did I get too much sun and fall asleep? That's possible, but I don't remember seeing Jackson this afternoon.

Wait, he was running late. He was running late, so I biked to the marina to wait for him. I brought the book I'm reading with me. I was going to read while sitting on the boat, getting some sun until he finished work. But he didn't come.

Why am I asleep in the boat with a hangover in the middle of the day? Without Jackson?

I hear movement to my right and hold as still as possible.

Whoever it is, they are grumbling something under their breath and moving a heavy object around, causing the boat to rock more. I think I recognize the voice, but I can't completely place it. I know it's not Jackson.

I risk opening my eyes slightly and regret it immediately. I can't hold in the groan that escapes as the sun assaults my sensitive retina.

"Oh, good, you're awake. This wouldn't be as much fun if you were unconscious for it." I open my eyes further and am met with pure anger radiating off Rick.

Rick?

"What's going on?" I ask. I have some sort of memory of Rick being in his boat when I got to the marina, but why would we be in the middle of the lake alone right now?

"What's going on is your little boyfriend is finally going to get what's coming to him."

What is he talking about? Both Jackson and I haven't exchanged more than simple pleasantries with the guy all summer. Do they know each other?

"What?"

"Oh, come on, Lillian, you seem like a smart girl. Too bad you had to fall for a crook like Jackson. I didn't plan on hurting you, but you're just so important to him. It's the only way he will really pay." Rick turns away from me, continuing to fiddle with something in front of him. I take inventory of my surroundings.

We are on Jackson's boat for sure. It seems as though he left me lying on the bench at the back of the boat. I'm not tied up, which I guess makes sense. He must have drugged me to knock me out, but there's nowhere for me to go besides the lake, so tying me up probably seemed unnecessary. How did we get out here?

I don't have keys. Does Rick have keys to the boat? He's always tinkering with his boat; I guess it's not unreasonable that he would know how to hotwire one.

I have no idea why he is so mad at Jackson or what his plans are for me, but I think it's safe to assume he doesn't plan on returning me unharmed.

Aspen loves to watch true crime shows and is fully prepared to defend herself should she end up in trouble. I remember her telling me to keep a captor talking. I'm not sure if it was for information or to buy time, but it can't hurt either way.

"What did Jackson do to you?"

Rick huffs out an annoyed breath. Without looking back at me, he says, "He stole my family."

As far as I know, Jackson doesn't have a secret family some-where. I have no idea what he's talking about, but he continues, "We used to spend every summer at my family's cottage, making memories, bonding. But Mane Construction swooped in and tricked my parents into selling it to them. Without the cottage, my family crumbled, and my wife left me and took the kids. I haven't seen my girls in weeks. Weeks!"

Okay.

I doubt Jackson did any tricking to purchase his family's cottage, but I don't say that. He must be delusional. He grew more and more agitated as he continued to explain. I don't want him to lash out at me, so I need to tread carefully.

"I'm sorry that happened to you," I say instead. "How does kidnapping me fix the problem?" This may agitate him, but I want to at least know if he plans on killing me or not.

"Well, you see, Lillian," he seethes, "kidnapping you does very little. I want Jackson to hurt like I hurt. Kidnapping is too simple, and not enough pain is felt. And for that reason, I plan to kill you."

My stomach drops and I struggle to pull a breath into my lungs. A part of me wondered if he was going to hurt me. But to say he's going to kill me with the same nonchalance you would have while ordering a pizza? There is something seriously wrong with Rick.

He continues working on whatever he's doing, so I take a closer look at what's in his hands. Rope. He's tying knots around something else. I shift a bit to the left and can see cinder blocks.

He's going to drown me.

I want to distract him from his task to buy myself more time. Either to figure out a way to escape or hope help is on the way.

"What will you do after you kill me?" I try to keep my voice even. I don't want to give him the satisfaction of knowing I'm scared.

"I'm going to take the boat across to the US. I have a buddy who lives in Michigan. I figure I'll stay with him for a bit. It should take a while for them to find your body and even still, my fingerprints will be gone from your corpse. They won't know it was me."

His words send a chill down my spine. Referring to my corpse like I'm already dead... I need to get out of here.

We are far enough away from the shore that I can't see any landmarks. I'm a good swimmer, but there's no way I could make it to shore. Even with the adrenaline pumping through me, whatever Rick used to knock me out is still in my system, and I don't think my coordination is intact.

With Rick still looking away from me, I look around the boat. I know there are a lot of safety items in the compartment under the seat I'm on. If I can shift my weight enough, I should be able to reach in. But then what?

There should be a flare gun, but that's hardly a real weapon. If it didn't do enough damage, it would just make Rick angrier and probably send me overboard sooner.

A thought occurs to me. "Why are we stopped?"

Rick growls. "Your stupid boyfriend left the tank almost empty, so we are out of gas. I texted my friend Frank to bring me enough to get to Michigan."

Frank. Rick knows Frank. Were they working together the whole time? Frank wouldn't own up to all of the things he put us through. Maybe he wasn't to blame for all of them. If he was working with Rick, it's possible he didn't do it. I don't think the thought occurred to anyone that we should have been looking for more than one person.

Rick must not know Frank got caught. Jackson didn't want the media to pick up the fact that someone working for him was also trying to hurt us. Since it only affected us, we asked anyone who knew to keep it as quiet as possible. I guess it was quiet enough that Rick doesn't know his crime partner has been caught.

The sound of a motor in the distance draws Rick's attention away from both the rope and me.

As quietly as possible, I flip open the seat and pray I can find the one thing big enough to help me out of this situation, a fire extinguisher. After reading the boater's instruction manual, I made Jackson show me all the safety features on his boat.

The adrenaline running through my body drives me to my feet, and using all the strength I have, I hit Rick in the back of the head with the extinguisher.

He wobbles a little before tumbling to the floor by my feet. I take a deep breath but don't stop moving. My fingers move quickly, even as they shake, to untie as many of the knots Rick tied the rope into as possible. All those days mindlessly practising boater knots has paid off. I let enough length free to tie up Rick's hands and legs, leaving the cinder blocks attached at the end, hopefully weighing him down in place. And if not, he may meet the fate he had planned for me.

I take a moment to catch my breath. Whoa. Bending down cautiously, I feel for a pulse in his neck. It's there, but possibly weaker than normal. As much as I hate this guy, I don't want to kill someone who so clearly needs help.

I can't believe that worked. If I had grabbed anything else, I don't think I would be safe right now. My head throbs again. I think the energy I just exerted may have been too much. I need to stay focused. I may be safe for now from Rick, but I'm still stranded in a very large body of water.

The boat is out of gas, so I am stuck here until someone comes for help. Looking around again, there are a lot of boaters flying around the lake, but they are all too far away to hear me yell. The motor noise that had Rick distracted is gone, leaving me to figure this out alone. I stop and think for a moment, willing my heart rate to return to normal. I've gotten this far;

I need to think logically. The boating course I have been taking has taught me a lot that I didn't know before. What started out as research for my books, and a way to bond with Jackson over something he so clearly loves, may just save my life. I go back to the compartment under the bench seat where I found the fire extinguisher and take inventory. First aid kit, bailer, flashlight, flare gun and life jacket. I pick out the items I need and grab the radio beside the steering wheel.

I am getting off this boat. Alive.

Chapter 34

Jackson

We've been searching for ten minutes, but it feels like hours. There's a lot of boats on the water today, and slowing down to check every one of them is taking forever. I know we have to follow protocol, but the longer Lillian is missing, the more my heart crumbles. Just as I'm about to ask when the helicopter should be getting here, a flash of colour in the distance catches my eye and the radio picks up a message. Peters takes off in the direction the flare came from as the sweetest voice fills my ears.

"MAYDAY, MAYDAY. Um, I just sent off a flare. I need help. Please."

If I wasn't so relieved to hear her voice, I would laugh. I don't know exactly what she has gone through, but no matter what, she can't seem to turn off her manners.

Peters heads towards Lillian, full throttle, and I feel like I'm either going to puke or pass out. I have no idea what we are going to find when we get there. I pray she is unharmed, but I'm trying to mentally prepare for the worst. We slow down when we're twenty feet away so we don't rock the other vessel too much. The second we are within distance; I jump from the police boat onto the bow of my boat and grab Lillian into my arms. Feeling her breath against my neck heartbeat against my chest eases some of the tension in my body.

"Are you okay?" Lillian nods her head in my chest but doesn't look at me. Her whole body is shaking, either from shock or something else, but it seems as though she's in one piece and seemingly unharmed.

A throat clears behind us, and Constable Peters motions for us to get back into the police boat. I was so focused on Lillian that I didn't even see Rick crumpled and hogtied in the corner. Another boat approaches us, holding paramedics and more constables. One joins us on the police boat, the other staying in place as they load a now conscious Rick into it. I know there are procedures and rules that should be followed right now, and my boat is now a floating crime scene, but I want Lillian back at the cottage, safe with me. The paramedic checks Lillian out. I am relieved to hear that aside from drugging her initially, Rick didn't touch her.

"We are going to take your blood pressure and check for signs of concussion. You will need to see a doctor either tonight or tomorrow for blood work. He most likely knocked you out with chloroform, but if it was something else, it's important to know for police records."

Throughout the examination, I barely let her out of my hold. The paramedic is visibly annoyed to be working around me, but she doesn't say anything.

Constable Peters tells me that they will handle my boat, and it will be brought back to my slip after being processed through evidence. At this point, I wouldn't mind never seeing my boat again. If it holds too many bad memories for Lillian, then it's as good as sold. And if Lillian never wants to step foot in this lake again, I will find a new hobby. Peters leaves on the boat with a handcuffed Rick, who is surprisingly quiet right now, and we head back to shore with another constable.

I get Lillian back to her cottage, wrapped in a blanket on the couch. Just as her tea is finished steeping, Constable Peters knocks on the door. I let him in and he gets straight to business.

"Rick's not talking. He requested a lawyer, but I don't expect anything from him anytime soon." He pauses a moment and looks at Lillian with apprehension. "I know you don't want to relive what happened, but I need to ask while it's still fresh in your mind."

Lillian takes the mug of tea as I hand it to her, taking a sip before she gives us a play-by-play of what happened, from her getting to my boat early and waiting, up until we found them in the middle of the lake, and Frank's involvement in everything that happened. I will forever regret having her meet me there instead of picking her up like I always do, but I am so proud of her. My little sailor, tying him up like she did. She's the hero of her own story.

Constable Peters takes down all the information before excusing himself to make a call. With us being alone again, I take the opportunity to sit next to Lillian on the couch, pulling her into my side. I always like to be touching her, but the need to feel her breathing, feel her heartbeat, is so strong right now, that

I'm not sure how I will ever let her out of my sight again. We stayed mostly silent on the trip back to my truck and then back to the cottage. I don't want to force her to talk if that's not what she needs. I will do whatever it takes to make her feel safe and comfortable again. I squeeze her even tighter against me to remind myself she's okay.

"I'm okay," she says, reading the tension coming off my body. "Really, I am. It was scary, I won't lie about that. But it's over. I'm safe and we can put this all behind us. Well, we can put it behind us after I talk to Miranda about it."

"I could have lost you, Lil," I croak. "I don't want to live in a world without you."

She places a light kiss on my lips. "You don't have to. I'm here. And we have forever right in front of us."

If I had a ring, I would get down on one knee right now, but I put that thought on hold as Constable Peters enters the room, putting his phone back in his pocket. "I just got off a call with a friend from London. Turns out Rick has been spiralling ever since his wife asked for a divorce. She had a protective order against him for herself and their kids. I guess he was stalking her, and showing up at the girls' school in the middle of the day. She was under the impression he was spending the summer in a treatment centre. If I had to guess, he's been taking trips to London to watch them and then sleeping on his boat here when he needs to lie low. That's why the crimes were so sporadic."

"Oh, gosh. I hope he gets the help he needs now." I pull Lillian impossibly closer to me. Even after everything that just happened, she's still able to wish for the best for him. I don't think there is anyone in this world with a kinder heart than hers.

I would like to see him rot in a jail cell for the rest of his life, but I don't voice that out loud.

Peters nods his head a couple of times, agreeing with her. "I need to get back to the station. Please call if you need anything. I'll check in tomorrow regardless. Don't forget to get to the doctor soon. The one here in town will make time to see you. I've already talked to her."

Lillian extracts herself from my arms, dropping the blanket from her shoulders as she stands. Rounding the couch, she steps in front of Peters and pulls him into a gentle hug. He hesitates a moment before wrapping his arms around her, too. When he steps away, I notice a light blush on his cheeks, and if the moment wasn't so serious, I would call him out for it.

"Thank you, Dylan. For everything." Lillian takes a step back as Peters puts his serious cop face back on.

"Just doing my job."

"Even still, thank you."

He puts his hand on her shoulder and squeezes lightly. With a head nod in my direction, he takes off towards the door, leaving us alone once again.

Lillian looks at me and I angle my head towards the staircase. In silent agreement, we make our way upstairs and get ready for bed.

We move in practised silence. I don't remember most of the steps I took, but when Lillian curls up into my arms under the covers, I'm brought back to the present.

Lillian kisses up my neck, so lightly it tickles. She hooks her leg around my waist. Her kisses turn from innocent to something else when I feel her nibble on my ear.

"Lil," I murmur, breathing in the citrus smell that is all her. "You need to rest. Your body was under a lot of stress today."

"No." She shifts her body until she's on top of me, straddling my hips. Even though I just tried to get her to stop, my cock did not get the message and is making its presence known.

"Lil," I try again. "Sleep."

"Jackson, I could have died today. He planned on killing me." She takes a deep breath, holding tears in her eyes. "I let so many things pass me by because of anxiety and fear. And what happened today isn't going to cure that, but it sure is a great motivator to fight back. I want to live. I want to feel." She shifts her hips, grinding into my growing erection. "Let me feel. Let me live."

There's no way I can argue with that, not that I really want to anyway. I grab Lillian's neck, pulling her down into an all-consuming kiss. Our tongues tangle as she continues to grind into me. I put her there, pushing my hips higher into her, causing a moan to escape her lips.

"I love you. I need you, Jackson."

I break the kiss to rip her tank top over her head as she slides those pesky boxers off her legs. She reaches for the waistband of my boxer briefs and slowly slides them down my legs. With nothing between us now, I take her perky breast into my mouth, swirling my tongue around her nipple until she is writhing in my hands. She takes my cock in her hand, squeezing from base to tip, causing a hiss to break through my lips. Knowing that if she keeps going, I won't last, I flip her over, moving my mouth to her other nipple and then continuing my descent.

When I reach the apex of her thighs, I lightly blow on the

sensitive skin. Lillian's skin is covered in goosebumps as she tips her head back into the pillow. I nibble at the skin on her thighs and hips, putting my mouth everywhere except where she wants it most. Lillian whimpers, taking matters into her own hands. She scratches her nails through my hair, grabbing on hard, and pushing my face exactly where she wants it. I nibble, lick and swirl my tongue, Lillian squirming underneath me. When I think she's had enough, I add my fingers, causing her to reach her peak immediately.

I stay there a moment, intending to let her come down from her high, but Lillian has other ideas. She pulls me up to her, kissing me hard, tasting herself on my tongue. I settle both my elbows on either side of her face as I continue to kiss her. Our movements are less frantic than when we started. I pull away for a moment, reaching towards the nightstand to grab a condom when Lillian stops me.

"I've been on birth control forever, and I know we've both been tested." She hesitates a moment. "I want to feel you with nothing between us."

I pull my arm away from the drawer, nodding at her. A bashful smile paints her lips, so I kiss them again.

I've never been with anyone without a condom, but it feels right with Lillian.

"I don't want anything between us either," I tell her.

Easing slowly between her legs, I grab each one to wrap around my waist.

"I love you, Lillian. Forever." I drop my forehead to hers as I begin to thrust.

"Forever," she echoes. "I love you, too."

We repeat those three words, well into the night, as we continue to show each other just how much we mean them, falling apart together, knowing the other would put us back together again.

Chapter 35
Lillian

It's been five days since I was kidnapped, and it's been a whirl-wind. Not only have my parents, brother, Noah and Aspen all been staying at the cottage with Jackson and me, but word spread around town quickly and there has been a revolving door of Bluefield residents showing up at the cottage. Some of them we know, like Mrs. Langley and Ron, others we've met at the café or hardware store briefly, but some were complete strangers who wanted to make sure I was okay, and to show their support to Jackson and his business.

One of the good things to come out of everything that hap-pened is the town council fast-tracked the approval process and

Jackson will be building a new subdivision next year in town. There will be a mixture of rental properties, housing for seniors, and starter homes for young families. Jackson wants to make sure we are supporting the local economy by providing housing for them, while also catering to the tourists that drive most of the local businesses' success.

After a week of being fussed over, we politely asked everyone to leave. Ben needed to get back to the city for work and Noah for summer camp, so he left willingly. My parents put up a bit of a fight but eventually caved, and Aspen left us with a smack on the ass and a wink, assuming we needed some privacy. She's not entirely wrong; the cottage is old with thin walls.

The main reason I wanted the quiet is because Christopher is coming to visit. Not only were we due for a meeting about my books, he also heard about what happened, it made the news, and he wanted to check on me. Jackson offered to leave and give us privacy, but I could tell the whole situation made him a bit uncomfortable. Jackson is so great that I often forget this is his first relationship, and he's allowed to have insecurities. I know he trusts me, but I also know he will feel more at ease being able to at least be in the cottage, if not in the room, when Christopher is here.

Christopher pulls up at the cottage in his sporty car and fancy suit, just the way he always did when we were dating. It never seemed weird to me at the time, but everything about Jackson being here feels more natural than it ever did with Christopher.

He greets me with a friendly hug and introduces himself to Jackson with a firm handshake. After we get over the formalities of the kidnapping and what I've been up to this summer, we settle in the living room while Jackson sits in the dining room, working from his laptop.

I give Christopher a progress report, outlining the three stories I have completed and the planning diagram for the remaining two. I also show him the draft illustrations and marketing plan I have been given.

"This is really great work, Lillian. I know it took you a bit longer than normal, but it's great."

With our breakup, I worried it would affect our working relationship, but I can see that it hasn't. Christopher and I were always friends first, so I hope he will be on my side with what I'm about to say.

"I appreciate your compliment, but I do want to talk to you about something." I pause, and his face grows serious.

"You aren't about to quit, are you?" he asks nervously.

"NO. No." I take a deep breath. "I cannot write another book in this age group. I managed to get some inspiration this time." I look towards Jackson, who is now in the kitchen, pretending not to listen, but the smirk says he clearly is. "This is the only company I have ever been published with, and I am so appreciative of your parents taking a shot on me right out of school, but I need more freedom and choice if I am going to stay working here. I need to have a say in how my career progresses. I feel like it's been stagnant recently and I do take responsibility for that. How would anyone know I was unhappy when I wasn't telling them I was?"

"Okay, wow. That makes sense. I had no idea you weren't happy being assigned projects."

"That's not that surprising because I didn't know I was unhappy. Not until recently, but I am. I plan to meet with my department head next month to discuss everything I'm saying to you now, but when this meeting ultimately gets back to your parents, I am hoping you will support me."

Christopher puts his mug down and takes my hand, squeezing it quickly before releasing it again. "Lillian, absolutely. You have a talent, and I want you to feel like you're using it. Whatever you need, I'm on your side."

I feel like I could fly. I still need to have the conversation with my department manager, but I was more worried about Christopher's reaction than theirs.

A giant weight has been lifted off my shoulders. I knew after the kidnapping, I needed to make some changes in my career. The midlife crisis I thought I was having was of my own creation. I let my life happen; I wasn't the one driving it. And although this is just one step in correcting it, it's one of the most important ones for me. I need to know my work is valued, but I also need to feed the creative being inside of me. When I smother it, it withers and then I become lost like I was at the beginning of the summer.

Checking his watch, Christopher mutters, "Shit," under his breath. "I don't want to cut this short, but if I don't leave now, the traffic is going to be horrendous on the highway."

Standing, I say, "Not a problem. I think we've covered everything I wanted to get through today."

I walk him to the door. He nods goodbye to Jackson on his way past and Jackson smiles in return. When we reach the door, Christopher stops me. "You seem happy. That's all I ever wanted for you."

"Thank you, Christopher. I hope you find this, too." And I genuinely mean it. I may have been surprised when he broke up with me, but it was the right thing for both of us.

"I think I may have actually. I met a girl at my gym a couple of months ago and it looks promising. I'm happy, too."

Suddenly feeling a bit emotional, I will the tears to stay in my eyes, not allowing any to fall. Is this what happy people do? Cry over other happy people?

I walk Christopher to his car, but before he opens the door, he pulls me into a hug. It's familiar and comforting in the same way a hug from my brother would be.

"Take care, I'll be in touch soon. And don't worry about my parents, I've got your back."

"Safe drive," I say as he climbs into his car, waving as he backs out of the driveway. Jackson appears behind me, wrapping his arms around my shoulders and chest and pulling me into him.

"You know, I was fully preparing for a pissing contest with him. I thought for sure he was going to try to get you back and we were going to fight."

A full body laugh erupts from me.

"One, Christopher has never thrown a punch in his life, so that wouldn't be a fair fight. Two, we are meant to be friends, nothing more. After how long we were together, all I ask is that he supports me at work, which he does. He wants me to be happy and I want the same for him. And three, I'm yours, Jackson Mane. It's a fact, so you better get on board."

"Oh, I'm on board," he says as he grabs me around the waist and throws me over his shoulder. He carries me all the way upstairs and shows me just how on board he is late into the night.

Chapter 36
Jackson

If you told me a year ago, six months ago, or even three weeks ago that I could be this happy, I would have called you a fool. Turns out, I'm the fool.

I do not want to jinx things, but it seems like everything is coming up Jackson and Lillian now.

Lillian had a meeting with the head of her department, and they have given her as much creative freedom as she asked for. She now gets to choose each project she works on, from age group to subject matter and illustration direction.

I'm not sure if Christopher had to step in to help get her there, but regardless, she's ecstatic. I'm choosing to believe she didn't need his help. I know my girl is powerful when she puts her mind to something.

She earned this.

With most of my projects wrapping up this fall, I'm prepared to sit back and be a stay-at-home boyfriend for my breadwinner girlfriend. First, I need to convince Lillian to live with me. Permanently.

I mean, she can leave at any time, but I'm hoping she stays forever.

After everything that happened on my boat, I decided to sell it. Lillian insisted she was fine with me keeping it and would still enjoy using it, but I couldn't do it. Every time I got to the slip, I got an unsettled feeling in my stomach. When I would close my eyes, all I could see was Lillian standing there with the radio in one hand, the flare gun in the other, and Rick tied up at her feet.

Needless to say, we've both been attending weekly therapy sessions. Sometimes together, sometimes individually. We are both working through the trauma that both Frank and Rick caused us, but ultimately, I needed that boat gone.

Simon offered to make it a joint investment, which I happily accepted. We are the proud owners of a seventeen-person Wakesetter. It's about twice the size of my old boat. More room for friends and family. More power to pull Noah on his tube or Aspen on the wakeboard. More possibilities for new memories.

It's a bit of a flashy boat. Especially considering most of the marina is full of small sailboats. This is something you would see all over the lakes up in the Muskokas or Kawarthas, but I don't care. It will be perfect for us, our friends and family.

I can already see us taking the girls out and waiting on them all day in the sun. Or having Aspen show up Simon, Ben, Dylan and me at wakeboarding and water skiing, since she's good at everything.

We can take Lillian's parents out for leisurely cruises, too. I'm most looking forward to sunset dates with Lillian, though. I see this boat and a lot of those in our future. Who knows, maybe one day there will be little Lillians and Jacksons running around who will learn their love for the water on this boat.

Lillian knows I was looking for a new vessel, but I didn't tell her that I bought one and it's ready and waiting for us. It's all part of the surprise.

I have Lillian in the passenger seat of my truck with a blindfold on. I don't know where she thinks we're going, but she seems pretty content in letting me surprise her. I pull up to the marina and park near my new slip. After everything that happened, I was able to convince someone else to trade slips so we wouldn't have to be anywhere near where everything happened.

I open Lillian's door and take her hand, guiding her out of the truck and to the edge of the shore, just before the dock.

"Okay, take your blindfold off," I instruct.

Lillian swipes it off her head, almost elbowing me in the gut in the process. "Whoops." She giggles before looking at the beauty of a boat in front of us.

"Jackson? Whose boat is this?"

"Mine and Simon's?" I don't know why that came out like a question. It was a big purchase, but with the trade-in, plus Simon paying half, it is an investment we can afford.

"It's huge! I love it!" Whew. I wipe the sweat that started to form on my brow and take Lillian's hand. I guide her onto the dock and help her into the boat. It is a bit huge. At least in comparison to a lot of the boats around us and my old one. "Noah is going to freak. Actually, Ben is going to freak. No, no, Aspen is going to freak. There's so much space on this thing. We could throw a party. Actually, trash that thought. No parties. Just us and our close, close friends."

"I agree. I can't wait to have everyone out here for a boat day soon." I pause because I'm not sure how she's going to take the final surprise. "One more thing. You need to see the name."

"You named the boat?" she asks.

"I wish I could take credit for it, but this was actually all Simon. I've never been big on the tradition, but Simon swears by it. There's a superstition that naming a boat after a god or goddess brings you good fortune. They probably didn't have pleasure crafts in mind when that came to be, but he insisted we needed a name."

"That sounds like something Simon would do." Her nose

crinkles a little as she chuckles. "Okay, okay. So what god or goddess did you name it after? Apollo? Neptune? Athena?"

"Why don't you see for yourself?" I direct Lillian off the boat and back to land so she can see the side of the boat. I wasn't hiding it when we arrived, but she was so shocked she wasn't paying close enough attention. I stand behind her with my arms wrapped around her shoulders. I wish I could see her reaction, but if she hates it, at least I can hide my face in her neck.

"What? Jackson? Why is your boat named 'The Wild-flower'?" She spins in my arms and that's when I see the tears falling down her face. "Simon calls me Wildflower. He told me you called me that once, too." I wipe the tears from her cheeks with both my hands.

"He named the boat after you."

"WHY?!"

"Lil. Do you not know how amazing you are? You survived a kidnapping. Well, not only did you survive, you overtook him. You are a rock star author. You inspire children with your writing. You love your family fiercely. You put up with me somehow. You are a goddess among us mortals. When Simon suggested we name the boat Wildflower, I couldn't think of anything more fitting. You are my goddess, my good luck. My everything."

Lillian just nods her head as the tears continue to stream down her face. "I love you, Jackson."

"I love you, too, Lil."

Okay, here goes nothing. The reason I actually brought her here.

"Hey, Lil. Do you want to be my roommate?"

"Jackson," she laughs out. "You asked me that, like, four

months ago and we've been living together ever since."

"Okay, fine. Do you want to be my roommate, like, forever?" I lift one shoulder, trying to act casual about it, but I know she can probably feel my heart beating way too fast in my chest.

"Is this you asking to move in together in Toronto?"

"Toronto, here. Basically, anywhere you are…"

"Yes! Of course. You said all those months ago that I get to decide when you leave. And I'm pretty set on forever at this point. We will need to get rid of one of our condos, though."

I plant a kiss on her forehead, each eyelid and then finally her lips.

"We'll figure it out. As long as we're together, we'll figure it out."

Epilogue

Lillian

My family vacations have always been fun, but with Jackson joining our group, I don't think I have ever enjoyed myself this much. Sometimes I forget what a charmer he can be, but I'm pretty sure every person we have encountered, from the flight attendant to our taxi driver, the hotel concierge, our cooking instructor and our jungle guide, is smitten with him. Luckily for me, he's all mine.

Jackson met my parents shortly after my kidnapping. He was nervous but for no reason.

My parents love him.

We took them out on his new boat, he showed off all the renovations he was working on, helped my dad with maintenance around the cottage and by the end of the day, my mom was booking him on our flight to Thailand. Christopher was never once invited to join us.

I guess our parents really do know better.

Jackson has now firmly cemented himself as part of the family and I couldn't be happier. Things with his dad will never be amazing, but Jackson has come to terms with that.

He is okay with their relationship being mostly professional and I support whatever decisions he makes with that.

Aspen assumed that Jackson would be taking her place on my family vacation, but there was no way that was happening. She's here with us, the only difference being she got her own room. It's worked out well for everyone because when Aspen gets a crazy idea and wants to take off on her own, Jackson tags along. He's better at keeping her in line than Ben or I ever was.

Somehow, she has roped the whole family into Muay Thai lessons, with tickets to the professional fights afterwards. This is not my thing at all, but I've been stepping out of my comfort zone lately, with the help of Miranda, Aspen and Jackson, and

I'm willing to try most things once before I make a judgment now.

As we walk the streets of Chang Mai, Noah walks ahead with Jackson and Ben on either side of him, holding his hands. Aspen and I trail behind a couple of paces, wanting to take a photo of the three of them. Just as I get the best shot, an elderly woman approaches the three boys, says a couple of words and then continues on.

Based on the flush to both Ben's and Jackson's cheeks, I am thoroughly curious.

When we get to the building where our lesson is to be held, Aspen goes ahead to get us checked in, so I go to stand next to Jackson.

"What did that woman say to you?"

Ben looks away, chuckling, Jackson won't make eye contact, and neither of them answers my question. I look between both of the men and then down to my nephew. I love the kid, but he can't keep a secret.

Bending down to his height, I ask him the same question Ben and Jackson are avoiding answering.

Noah giggles before whispering to me, "She thought Uncle Jackson was my daddy." I look up at the two men, still confused as to what the big deal is.

"Why is that funny?" I ask Noah.

"She thought my daddies were cute." Okay, the kid can't keep a secret, but he's not great with his explanations either. I stand up and face my brother, planting the little sister pout I've perfected over the years on my face. I know I could get Jackson to cave just as quickly, but messing with my brother is too much fun.

Ben groans, finally filling me in. "She thought Jackson and I were a couple and Noah was our kid... She told Noah, 'You are very cute. Almost as cute as your two daddies.'"

I can't help but laugh, taking a step back. Looking at the three of them, I can see it. Jackson and my brother get along great. Sometimes I feel like the third wheel when they start talking about hockey, action movies, or some band I've never heard of. And with the way Jackson dotes on Noah, the three of them do look like a happy little family. It's all very cute.

Being here with my family has me already excited for next summer.

I never thought I would say this, but I miss all the kooky seniors in Bluefield. I feel like we now have ten extra sets of grandparents to look after.

For now, we will enjoy the warm weather of Southeast Asia, because when the trip is done, we will be heading back to Bluefield for the winter, at least on a part-time basis. And a winter on Lake Huron? Freezing.

Jackson and I had every intention of going back to Toronto for the winter, but then the deal fell through with the Waldens' property. After the place was subject to multiple vandalisms, the clients that were going to buy the place backed out, not wanting to deal with any future problems, even though there won't be now that Rick and Frank are sitting in prison, awaiting trial. Normally, Jackson would call the next client on the waiting list to see if they wanted to take over the buying agreement, but he decided to sign his name on the dotted line instead.

Yeah, Jackson bought the cottage next door to my grandparents' place in Bluefield. Since he had to sell his condo to make it work financially, we decided to keep mine for when we needed to be in the city but plan to spend as much time in Bluefield as possible. If everything goes according to plan, our friends and family will be there with us. It's our home now.

It's where our story started and will continue to be written.

The Bluefield Beach Series continues with
Aspen and Simon's story, *Staged River*.

More by Heather

Want more Lillian and Jackson?
There's a bonus epilogue available on my website.

Head back to Bluefield with Aspen and Simon in
STAGED RIVER available now.

THE BLUEFIELD BEACH SERIES
Inky Water - Lillian & Jackson
Staged River - Aspen & Simon
Scattered Acres – Julia & Elliot

Content Warnings

The content warnings for *Inky Water* include discussion of toxic childhood environment and parental relationships, kidnapping, animal blood, mentions of anxiety, and explicit sexual content.

About the author

Heather is a Canadian author with a passion for romance—and just the right touch of suspense. After years spent in the financial world, she traded in spreadsheets for storylines and now crafts stories with love, drama, and a little mystery into every page.

When she's not writing or dreaming up her next plot twist, you'll find her curled up with a book, surrounded by her beloved pets, enjoying time with friends, or exploring the outdoors with family.

To stay up to date on Heather's upcoming projects, connect with her on social media @authorheathergrey

Acknowledgements

Wow. I can't believe I wrote a book and now get to write acknowledgments.

First I would like to thank my husband. Thank you for reading other romance books so that you could tell me whether this book was good enough to publish. I would have done it regardless, but I appreciate your support and encouragement.

To my mother: Thank you for supporting me in every life decision I make. I know a lot of authors don't let their parent read their work, I appreciate that you were okay with skimming through certain chapters.

To my Beta Readers: Thank you for not running away from the disaster document you first received, we've come a long way from that draft.

To my Editor, Bobbi: Thank you for your support throughout this entire process. Having you in my corner put me at ease during this scary journey.

To my ARC Readers: Thank you for taking the time to read *Inky Water* and offering me your support and kind words. Getting to experience Lillian and Jackson's story through your reactions is something I will treasure, always.

To everyone who has supported me on social media: Thank

you for welcoming me into the bookish and indie author community with open arms.

To the person reading this book: Thank you. Publishing *Inky Water* is one of my life's most nerve-racking and exciting experiences. Thank you for being a part of my author story and I hope you will join me again in Bluefield, very soon.

www.ingramcontent.com/pod-product-compliance
Lightning Source LLC
Chambersburg PA
CBHW030935120726
47906CB00002B/573